THE
GARDEN

THE GARDEN

A NOVEL

NICK NEWMAN

G. P. PUTNAM'S SONS
New York

PUTNAM
— EST. 1838 —

G. P. PUTNAM'S SONS
Publishers Since 1838
An imprint of Penguin Random House LLC
1745 Broadway, New York, NY 10019
penguinrandomhouse.com

First published in Great Britain in 2025 by Doubleday, an imprint of Transworld
Publishers. Transworld is part of the Penguin Random House group of companies.

Book design by Angie Boutin
Title page and chapter opener illustrations by Merfin/Shutterstock.com

Library of Congress Cataloging-in-Publication Data

Names: Newman, Nick (Pseudonym), author.
Title: The garden / Nick Newman.
Description: New York: G. P. Putnam's Sons, 2025.
Identifiers: LCCN 2024027839 (print) | LCCN 2024027840 (ebook) |
ISBN 9780593717738 (hardcover) | ISBN 9780593717752 (epub)
Subjects: LCGFT: Gothic fiction. | Science fiction. | Novels.
Classification: LCC PR6102.O949 G37 2025 (print) |
LCC PR6102.O949 (ebook) | DDC 823/.92—dc23/eng/20240715
LC record available at https://lccn.loc.gov/2024027839
LC ebook record available at https://lccn.loc.gov/2024027840

Printed in the United States of America
1 3 5 7 9 10 8 6 4 2

The authorized representative in the EU for product safety and compliance is
Penguin Random House Ireland, Morrison Chambers, 32 Nassau Street,
Dublin D02 YH68, Ireland, https://eu-contact.penguin.ie.

For Laura

Th' world's all fair begun again this mornin', it has.
An' it's workin' an' hummin' an' scratchin' an' pipin' an'
nest-buildin' an' breathin' out scents, till you've got to be
out on it 'stead o' lyin' on your back.

THE
GARDEN

1

Somebody had moved the beehive. Evelyn couldn't understand how it had happened. It was at a slight angle to the others, like it had been shoved, and beneath each of its wooden feet there was a shallow red trench in the earth. An animal? A storm? It couldn't have been. They wouldn't have slept through a storm, and if they had they would now be under a foot of dust, along with the rest of the garden.

Evelyn pushed the hive back into place, clung to it for a moment, caught her breath. She felt the hum of the bees against her ribs. Perhaps they could tell her what had happened? She pressed her ear to the wood, warm and wind-smoothed, and listened. They droned on, not caring whether she was there.

She checked the combs for disease and mites, found the

queens and counted the eggs. She tasted a little of the honey on her fingertip. The bees came and went like snatches of conversation. She brushed them from her ears, her hair, the backs of her hands. One of them stung her knuckle and she just nodded.

"I know, I know," she said. "Keep your hair on."

She replaced the roof of the last hive and went up the garden to the house, following the path past the willows, magnolias, rhododendrons. The hydrangeas had started to bloom, their flowers round and heavy like fruit. In the shadow of the house she went to her sister's little vegetable patch and picked rhubarb and blueberries and put them in the pocket of her apron. When she passed the pond, she got to her knees and dipped her swollen finger in the water.

She trailed her hand back and forth among the weeds, noticed, with surprise, the tightness in her brow.

Had she moved the hive and forgotten? She knew her memory was not what it had once been. She was out of practice, remembering. There was no reason to remember anything, not really, not anymore—except when to water the plants, when to refresh the soil, when to check on the bees.

Perhaps Lily had moved it?

No. The hives weren't Lily's responsibility. They always laughed about how scared she was of the bees. And with Lily's joints the way they were, she was in no fit state to be hauling heavy wooden boxes around.

Evelyn's hand was numb now and turning white. The sun had gone behind the vast battlements of the house, the jagged shadow of its many gables and chimneys creeping almost beyond the edge of the lawn. She shivered and flexed her fingers and went inside.

Lily was in the kitchen, chopping potatoes in almost total

darkness. Their old windup lamp lit half of her face, the edge of the knife, the pale yellow skins she'd discarded on the work surface. She was wearing their mother's ball gown, and she shimmered like some black and bony fish raised from the deep. Behind her, the rest of the room seemed to go on for miles. It was kitchen, living room, bedroom, and storeroom to both of them, and still felt too large. The darkness echoed each time Lily's knife struck the wooden board.

"Hello," said Evelyn.

Lily turned and smiled. Evelyn went to her, held her, laid her head in the warm curve of her sister's neck and shoulder. She heard Lily's blood humming inside her, like the bees in the beehive.

"Your rhubarb is looking magnificent," she said, taking the red stalks from her apron.

"You sound surprised," said Lily. "I am not completely clueless, you know."

"Blueberries are on the way, too. A bit sharp."

Lily nodded and turned back to her potatoes. She cut a few more slices, then said, without looking up: "What's the matter?"

Of course she'd noticed. She would have felt Evelyn's discomfort before she even entered the house—had registered the slight change in the rhythm of her footfall, the tightness of her breath. She tucked a strand of long silver hair behind one ear, as if to hear Evelyn better.

"Did you move one of the beehives?"

"Me?"

"One of them's moved."

Lily laughed and scraped the potatoes into a dish. "Oh, yes, your little sister up to her old mischief. I hid all the honey, too, so I can guzzle it when you're not looking."

"Really?"

"Of course not! I wouldn't touch those things with a barge pole."

"So you didn't move it."

"I'm surprised you suddenly think me so capable."

"Then who did?"

"You probably did."

"I didn't."

Lily shrugged. "You must have."

And that was that.

Evelyn watched her sister hobble over to the stove and arrange the tinder. She fumbled with the flints for a moment, dropped them, cursed. Evelyn joined her and helped to rake through the cinders. She found the flints and began to strike them herself.

"I can do it," said Lily. As if they were children still and Evelyn was offering to help her with a jigsaw or a drawing.

Lily snatched the flints back and tried again. Her hands shaking. The light from the windup lamp showed every line and knot on her long fingers. They were far more graceful than Evelyn's, or at least they had been. A pianist's hands. A magician's. They were too good to spend their days thrust in the soil, but even so, they had conjured miracles from it. Now they were shaking.

We are old, thought Evelyn, without contemplating much beyond that simple fact.

The matter of the beehive wasn't mentioned again. Of course Lily was right. It must have been Evelyn who had moved it because there was simply no other explanation. She'd moved it and forgotten. It had been silly to imagine anything different.

When the fire was lit, they had to wait some time for the

stove to heat. It was a monumental thing—two hobs and four doors, all in cast iron. They had run out of coal a long time ago and heating it with wood required hours of attention and the temperature was wildly inconsistent.

They fried the potatoes with onions and herbs and ate them under a blanket, straight from the pan.

"We should have got something from the icehouse. For a treat."

"You'd eat nothing but treats if you could."

"Guilty as charged." Lily shoveled another mouthful. "Well? It's not too late."

"It is too late. It's nearly your bedtime."

"It's nearly *your* bedtime."

They fell to eating again.

Evelyn had not visited the icehouse for some time. It was a few moments' walk from the kitchen, a brick dome cool enough for curing and keeping meat all year-round, but she wasn't sure its contents were getting better with age. What did? They hadn't added to their meat store since their mother had gone, and she had been the only one who knew how to preserve things properly. Some of the stuff down there was positively ancient, but Evelyn and Lily still occasionally cut off the leathery strips and chewed at them like dogs. When the seasons conspired against them and the garden was barren, it was almost all they ate.

Lily finished first and licked her fingers.

"Do you remember Mama's bacon and beans?" she said.

"I think so. No idea what the recipe was."

"I suppose I could work it out. Dessert?"

"Always room for dessert."

Lily got up to check on the rhubarb, which they'd left

stewing on the hob. It was freezing outside the blanket. She prodded at the pot, tasted a little from the end of the spoon, and added some more honey from their stores. She brought back two bowls, and they both ate it too quickly, "hoohing" and "hahing" and frantically sucking in air to soothe their scalded tongues. They laughed. It didn't stop either of them going back for seconds.

They curled up under the covers in warm, comfortable silence. Lily was snoring before the embers had gone cold, but Evelyn continued to stare into the darkness for a long while afterward, thinking. Her finger was still gently throbbing from where she'd been stung. Outside, the garden sang into the night.

2

Evelyn was up at sunrise to collect eggs. She left Lily under her heap of blankets and went barefoot around the great western wing of the house and the ruins of the sunroom. The chickens were already awake and waiting to be let out. Just three hens now, and an elderly rooster, in the same coops that had stood there for decades. Their father had built the wooden hutches to last, and it seemed they were destined to outlive the chickens' entire lineage. They'd had no chicks for a long time.

She let the hens out and they came down the little wooden ramp and clucked and pecked at the ground uncertainly, every morning exercising the same caution, as if encountering the world for the first time. She left them prowling through the grass and opened the back of the hutch. There were two eggs hidden in the straw, one each for her and her sister. They felt like a pair of large, sun-warmed pebbles in the palms of her hands. She put them into the front pocket of her nightdress and looked up into the cold blue haze and there found most of a full moon hanging where she had not expected to see one. She'd forgotten where the month had got to. She stood and thought, counting the days and nights on her fingers, then went inside.

Back in the kitchen Lily was still asleep. She always rose later than Evelyn. Evelyn didn't particularly mind. It seemed as much Lily's duty to sleep in as it was Evelyn's to collect the eggs.

She stepped quietly over her younger sister and crossed the kitchen floor, the soles of her feet numb from the dew. She placed the eggs carefully in the cast-iron egg tree and then came back to the dresser and opened the topmost drawer. She took out the almanac and laid it open on the table.

"You're back early."

Evelyn turned. Lily was sitting up like one of the hens in her nest of blankets.

"I'm just checking something."

"Checking? Now there's something I never thought I'd hear. First the beehive, now this. You losing your marbles, Evie?"

Evelyn smiled but said nothing and turned back to the pages spread on the tabletop.

The almanac was their mother's work, a large ring-bound diary whose damp and wadded pages contained all that she knew and all that she had instructed her daughters to know. There was not half an inch of blank paper between its covers. The first dozen pages showed a bird's-eye view of the house and the gardens, front and back, with plans of the plots and the beds. At the back was an appendix of recipes and remedies that could be made from the things they grew, a kind of apothecary's miscellany. In between, the lion's share of the almanac was given over to timetables for planting and growing and harvesting. Sections headed *Spring, Summer, Autumn, Winter,* though these meant little nowadays. The garden kept its own seasons. Each new year seemed overlaid rather than joined consecutively, a jumble of cycles within cycles. It was not unusual for Evelyn to be digging potatoes out of earth that was scattered with apple blossom.

She turned a few of the pages and traced a finger over the minuscule writing. The words had been etched deeply into the paper and were covered with a thin patina of dust, giving each page the appearance of some ancient stone tablet. She found the section headed *Autumn, first moon, gibbous, waxing,* flattened the almanac, compared her mother's list to the list she held in her head. There was more to do than she had thought.

"I thought that thing was useless, anyway," said Lily.

Evelyn felt the slightest shiver of indignation on their mother's behalf. "Not useless. It's just a little out of step."

"What is it today then?"

"Brassicas. Onions and garlic. More beans."

"More beans? I feel like I should have some say in this since I'm the one doing the cooking."

"They're good for the soil."

Lily didn't reply, but Evelyn knew she was rolling her eyes.

"I think the roses need deadheading."

"Oh! I'll deadhead the roses."

"Mama doesn't mention it, though."

"So?"

"So maybe we shouldn't."

Lily got up from her blankets with a groan and came and put her arms around Evelyn's waist. She pressed her chest against the back of Evelyn's ribs, and Evelyn felt her sister's heart beating through her thin bird-bones.

Lily peered over her shoulder and said, "I don't know why you don't just give up on that and write a new one."

It was not the first time she had said it, not even the hundredth time, but the suggestion still seemed a wild one. Of course the almanac couldn't be replaced. Evelyn wouldn't know where to start. Besides, they had no more paper, and their one pencil belonged to Lily, and Lily didn't like to part with it. It was little more than a nub now, and writing anything so extensive would wear it down to nothing.

"I'll ask Mama about it," said Evelyn. "Later."

Lily went to the back of the kitchen to make their porridge. Evelyn closed the almanac and looked at the cover for a moment. It was curled and liver-spotted and showed another timetable, a daily schedule that did not shift beneath their feet as the seasons did. Lunchtime, teatime, bathtime, bedtime. Beside each entry were numbers that seemed to refer only to themselves rather than any objective measurement of minutes and hours. The handwriting was larger but still recognizably their mother's, the words more forcefully imposed, somehow, than the almanac's contents.

"Oh dear," said Lily, from back in the darkness.

Evelyn returned the almanac to the drawer and looked over at her. "What's oh dear?"

"Just two eggs today?"

"Better than yesterday."

"Not much. How are the old girls?"

"Fine. Bad-tempered."

"Wouldn't you be? Having to live with that cockerel."

The remark was more a ritual than a joke, but they both laughed anyway.

Lily brought over their bowls of porridge and they ate it wordless and smiling. The kitchen door was ajar, and a wedge of yellow sunlight fell across precisely half of the table. Birdsong and bristling leaves outside. Lily's jaw clicked when she ate, and Evelyn liked the sound. She liked all the sounds of her sister's body. They were more in keeping with the other sounds they heard in the garden, she thought; much more so than speaking, which seemed to belong there less and less these days.

Lily pushed her bowl away and got up first, as if steeling herself for something.

"What will you do today?" said Evelyn.

"I shall fetch the water," said Lily. "Then I shall wash the dishes. Then I shall go to the gazebo to practice my steps." She paused. "What about a game after lunch? We haven't played a game for months. Not a proper game."

Evelyn thought of her list of tasks. "Yes," she said. "If I have time."

Lily shrugged. "Well, I'll play by myself if I must," she said. "Although I don't know why you keep yourself quite so busy all the time."

Lily always seemed surprised that there was work to do; had not twigged, after all these years, that work was all that there was.

Evelyn got up herself and squeezed her sister's hand. She

put on the same outfit she always wore—plaid shirt, jeans, holes at the elbows and knees, and cinched in the middle with their mother's cracked leather belt. She took the waxed jacket from the hook behind the door and put on her Wellington boots and went out into a day that was, she thought tiredly, already well ahead of her.

3

The sun was up and the garden was dazzling. Evelyn stood for a moment on the doorstep and closed her eyes. The skin on her brow softened like wax under a warm thumb. She went to the toolshed and took down the spade and the fork and the largest of the wicker baskets. In the basket she put a smaller bucket of chicken manure, a plant pot full of broken eggshells, and a small paper packet of speckled beans and then set off for the beds at the bottom of the garden.

She took the long way around, to check all was still in order. She approached the beehives with some apprehension. She found them as she had left them the previous evening, the hive closest to the house a little skewed, despite her best efforts.

From there she passed through the green shade of the

orchard, inspecting the swelling clusters of apples. Many were already windfallen and were lying in the grass, brown and spongy underfoot. The faint sweetness of rot in the air. The day for wassailing had not even come, and the harvest was already going to waste. She would have to consult their mother about that. The avenue of roses looked slightly better than she remembered, but there were fresh blooms inexplicably growing among others that were brown and limp. She would have to ask Mama about that, too. She wondered how she would take the news.

By the time Evelyn reached the bottom beds, the sun was high and the garden exhaling in the heat. The wall was perhaps a hundred paces away, but still she turned her back to it, just in case. She cleared the spinach of slugs, reprimanding them as she went, and scattered the soil with the broken eggshells to ward off their return. She heaved at the earth, plucked the weeds by the root, planted the beans in neat rows. Back to the toolshed, another handful of seeds, then on to the next bed. She hardly looked up from her work, sweat running down the sides of her nose, the shirt clinging to her bones underneath the heavy waxed coat. Not as fast as she used to be, but no less dogged. A dull ache bloomed in her knees and elbows that she always assumed was early-morning stiffness but that never left her these days, however warm she got. In between forkfuls of earth she heard only her blood thumping, and occasionally, distantly, the sound of Lily practicing her routine in the gazebo on the other side of the house.

She was glad to be working. When she was working, she was not thinking.

At midday her sister came down to the bottom of the garden with a pot of black tea and lemon. She was still wearing the sequined ball gown, as well as an enormous sun hat and almost all of their mother's jewelry. She clinked like a chandelier when she walked, earlobes pulled so low that the earrings nearly rested on her shoulders.

Evelyn leaned on the fork. Lily smiled broadly and set the tray on the grass.

"Tea's up," she said.

"How did it go today?" asked Evelyn.

"Coming together nicely," said Lily.

"I don't suppose you're ever going to let me watch, are you?"

"Oh, I daresay. One of these days. It's not quite there yet."

She perched on a stone by the edge of the vegetable plot and wiggled her toes. Then she looked up at Evelyn and pouted.

"Don't say it," said Evelyn.

"I wish I had my shoes," said Lily.

Evelyn didn't reply. Her sister had been lamenting the loss of her ballet shoes for as long as they had looked after the garden. She'd had them as a little girl, and by now they would be far too small, but Evelyn knew better than to remind Lily of that. Besides, the shoes were in the house along with everything else. And they never went into the rest of the house.

Lily sighed and bent over the teapot. She poured two cups and said: "A resounding victory against the slugs."

"They gave as good as they got," said Evelyn. "I still haven't got the slime off me." She scrubbed her palm against her hip.

"How's the soil?"

"Heavy. I did my best. The beans are in, at least."

"Well, hurrah for that."

They drank their tea and then lay side by side on the hot lawn and watched the sky. Evelyn listened to the insects and the birds and the slow creak of things growing. She tried to make a list of all the things that she had to do: tasks left over from the day before; tasks yet to come; tasks that, according to the almanac, she wasn't supposed to be doing at all but that were upon her nonetheless. She thought of the chickens and the roses and the apples already turning to mulch in the orchard. She thought about the beehive and tried to forget it but couldn't. Eventually Lily squeezed her hand and rolled over and got slowly to her feet.

"So, then," she said. "Are we playing a game, or aren't we?"

"Now?" said Evelyn. She propped herself on an elbow. "I'm not halfway done here."

"It's too hot for work," said Lily. "Even Mama would say that."

That was not true, but Evelyn humored her. "What would you like to play?"

"I don't know."

"I fixed the croquet hammer."

"No, not croquet. I need to use my body. Hide-and-seek."

Evelyn looked at where she'd stuck the fork in the ground. There was so much to do, and Lily could happily make these games last for hours.

"We'll play hide-and-seek as long as you help me with the watering afterward."

"Deal."

Lily stuck out her hand, fingers covered with their mother's rings almost to their tips. Evelyn shook it.

"You'd better take all of that off or you'll be ever so easy to find," said Evelyn, gesturing at the jewelry.

"Yes, yes, I know," said Lily, already unhooking the earrings and the necklaces and placing them one by one on the tea tray. She threw off the hat, too, and tied her long hair up in a gray bun so tight it looked like the whorl of a tree trunk. She stood to attention in front of Evelyn.

"What am I counting to?" said Evelyn.

"One hundred. And face the wall."

"I won't face the wall. But I'll put my hands over my eyes."

"You'll look. You always look."

"I promise I won't."

"Fine. And don't count too fast."

Evelyn placed her muddy hands over her eyes and started to count out loud. She listened to her sister's footsteps recede over the grass and then opened her fingers slightly. She watched her go up the garden path. Always the same—Lily's gleeful hobble to the back of the house, Evelyn's terror at the thought that this time would be different, this time she would hide somewhere new and Evelyn would not be able to find her. She counted a little quicker, skipped the numbers from ninety to one hundred, announced she was coming.

A Party

Her sister had hidden in the attic once, and hours had passed before anyone noticed she was missing. They were both very small at the time. Evelyn eventually found her wandering the landing wearing only one shoe, her face red and glazed with tears and snot. She held her little white sock balled up in one fist. On her bare foot, a single pink welt that blinked in time with her pulse.

What happened? Evelyn asked, but her sister just cried and shuddered.

Evelyn took her hand and led her downstairs to look for Mama. There was a party going on in the drawing room. Guests drifting quietly and stiffly through the vast space like souls in some dark limbo. A stale smell of wine and old-fashioned perfume. Beyond the bay window dozens of cars were pulled up in rows and glinting in the house's floodlights.

She could see her father in the center of the room, lit dimly by the chandelier. He was talking seriously with a woman who was not their mother, and Evelyn knew better than to interrupt. A few of the guests noticed her and her sister, but they only scowled or smiled encouragingly.

Mama was in the kitchen, perched on a stool and wearing a thick woolen jumper over her evening wear. She was gossiping with the staff and eating canapés from a tray that had come back half finished. When she saw Lily, she leaped up and pulled them both to her.

Oh, love, she said. Little love. What happened?

It's her foot, said Evelyn.

Let's see. Oh, Lils. Did something sting you?

Lily nodded.

What was it?

Lily just shook her head.

She was in the attic, said Evelyn.

Why?

We were hiding.

Hiding from what?

Each other.

Where's your father?

Upstairs.

Their mother paused and then took Lily and lifted her up onto the work surface, Lily's skinny legs dangling over the edge. She went to the other side of the kitchen and rummaged in a wicker basket and came back holding a bulb of garlic. She plucked out a clove and crushed it with the flat of a knife and peeled away the skin. She began to rub it into the sting.

Here, she said. My mummy used to use this. Good as anything from a tube.

Their father appeared in the door to the kitchen. His body seemed almost too large for it, as if he might end up wedged in the frame if he tried to come through. A teenager with a tray of champagne flutes took a step back and imperceptibly bowed.

Oh dear, their father said. Have you been in the wars, Lily-bear?

She was in the attic, said Mama.

Well. That was very intrepid of you.

There are wasps' nests up there. They're there all year-round now.

There was a general pause in the kitchen.

They got you, did they?

Yes, said their mother, straightening up. They got her.

Bad luck.

Weren't you watching them?

No, their father said.

Why not?

I was in the drawing room.

Yes, and they were meant to be in the drawing room with you.

I can't watch them and talk to the guests all at the same time.

The room seemed to darken and contract somehow. The staff slowed in their tasks to listen.

Yes, of course, their mother said. Heaven forbid you neglect your guests.

She snatched her glass by the stem, and the wine slopped over the rim and onto the work surface. She pushed past him to the back door. Their father looked at her and then at the rest of the staff. They became conspicuously busy. He turned back to Evelyn and Lily, rolled his eyes, and gave a smile that disappeared very quickly.

Mummy's a bit squiffy, I think. How's the old foot?

Lily peered at it and wiggled her toes.

Hope you swatted the little bugger. What's that you've rubbed on it?

Lily held out her hand to show him the crushed garlic clove.

Golly. I'm not sure that'll make you any friends smelling like that. Come on, Lily-bear, I'm sure we've got a cream somewhere.

He lifted her off the work surface and hefted her onto his shoulders. She started laughing as he carried her out of the kitchen. Evelyn watched them go and then turned to look out the opposite door, where their mother was standing on the gravel, holding one elbow to herself, her wineglass raised to the moonlight. The evening air was very warm and carried with it scents of jasmine and thyme from the herb garden. Evelyn sat for a few moments and listened to the gleeful muttering of the kitchen staff and then went to join her. They stood in silence for some time.

That man, said her mother eventually, not to Evelyn but to the world at large. At the time Evelyn did not even realize which man she meant.

4

 By now there were only four or five places where Lily liked to hide. She was too old and too stiff to get into the tighter spots she had once favored. Evelyn still tried to take her time, though, knowing that her sister would be disappointed if the game was over too quickly.

She set off up the lawn and looked in the toolshed and in the backseat of the ruined car. She looked around the sunroom. She looked in the stand of silver birch trees behind it, Lily's figurines spinning slowly on their filaments and glistening blackly with the bodies of ants. She looked in the icehouse, even though she knew Lily was as frightened of this as she was of the bees and had never hidden there in her life. It was better to be sure.

She rounded the west wing to the back of the house. Here

the garden was wilder. Lily thought of it as her domain, but it was really Evelyn's, like everything else was, and the wildness only persisted because Evelyn allowed it to. Here there were older and taller trees, and the grass was longer and scattered with wildflowers that even their mother had not found the names for. It was divided by a narrow black lake, the gazebo standing slanted on an island in the middle and connected to the bank by a wooden bridge. Lily once said she'd seen something that looked like an eel in those dark waters, a monster ten feet long with yellow eyes like dinner plates, and Evelyn had never been able to tell if her sister was joking or not.

She skirted the edge of the lake and searched the grotto and the rock garden. Nothing. She searched the pampas grass and found broken stems and feathery heads trodden in the dirt. She hollered her sister's name and said, "Found you!"—as if by saying it she could make it so—but Lily did not appear.

Evelyn made another lap of the lake, then crossed the bridge to the gazebo and sat on the little bench. The boards were scuffed and dented from Lily's heels. A few stray sequins were scattered there, along with a pile of discarded dresses and leotards and one inexplicable fur coat. The garden felt very quiet. In the silence she caught a glimpse of what it might be like to live there alone, and she shivered in her bones.

Something fluttered in one of the windows of the house and she looked up. She could not be sure where she had seen it. She surveyed the west wing, east wing, attic, chapel, sunroom. The house spanned the horizon like a mountain range, vast and silent. A stately home, Mama had sometimes called it, though there was nothing stately about it these days. There was hardly a square foot of brickwork that was not concealed by ivy and roses and clematis, so that now the house was more a feature of the garden than the other way around. Her mother had always wanted it that way. Would happily have seen it consumed entirely, Evelyn thought.

She saw it again. Something moving between the branches that covered one of the third-floor windows. A flicker of daylight, off and on again, as though someone were pacing around behind the window frame.

Relief was quickly overlaid with panic. How had Lily even got up there? Everywhere was locked or boarded up and always had been. Their mother forbade them from even thinking about exploring the countless halls and rooms that made up the rest of the house. There were black and poisonous things in there that were best left undisturbed. Admittedly it was only Evelyn who still followed Mama's instructions to the letter, but even Lily had never shown an inclination to go beyond the bounds of the kitchen.

Evelyn went quickly back to the kitchen, hitching her belt up around her hips. Her ankles rattled and chafed in the Wellington boots. She shooed the chickens on her way and came inside without wiping her feet.

"Lily?" she called.

The house answered with a distant, almost inaudible creak. How could Lily have been so stupid? Had she forgotten how dangerous it was? Ever the wayward little sister. Sometimes Evelyn thought that the handful of years between them, rather than dwindling to insignificance, yawned ever wider as they got older.

"Lily, please! Come out here right now!"

Again, there was no answer. She went into the depths of the kitchen and found the wardrobe squarely in front of the inner door, as it always had been. There was no other way into the rest of the house unless Lily had somehow climbed through a window from the outside. Evelyn stumbled back toward the light, calling her sister's name, and when she reached the doorstep, Lily leaped out in front of her.

"Boo!" she said.

Evelyn gripped her sister's shoulders and pulled her into the kitchen. There were leaves in her hair and mud on her knees.

"Where have you been?"

"Ouch! You're hurting me!"

"You stupid girl!"

"It was just a joke! For goodness' sake, Evie, what's got into you?"

"Have you been up in the house?"

"When?"

"Just now."

"No."

"You weren't hiding behind one of the windows?"

"Of course not!"

"Then where were you?"

Lily looked proud of herself. "I moved around. I heard you coming and I *moved*. I was in the front garden, in the orchard, all this time."

Evelyn went back to the inner door and listened at the wardrobe but heard nothing.

"Wasn't that clever of me?" said Lily.

Evelyn ignored her and went back outside, around the green wreck of the car and beyond the chicken coops, and looked up at the window she'd watched from the gazebo. Lily followed a few feet behind, talking all the way.

"What is all this hollering about, Evie?"

"I saw something," said Evelyn. She pointed at the window. "In there."

Lily laughed. "And you thought it was me?"

"Yes."

"Why?"

"Who else would it be?"

"Any number of pigeons, for starters."

"It was bigger than a bird."

Was it, though? Evelyn struggled to remember exactly what it had looked like, why it had struck such panic in her.

"Some of those pigeons are very fat fellows. They eat more of our vegetables than we do."

"It moved across like this." She waved her arms stiffly to demonstrate.

"Must have been a branch. Or the reflection of a branch. That's the window that's still got some glass, isn't it?"

"It was inside, though."

"Are you sure?"

Evelyn wasn't. She shook her head. She felt suddenly very tired, as if she and her old shirt were made of the same damp and flimsy material.

"Well," said Lily. "It wasn't me."

A moment passed before Evelyn replied: "I know. Of course it wasn't."

"But don't give me any ideas."

"What? No, Lily, you can't!"

"Oh, take a joke, Evie!"

Lily laughed and put a warm hand to Evelyn's cheek. Evelyn shivered. She looked at the window again. Maybe this was how it started. Maybe she was going to go the way of their mama, seeing and hearing things that weren't there, until she was no longer in the world at all. Poor Lily would have to care for her, as they'd had to care for their mother. She would have to care for the garden, too. And if she couldn't? If she wouldn't?

"Another round, then?" said Lily.

Evelyn looked back at her and blinked. "What?"

"You can hide this time."

"I don't want to hide. I want to get back to work."

"But we barely played at all! And you didn't even find me."

"No."

"Please?"

Evelyn took a deep breath and tried to smile. "You're a mithering little thing," she said, fixing a loose strand from Lily's enormous bun. "And you need a haircut."

"Never!"

"You'll have pigeons nesting in *there* if you're not careful."

Lily swatted her hand away. "Stop it. Come on, then. One more game."

"Not today. I've got work to do. And you owe me some watering."

"Well. You're no fun at all." Lily removed the paintbrush that she had used to pin her hair, and it tumbled down her back and shoulders. "Show me, then."

They linked arms and walked over the lawn. Evelyn took a last look at the window. There was nothing there, though she wondered, for the first time in an age, what might have been left inside the house when they abandoned it. What might have grown there in their absence.

5

They spent the rest of the afternoon lugging water from the lake to the vegetable beds. Evelyn carried the big plastic bucket, though these days she was only able to lift it when it was half full, while Lily insisted on using their mother's old tin watering can. "Such a pleasing object," she said, every time she brought it out of the shed, caressing its dented sides. Lily used it like a theatrical prop, the watering itself another kind of performance. She tended to each seedling slowly and deliberately, visibly delighted to see the water sparkling from the spout each time she tipped the can.

When their work was done, they leaned against each other and staggered back toward the kitchen. The sky glowed like a furnace behind the battlements. Evelyn glanced up at the top floor again, but on this side of the house the windows were completely covered with foliage and there was nothing to see. The bats emerged from under the eaves and snickered around their ears.

"Good evening, everyone," said Lily. "Gnats for dinner tonight. Gobble gobble gobble."

She stopped to watch them dance in the twilight, but Evelyn went inside. She slumped at the kitchen table and wound up the lamp and stared at the halo it cast on the ceiling while she waited for her sister. Lurking behind her worries about the window and the beehive was the other, larger worry, which was there every night: she was completely exhausted. There was a time when she could have done all the watering herself and still had energy left for sewing, or fixing and sharpening their tools, or collecting water for the next morning. She could feel herself running down like a clock from day to day.

Lily went on chatting happily to the bats. She obviously did not share Evelyn's worries. But then Lily simply wasn't a worrier—because she was the little sister; because she did not know the things that Evelyn knew, and had not seen the things that she had seen.

Eventually Lily came back whistling and collapsed opposite Evelyn. She laughed, amused at her own decrepitude. They sat and caught their breath in silence.

"Eggs for supper?" Lily said

"I'm surprised you have the energy to cook after all that work."

"You're making fun of me."

"I'm not! You watered half the garden while I was sloshing around with that bucket."

Lily considered this and nodded. "I think," she said, "I am getting stronger. It's all my practicing, I suppose. You should see my arabesque, Sissie! I have to hitch my skirts up, and it looks quite obscene, but I'm nearly as good as I used to be."

"I wish you *would* let me see it."

"As I said. It's not quite ready."

Lily had never been quite ready. Not in years and years. The rehearsals had started when she'd found a bronze figurine of a dancer half buried in the grotto behind the lake. They were old even then. Lily had claimed, suddenly, that she had always wanted to be a dancer. That Mama had given her lessons once upon a time, and a strange, stiff skirt that looked like a water lily. There were special shoes, too. Evelyn had thought it all very suspect, particularly Lily's description of the costume, but her sister had not let the idea go. Before long Lily was remembering the steps and going out to the gazebo to practice in secret.

Evelyn suspected she would never see "the routine," as Lily called it. Wondered, in fact, if she had ever been the intended audience.

"Eggs, then?"

Evelyn looked up. "Yes," she said. "Lovely."

"And soldiers?"

"But of course."

Lily gave a military salute, then took the lamp and went back to the stove. She began hacking at one of their plump, round loaves.

Evelyn rose from the table and went to the kitchen window and stood staring out at the garden. In the dregs of the daylight things became unclear. She found shapes and figures in the bushes that fringed the lawn, slender arms and legs in the branches of the camellias and the rhododendrons. She saw small, pale faces in their flowers, rising and falling in the breeze like something patiently breathing.

"You forgot to talk to Mama about the almanac," Lily said.

Evelyn jumped at the sound of her voice. "What's that?" she said, though she had heard very well.

"The almanac. You were going to ask Mama if you could change it."

"Oh, yes," she said. "Well. There's always tomorrow."

"Tomorrow and tomorrow and tomorrow," said Lily, affecting a strange baritone that Evelyn did not understand.

"I'll ask," said Evelyn. "I won't forget."

"Tell me," said Lily, "what does the almanac say about apples?"

"Why? What about them?"

"Well, I saw them all while you were making a pig's ear of finding my hiding place. We haven't picked any for months, and the wasps are having a field day out there."

Evelyn paused a moment. According to the almanac, the apples should not be picked until the next new moon.

She opened her mouth, but Lily interrupted.

"You see?" Lily said. "The thing's useless. No point sticking to the rules if we're just going to end up with piles and piles of rotten fruit."

Evelyn conceded the point with difficulty. "I suppose so," she said.

"So then. We should pick them tomorrow."

"If there is time."

"There will be time. If we do, I solemnly swear I shall make us a pie."

Evelyn brightened a little. At the thought of the pie, at the thought of her sister trying to cheer her up. "That's a lovely idea."

"We can devour it in bed tomorrow night. I'm going to eat it with my hands, and you're not allowed to tell me off because I'm the one making it."

Evelyn smiled. She watched her sister place the eggs carefully in the saucepan with a teaspoon and listened to them click and roll in the boiling water. She turned briefly back to the window, but even in those few moments the last of the light had been leached from the lawn and there was nothing to see but her own reflection.

"Very well," she said. "But if we're picking apples early, then we're wassailing, too."

Lily let the spoon drop beside the pan. "Do we have to?"

"Of course. You're the one who suggested the pie."

"I feel like I spend half my life talking to those trees."

"With good reason!"

Lily grumbled and went back to poking at the eggs. A minute later she carried them over, still steaming, in two chipped eggcups, and put one in front of Evelyn. She went back and brought two plates of bread cut into fingers. On Evelyn's plate were also the crusts that Lily wouldn't eat. Evelyn tapped the top of her egg with the spoon and picked off the shell. The yolk was as thick and as bright as yellow oil paint. She lowered her nose to smell it as Lily decisively sliced the top off her egg with a knife.

"Oh no," she said.

Evelyn looked up.

"Oh dear," said Lily.

"What is it?"

"Did you not candle these?"

Evelyn had not. Why had she not? Another thing she had forgotten. Though there had been no need for many, many months.

She came around to the other side of the table and brought the lamp closer. Nestled in the opaque jelly of the egg was the beginnings of a chick, tiny and pink, with one huge, misted eye that stared up at them.

"It must have been in the straw for days. I must have missed it."

"It happens."

"I don't know how I didn't notice."

"Don't worry, Evie."

There was a long silence. Evelyn looked at the aborted bird and felt a loss far deeper than such a small creature seemed to merit. Her heart shrank a little.

"We've been waiting for so long for another chick," Evelyn said.

"I know."

"I bet the chickens have as well." She sighed. Lily squeezed her shoulder.

"But gives us hope for the future, though, doesn't it? If there's one, there'll be more."

Evelyn nodded, though she couldn't think of it as anything other than a black omen.

"What do we do with it?" said Lily.

"It's special," said Evelyn. "It's a special thing. We should bury it near the wall."

"Yes," said Lily. "Good idea." She got up and went to the coat hooks, but Evelyn just sat and looked at her.

"Now?" she said.

"Yes. Why not?"

In the circumstances Evelyn found the idea of crossing the lawn or going anywhere near the wall unthinkable.

"Because it's suppertime. And soon it will be bedtime."

"But we can't keep it in the kitchen. I don't want to sleep in the same room as it."

Evelyn didn't either. She got up and found a tea towel and laid it over the eggcup, as if this afforded the unborn thing some kind of dignity. Then she went and unbolted the back door and, without looking into the garden, placed it carefully on the step and closed the door behind her.

"We'll bury it first thing tomorrow," she said, sliding the cold remains of her own egg between the two of them.

They went to bed with their stomachs rumbling. Evelyn nestled down beside her sister and turned out the lamp. They lay together, twitching and rustling and sighing. Lily reached over and turned the lamp back on.

"I don't feel like sleeping yet."

"Neither do I," said Evelyn.

"Thinking about that poor chick."

"Yes," said Evelyn, though she was thinking about a good deal more.

They sat a little longer in silence.

"What about a bit of the book?"

"Yes, why not."

Evelyn dug under the pillow, found the bundle of pages, and untied the garden twine that held them together. The book had once had a cover, but that was gone now and the paper had curled into a fragile, yellowing scroll. Their sacred text. Evelyn paused.

"Well?" said Lily.

"I'm thinking of where to start," Evelyn said.

"Start at the beginning. I can't remember where we got to."

"All right."

Evelyn carefully peeled back the first page. It trembled, though she thought her hand was perfectly still. She cleared her throat.

"*There is no one left . . .*" she began, and Lily pressed herself a little closer against her sister's side.

6

Evelyn dreamed of the egg in the small hours of the morning. She could hear the chick stirring in its shell from where she lay on the kitchen floor. A sticky sound like dry lips opening and closing. She got up and found the chick rolling about on the back step, oaring the air feebly with its tiny featherless wings. She fed it Lily's unwanted crusts and gave it a saucer of milk, though somewhere in her waking mind she knew the pair of them had not had any milk since they were children. The chick quickly grew to be enormous, though it remained pink and veiny, its head too big for its body, its feathers sparse and matted. Its beak gaped, but Evelyn didn't know what it was asking for. As it grew, it began to move quickly and erratically, and it became demanding, nipping violently at Evelyn's feet and hands and chest, and she felt a sharp pain and then was awake without realizing, a hand at her heart, the light gray at the kitchen window.

She got up and retrieved the almanac and studied the map that spanned the first dozen pages. The line that marked the old wall of the estate was heavily penciled where they had buried previous omens and prodigies, so many crosses and lines it looked like a suture inexpertly stitched around the edges of the garden. There was a little space along the east side, she saw, a patch of undisturbed ground beyond the beehives and the lilac and the laburnum where they might lay the egg to rest.

She shook her sister gently.

"Are you coming?"

Lily muttered something inaudible and pulled the blanket over her head.

"I can do it by myself if you want."

Her sister flung back the blanket, sighed, and stretched. She had slept in two of their mother's summer dresses, one on top of the other, and a pair of misshapen leggings that sloughed at her knees and ankles.

"I'm coming," she said.

"I think you should wear something more practical than that," said Evelyn.

"Yes, yes," said Lily.

"And the glasses."

"If you insist."

"I do."

Evelyn kissed the crown of her sister's head and went back to the dresser. In the smaller drawer next to the one where the almanac was kept there were three pairs of sunglasses. Evelyn took out a pair with tortoiseshell frames and another in luminous yellow plastic and put both in the pocket of her apron.

Even if you weren't planning on looking over the wall, it was a good idea to wear them, in case you accidentally saw something while you were working. The land outside was so dry and so bright it could blind you at a glance, Mama had said. It was not a claim either of them had ever wanted to put to the test.

Lily wriggled out of the two floral dresses and made a small pirouette, searching for something else to wear. Evelyn looked at her sister's body. Lily was slighter than Evelyn and had lost whatever sinewy hardness she'd had when their mother had put them to work. Her hair was long enough to reach the small of her back, and she stood like some aged nymph in the pool of her clothes. A beautiful thing, for all her folds and wrinkles. Evelyn thought herself a twisted old root beside her sister, and always had. Her hair cut back to a few scant inches, as short as she could get it with the shears. "Tough as old boots," their mama said. She had meant it as a compliment.

Lily stepped into some filthy dungarees and pulled them up over her shoulders.

"Ready?" Evelyn said.

"Ready."

Evelyn opened the back door and found the egg lying unmolested under its tea towel. She handed it to Lily while she went to fetch the spade, and then the two of them set out together toward the eastern side of the garden. The morning was chilly and hushed. A low mist over everything, as if a levee had broken somewhere and the garden had been flooded up to their ankles.

When they got to the lilac bed the sun came up very suddenly, as if rising from behind the wall itself, rather than the distant and unseen horizon. It shone upon a litter of broken stones, seemed to single them out for illumination, bright and harsh.

The wall was broken. Where it had once stood at head height, there was now only a yawning space and beyond it the blank and dead vista of the world outside. Evelyn's heart convulsed and she turned away quickly and fumbled in her pocket for the sunglasses. She held out Lily's pair.

"Did you see it?"

"See what?"

"Outside."

"I don't think so."

"You don't think so?"

"I think I closed my eyes in time."

Evelyn took a couple of breaths and then turned back slowly, her eyes fixed on the ground. She crouched and rubbed a hand over one of the fallen stones, and the ancient cement turned to dust on her fingertips. She felt the contours of the wall itself. There was an irregular V-shaped gap, and at its lowest point the wall was only about a foot high.

"How long has it been like this?" said Evelyn, and found her voice quieter than expected.

"I don't know," said Lily.

"What do you think happened?"

"Your guess is as good as mine. It's a very old wall. I'm surprised it lasted this long."

Evelyn looked at Lily. Unconcerned as ever. And wasn't that Evelyn's own doing? Keeping her sister in the dark as she had done; or rather, keeping her from the dark.

She sheltered where the wall was unbroken, her back to the stones, a hand to her sternum, as if to calm the wildness beneath. The wall had stood as long as the house. She'd never known any part of it to fall down, not since the storm.

Evelyn looked over at her sister and found her studying the loose stones.

"No need to get your knickers in a twist," Lily said. "These aren't so big. I'm sure it won't be difficult to put them all back. Two big strong girls like us."

Evelyn took another few breaths. "What if it's too late, though?"

"Too late for what? We've only just woken up."

"No, I mean what if something got in?"

Lily looked at her, eyes hidden behind the sunglasses. They were slightly too small for her face, and the arms bent outward to accommodate her skull. It was hard to read her expression.

"Got in?"

"Yes."

"Like what?"

"I don't know. Something from outside."

A pause. "There isn't anything outside, Evie."

"The beehive, though."

"I thought we decided you'd moved the beehive."

"Yes, we did."

"Well then."

"And the window."

"The window?" Lily frowned.

"When you were playing hide-and-seek," Evelyn reminded her. She thought again of the apparitions she'd seen in the bushes as she'd stared out the kitchen window.

"Come here," said Lily. She held Evelyn's hand. "What's got into you, Evelyn? Silly thing. How long have you spent trying to tell me there's nothing out there, and now you sound just like Mama! Monsters over the wall, monsters under the bed. Good thing I'm a big, brave girl these days or I might start to believe you."

She laughed.

Evelyn sat down, her body clutched like the husk of a spider. She did not care for the slight against their mother, nor for the suggestion that she was the one behaving like a child. Lily was only so blithely confident in their safety and their solitude because Evelyn had let her be so. The knowledge was just another burden she bore alone, as the elder sister. A memory so distant as to barely exist, but Evelyn had seen and smelled and tasted—yes, had she not tasted it?—what lurked beyond the boundaries of the garden, and she knew that their mama's monsters were quite real.

"You're right, we should try and put the stones back," she said.

"After lunch."

"Now."

"Heaven's sake, Sissie."

"I think we should be sensible about this."

Lily looked at her a moment and then levered herself to her feet. "Chop-chop, then," she said. "Otherwise we'll be overrun!"

Evelyn did not laugh at the joke.

The sun passed overhead and they worked through most of the day to put the wall back together, eyes always turned away from the outside world. Despite Lily's optimism, the stones were too heavy for them to lift by themselves. They strained on each one together, groaning and abandoning them when their muscles protested—Evelyn's back, Lily's fingers. They fitted them into place as best they could, though they couldn't work out the original order exactly. Even with their skin toughened from gardening, their hands bled.

The shadows in the garden were long by the time they finished. Lily massaged her forearms and admired their work. She wiped the sweat from her brow and looked very tired but was too proud to admit it. Evelyn stared at her raw fingers and began to worry anew. The whole day gone and she hadn't even started the tasks she was meant to be doing, or those that were left over from the previous day.

When she looked up she saw Lily had gone to the wall and was poking a long finger into the holes where the stones were not quite flush. Then she watched in disbelief as her little sister bent her knees slightly and put her face to a chink and spied through it.

"Lily! What are you doing?"

"I'm wearing the glasses, aren't I?"

"You still shouldn't look."

"It's awfully empty out there. If I were a monster, I'd want to be in here, too."

Lily did not turn around, but Evelyn saw the twitch in her jaw and knew that she was smiling.

"Have a look, Evie. It'll make you feel better."

"Don't be ridiculous."

"Just quickly."

Evelyn pulled her away. "Stop it!" she said. "And stop making jokes about things outside."

They stared at each other. Lily shrugged and one of the straps of her dungarees slipped from her shoulder.

Evelyn held out a hand. "Come on," she said.

"What?" said Lily.

"The bird," said Evelyn.

They dug a hole, and Evelyn unrolled the egg from its funeral shroud and planted it upright, as if it might sprout whenever spring reached that corner of the garden. Lily said a prayer, its words practically meaningless these days, before they piled the soil on top and patted it down. Evelyn stayed on all fours long after the service had finished, warm palms to the cooling earth, thinking, always thinking.

A Ritual

The soil she'd been digging in already had a hot, dry crust. A miniature desert with the apple tree quivering at its center no taller than Evelyn herself. She went about watering the sapling with her little plastic watering can. It had a face drawn on it so that the spout looked like a long nose. She stood up and held the watering can in both hands and watched the dark patches around the roots disappearing before her eyes.

She heard the sound of her father hammering at something on the far side of the house.

Mama came down from the other end of the new orchard, through the knuckled ranks of young apple trees that seemed already shrunken in the heat. The sun was directly overhead, and neither she nor the trees cast any shadows at all.

Well done, Evie, Mama said. They look happier in the ground than in the pots, don't they?

I've only done one, said Evelyn.

That's one more than none. You're making a darn sight more progress than your sister.

Evelyn saw Lily twirling around in the center of the lawn with an unwound ball of garden twine. She leaped and spun and threw the string into spirals and figures of eight, singing her accompaniment.

Come on, Lily, said their mother. Make yourself useful, please.

Lily looked at her for a moment and then carried on prancing. The lawn a vast green sea and Lily tiny and floundering in the middle of it. Behind her a dozen more men and women on their knees or leaning on forks and shovels. More down by the greenhouse. A figure pushed a wheelbarrow laden with bulbs across the lawn and had to steer erratically to avoid Lily's performance.

How long are they going to be here? asked Evelyn.

I don't know. As long as they want. Till things get better.

I wish they weren't here.

Her mother frowned.

Come on, Evie, don't say that. I had enough trouble convincing your father.

Don't they have their own houses?

They did, but they had to leave them.

Why?

Lots of reasons. But sometimes it's better when people live and work together, instead of struggling on their own.

Are they going to eat all our food?

It's everyone's food, Evie. That's the point. Don't you like having a few more people around? We could invite some of your friends from school.

Maybe.

What?

They'll make fun of me for being posh.

Her mother frowned. Is that what they say?

Evelyn nodded.

Are they unkind to you?

Sometimes.

What do they say?

They make fun of Papa. They make fun of me calling him Papa. They think we're in the royal family.

Her mother looked sad for a moment. She pulled Evelyn to her waist and kissed the top of her head.

Nobody can help the life they've been given. They just do their best with it. That's why this is the right thing to do. We should have done it years ago. Not everybody is as lucky as we are. All this land and this big old house. We can't just keep it all to ourselves, can we?

Evelyn shrugged.

Her mother took a handkerchief from the pocket of her dungarees and used it to wipe the sweat from Evelyn's forehead.

Thirsty work, isn't it? Whoops. You've got mud all over you now. Do you want a drink?

Evelyn nodded.

They started back to the house, the other gardeners' backs rising and falling on either side of them. They were all wearing shorts and T-shirts, some of the men bare-chested. A sweltering day under the sun, and spring barely even started. The man with the wheelbarrow had stopped beside Lily and was trying to start a conversation, but Lily was mostly ignoring him. He was older than the others. His hair was gray and thinning, and he wore a thick plaid shirt that was darkening under the armpits.

Lily, don't be rude, said their mother.

I was just saying, said the older man, we should get her wassailing. Been watching her twirling around like a dervish. About the right time of year, I think.

Evelyn did not understand what he meant.

What do you think, Lils? their mother said. Do you think you'd make a good wassailing queen?

Lily finally stopped dancing.

What's that? What's the wassailing queen?

Oh gosh, said Mama. Well, I think Jamie knows more about it than me.

You've got to wake up the apple trees, the older man said. Give them a bit of a song and a dance. Give them something to eat and drink. And in a few years' time we'll be up to our necks in cider and applesauce.

Lily looked at them all mutely.

It's just a bit of fun, the man said. I did it when I was about your age.

Can I do it, too? said Evelyn. She thought that the more people there were to sing, the more quickly and readily the apples would come. A few years seemed too long to wait.

How's your singing voice? said the man.

Evelyn clutched her mother's leg and didn't reply.

She's a bit more on the shy side, her mother said.

THEY GATHERED *in the orchard in the evening when the air was cooler. The guests and the gardeners and a few of the staff who still worked inside the house. Their father was there, too. Evelyn thought it was not really his sort of thing, but then he was also seduced by any kind of ritual. Everyone carried pots and pans and jugs, and they whooped and banged around the trees. Her father carried a bass drum on a leather strap, the skin of it yellowed and cracking. Evelyn had no idea where he'd got it from. There were so many of these ancient treasures in the house.*

At the end they lifted Lily up onto their shoulders and she sang a song that the older man had taught her. Everybody laughed and applauded. Her mother and father smiling so broadly. Evelyn was glad to see it, remembered their faces that way for a long time afterward, but at the same time she could not shake a feeling of discomfort as she looked around the group. Why are they all laughing? she thought. Why aren't they taking it seriously?

7

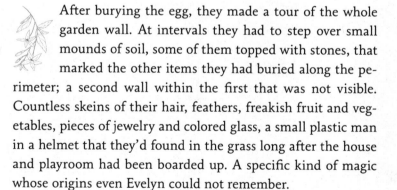

After burying the egg, they made a tour of the whole garden wall. At intervals they had to step over small mounds of soil, some of them topped with stones, that marked the other items they had buried along the perimeter; a second wall within the first that was not visible. Countless skeins of their hair, feathers, freakish fruit and vegetables, pieces of jewelry and colored glass, a small plastic man in a helmet that they'd found in the grass long after the house and playroom had been boarded up. A specific kind of magic whose origins even Evelyn could not remember.

When they were satisfied that both walls, real and imagined, were intact and that the garden was safe, they returned to the kitchen. Evelyn stood on the back step and removed her sunglasses. The sky overhead was the color of a ripe peach.

"I'm sorry, Lily," she said.

Lily looked surprised. "What for?"

"I don't know why I'm worrying so much," said Evelyn, though she knew well enough that walls did not fall down by themselves.

"I don't know either, Sissie," said Lily. "I don't know what's come over you."

"You wanted to practice your routine and now it's nearly suppertime."

"We've got an hour or so, I think."

"We're meant to be wassailing."

"Can't we give it a miss?"

"No, Lily. Please. I'd feel much better if we did things properly. What's the point of wassailing after we've picked the apples?"

Lily looked dejected but did her best to hide it. They were silent for a moment.

"I'm sorry," said Evelyn again.

Lily raised her eyebrows and wagged a finger at her. "Come on, Evie," she said. "Since when did we start using that word?"

Evelyn nodded. Lily was right to upbraid her, as strange as it felt. Neither of them had apologized about anything for many years. Attendant on apologies were fault and guilt and shame, and they had both made an unspoken agreement, a long time ago, that those things were their mother's and did not belong in the garden, not anymore.

"Come on, then," she said. "Let's give those trees a good talking-to."

Lily stuck a few spoons and spatulas in one pocket of her dungarees and a slice of bread in the other, then gathered up their two saucepans in her arms. Evelyn went to the store cupboard and took out two bottles of cider.

They made their way over the lawn and began their clamoring even before they had reached the edge of the orchard. They banged a saucepan each, Evelyn with a wooden spoon and Lily with a ladle, hollering and hooting as they passed beneath the branches. Evelyn found herself making more noise than usual. There was something frantic in her chanting, as if for the first time she really believed there might be some evil spirit that needed expelling.

After several rounds they met again at the largest of the apple trees. The same one Evelyn herself had planted, unless her memory failed her. Lily looked on despondently as Evelyn poured one of the bottles of cider around the roots, and then half of the other bottle into a saucepan.

"What a waste."

"Don't say that!"

"Why not?"

"They'll hear you and they'll turn the apples sour and rotten and there'll be no pie for anyone." Evelyn clicked her fingers. "Bread, please. You go and get the ladder."

Lily handed her a slice of bread, and Evelyn soaked it in the saucepan of cider while her sister went back to the shed. She was gone a long time. The shade in the orchard deepened, and Evelyn did not care to look up from the roots into the twilight that shifted among the trunks. She had never been a particularly imaginative child—certainly not as imaginative as Lily—but now, after all that had happened, her visions were rich and darkly colorful. A bird crashed and twittered among the leaves and the sound of it left her breathless.

When Lily returned, she was staggering slightly under the ladder's weight. Evelyn was relieved but did not say so. She took the ladder from her sister and stood it unsteadily between the thickest branches. Lily shook it slightly. She made a funny face at Evelyn, to disguise a genuine worry, Evelyn suspected. Too old to be climbing trees, both of them, and the ladder itself as rickety as they were.

Lily took the soaked bread and went up. The rungs creaked under her weight. Evelyn planted her feet and grasped the ladder's splintered sides, strained to keep it upright. At the top Lily reached up and placed the bread in the crook of two branches, then began to look for another she could sit and sing from.

Evelyn stiffened suddenly. As if her body had heard something before her ears had. She listened above and beyond her sister's protestations. Something lumbering among the trees. Bigger than a bird this time. She heard it twice and then heard nothing.

"Pay attention, Sissie," said Lily.

She heard it again. Evelyn glanced behind her and found herself looking at an absence. A dull imprint in the darkness, the echo of something that had recently slipped out of sight. She couldn't say if it was an animal or something else, if it had gone on four legs or two, if it had legs at all. She stared down the tunnel of hydrangeas toward the lawn, wanting and not wanting to see the thing again. Her eyes throbbed in time with her heart.

"What is that?" she said.

"What is what?" said Lily.

Evelyn let go of the ladder completely and turned around.

"Hold the bloody ladder!" cried Lily, but the thing was already wobbling, and by the time Evelyn had got her hands on it again it had tipped completely to one side and Lily was left hanging over the branch like a wet towel.

It was a moment or two before Evelyn turned from the darkness and went to help. She maneuvered herself beneath her sister and grasped at her calves, the skin papery and softly ridged with veins.

"I've got you, Lily," Evelyn said, though she knew she could hardly support Lily's weight if she fell. She could hardly support herself.

Lily gasped but said nothing.

"Can you get your legs a little lower?"

"I'm trying."

"Let yourself down gently."

"I said I'm *trying*."

Lily slithered backward until Evelyn was able to grasp her around her thighs; then she let go completely, and Evelyn yelped as the two of them fell entangled into the long grass. They lay there panting. Evelyn did not want to move, for fear she had broken an arm or a hip. For fear of what might be waiting in among the trees and the bushes, waiting to fasten upon her like carrion. Lily sat up first.

"What on earth happened?" she said. "Why did you let go?"

Evelyn rolled onto her front and then got to her knees but no further. "I'm sorry."

"Sissie! That word again. What was it?"

"I thought I saw something."

Lily sighed. Evelyn squinted at her and found a pitying expression on her face.

"What?" Evelyn asked.

"Nothing."

"Tell me, Lily. That face."

"It doesn't matter."

"It does. What are you thinking."

Evelyn waited.

"Well," said Lily after a moment, "you're not the first person to start seeing things that aren't there, are you?"

"Oh, please!"

Lily looked at Evelyn very seriously and then clutched her shoulders.

"I couldn't bear it, Sissie. If you started to go that way."

"I'm not going the way Mama went. Not yet, anyway."

But what if she was? That explanation was worse than the vision being real.

They extricated themselves from each other's limbs, and Evelyn bent her arms and fingers experimentally. She looked around the orchard and found it empty and still. They helped each other to their feet and groaned with the effort.

"Are you all right?" Evelyn asked her sister.

"I think so. You?"

"I'll survive. Come on. After all this nonsense we may as well get what we came for."

They left the ladder where it lay and went about picking the ripest apples and putting them in the front pocket of Evelyn's apron. They made their way quickly and wordlessly back to the kitchen. Evelyn was still trembling. Her mind conjured nightmare forms from the gloaming, and she cast her eyes down as they walked. Even here she thought she saw patches of grass that were flattened and smeared, though she couldn't say if it was their own footprints she was looking at, or if it was nothing at all.

AT THE EDGE of the lawn, the bright square of the kitchen door seemed to Evelyn like the refuge of a distant harbor. When they reached the kitchen table, the lamp set on top of it, Lily turned and gasped. Evelyn's whole body flushed and she spun around.

"What?" she said.

"You, Evie!" said Lily. She pointed at the pocket of Evelyn's apron, swollen with apples. "You're with child! At your age! A sign from God!"

Lily laughed, and Evelyn did, too, though it was more because she was relieved than because she found it funny. Lily pretended to be a midwife while Evelyn heaved the fruit onto the work surface, clutching her arm, telling her to push and breathe. The performance made Evelyn feel odd. She did not know where her sister had learned this act, or if it meant anything to her at all. It meant little to Evelyn herself. Like all of Lily's jokes, it had been hollowed out by repetition, but Evelyn heard in it the echo of something she half understood but was at pains not to understand any further.

They were not long making the apple pie. Evelyn chopped the apples she had recently birthed while Lily rolled the pastry and designed the lid: an apple with a worm poking out of one side. It was less intricate than it might once have been, but it still elevated the pie out of the ordinary. They put it in to bake, and while they waited they ate a supper of tomatoes and fat broad beans, and Lily gobbled up the leftover raw pastry. She

tried to teach Evelyn the harmony to a tune she'd been whistling, but Evelyn couldn't whistle, much less sing, and they had
a good laugh at this, too.

By the time the pie emerged from the oven, the evening
was as warm and convivial as any other and Evelyn was feeling
a good deal better. Lily stuck a finger in the apple pulp that had
oozed from under the lid, tasted it, proclaimed it a triumph.
The kitchen smelled heavenly. Lily brought over a knife from
the drawer and stood poised to cut into it. Evelyn swatted
her hand.

"Lily, behave! We can't eat it now. It'll be far too hot."

Lily pouted. "But it's nearly bedtime."

"Then we'll have to eat it tomorrow."

"After all that work? Go on, just a little bit."

"You'll burn yourself."

"I'm willing to suffer for my art."

Evelyn laughed again. She covered the whole pie tin with a
clean dishcloth and put it on the sideboard.

"Patience is a virtue," she said. "If it disappears overnight,
we'll know exactly who to blame."

8

It did disappear overnight.

When Evelyn woke, she went to check the tin and found the tea towel had been thrown to one side. A little of the juice had leaked from the bottom onto the work surface, and there were flecks of charred pastry scattered about. The tin itself was completely empty. She picked it up, turned it over, and then began to search the rest of the kitchen. She checked the cupboards, checked Lily's side of the bedding. Lily woke while she was rummaging through the blankets.

"What's got into you?" she said.

"What have you done with it?" said Evelyn.

"With what?"

"Don't play silly buggers."

"I don't know what you mean, Evie."

"The pie. Where've you hidden it?"

"I've not touched it!"

"You've hidden it, haven't you? Or maybe you haven't. I wouldn't be surprised if you'd scoffed the lot."

Lily laughed, but the sound of it died quickly. She got up and went over to the empty tin. She picked it up and popped out its base.

"I don't understand," Lily said. "Is this a joke, or are you trying to teach me a lesson?"

"Me?"

"You were up before me."

"Why would I want to teach you a lesson?"

"I don't know. Because you think I'm a greedy-guts."

They stared at each other for a moment.

"Well," said Evelyn, "if you don't show me where you've hidden it, then the ants will."

"Maybe the ants took it in the first place."

"Lifted it from the tin and carried it away? Clever ants."

"Or rats. Could be rats."

"We don't have rats."

"Of course we have rats."

She gestured vaguely at the ceiling, and Evelyn looked up, as if she might, at that moment, see the house swarming with vermin.

Lily went back to her bed and sat examining the cuts and grazes she'd received from the apple tree.

"Well. Let me know when you've finished doing whatever it is you're trying to do to me," she said. "I'm starving."

"Stop this, Lily."

"Stop what?"

"I'm serious."

Lily laughed. "I know, Sissie," she said. "That's always been your problem."

She licked the scratches on her forearm, and Evelyn went back to staring at the ceiling, not wanting to admit the other conclusion that lurked unspoken beneath their squabbling.

"I'm going to see Mama," she said at last.

"To dob me in?"

"No. To tell her about it. And about the wall. And everything else."

"I'm coming with you, then."

"You don't have to."

"I insist. I want to make sure you've got your story straight."

Their mother was buried to the west of the house, in a plot near their tiny patches of wheat and barley. A round stone marked the spot, like the stones in the wall, rough and etched with lichen. In front of the stone was a profusion of their mother's favorite flowers, transplanted from beds all around the garden: lupins, snapdragons, cornflowers, dog violets, pale colors that belonged in dreams. Lily had painted them once. Then a few years ago she had turned the canvas upside down and starting using it as a tray to carry tea and sandwiches.

It was another hot day, but the light was hazy and the sky seemed too low somehow. They were both still in their nightdresses, but Lily had decided to wear a beret, too, and her sweat was already beading beneath the headband. They were halfway to the grave when Lily said:

"I reckon we might get another storm soon."

Evelyn walked another few paces in silence before she replied: "Don't say things like that."

"Feels like it, though, doesn't it?" said Lily. "Dry heat. Maybe we'll just get a little one."

She stuck out her tongue and smacked her lips as though tasting the air.

"I hope not," said Evelyn.

"I wouldn't mind seeing one again. I mean, from afar. Like the last one. Jolly exciting, watching it racing along like that."

Evelyn knew Lily was trying to provoke her. She succeeded, too. It terrified her to remember it. A huge black mass seething along the horizon, as if some outer god were slowly rolling up the edge of the world. The storm had lasted a month. Lily had found the whole thing utterly captivating, and every evening had put on her sunglasses to watch the catastrophe unfold from behind the garden wall. They'd had a handful of dustings since, and each time Lily had seemed disappointed at how puny they'd been by comparison with the first storm. Evelyn hoped never to see anything like it again.

"Don't say that," she said.

"Say what?"

"You shouldn't wish for it. Even as a joke. It might just come racing in this direction, and we're hardly in the kind of shape to dig out this whole garden again."

Lily had a ready reply for this, but Evelyn chose not to listen and walked a little faster so that she was soon out of earshot. She arrived at their mother's grave first. Lily caught up and stood slightly behind her. They waited for a moment to compose themselves. Evelyn dabbed her brow. Lily removed her beret and held it before her. As if they were approaching an altar.

"Hello, Mama," Evelyn said eventually, and then could find no more words.

She wanted to tell her about the pie, the wall, the beehive, their troubled night of wassailing, but to state all these things out loud, all at once, seemed too troubling an admission. Evelyn herself would not be able to bear it, let alone her mother. And then there was Lily. If they really were no longer alone in the garden, her little sister would need to understand what that meant. Things would have to be explained to her that Evelyn had hoped never to explain. The facts of life, decades too late.

"I just wanted to say a few things," she said, then stopped again.

A bumblebee went about its business. The sisters watched it in silence, as though it might be eavesdropping. Their mother's flowers bowed their heads under its weight, and then it droned on its way.

"Listen, Mama," Lily said quickly, "Evelyn's going to tell you a whole lot of nonsense about how I stole an apple pie, but it has nothing to do with me and I'm sure I don't know why she is being such a *horror*."

Evelyn turned and looked at her and then turned back to the grave. "I was going to say no such thing."

"I think she's trying to punish me for something, but goodness knows what."

"Of course I'm not punishing you. I've never punished you for anything. More fool me."

"I've been watering the garden and fixing the wall and cooking all our meals. Doing everything I'm told."

"Please, Lily."

"What?"

"You're speaking very loudly."

Lily glared at her.

Evelyn thought she might approach the truth obliquely, and groped about for the words.

"We've planted onions and garlic and the cabbages," she said to the grave. "Did our best with the slugs, but I'm sure they'll be back."

"Tell her about the rhubarb."

"Oh, yes. We stewed Lily's rhubarb. It was quite something."

"Best we've ever had. No doubt about it."

"Petunias are late and the camellias are early. And the roses are both, somehow. I know we're not meant to be deadheading until next month but there are some rather sad-looking blooms on the trellis. Between the arches. You know the one I mean."

"You should ask her about the almanac."

"One thing at a time, Lily." Evelyn paused. "What else? The apples are very early. Some of them are rotting already. I don't know." She stopped again and began to feel nervous. "Things just feel a bit off."

"Oh, stop mincing your words! Mama, Evelyn wants to make some changes to the almanac."

"Lily! That's not what I'm getting at!"

"It doesn't make sense anymore. She said it herself. Summer's barely started round the lake. And it's autumn here."

"This is Lily's idea, not mine, Mama."

"So much for not dobbing me in."

"Why would I want to change it? All that work we put into it. That you put into it, I mean. There's nothing wrong with it at all."

"She said it was out of step, Mama."

"I didn't."

"She did. The whole garden's gone to pot. Everything's changing. She wants to write her own almanac, but she won't because she thinks if she replaces your one, you're going to shout at her."

Evelyn held her breath for a moment, and behind her breastbone rose a kind of cold dread she hadn't felt for a long time. She waited for it to settle. Around them the grass clicked with insects. An opalescent beetle crept steadily over the head-stone. Evelyn cleared her throat.

"I didn't come here to talk to you about the almanac."

Lily tutted. "Oh, here we go," she said.

"Some other things have happened that you should know about."

"Get it over with, Evelyn, we haven't got all day."

Evelyn turned and looked at her coolly. She was furious with Lily, but then was not in the habit of causing a scene as her sister was. She took a few deep breaths.

"Part of the wall fell down. We put it back up, though. Both of us."

She heard Lily shifting from one foot to the other.

"There was something with one of the beehives, too. It was moved. I don't know how."

"She moved it and forgot, Mama. Head like a sieve."

"And one of the eggs was . . . One of the eggs had some-thing wrong with it."

"She forgot to candle it."

"And then there was this business with the apple pie."

"Here we go. *Business*, she says. For crying out loud, Evie, listen to you! I'd rather you just accused me outright."

"I'm not blaming you. That's the point."

"What's the point? Spit it out, Evie!"

She did not. The thing could not be spoken aloud. *There is something else in the garden.* Evelyn shook her head and stared at the stone. Some days it seemed as if their mother was present to hear their questions and supplications, but not today. The grave was silent, and there was the feeling that she had abandoned the sisters to their squabbles. The bee returned and stayed this time, digging furiously in the purple depths of one of the lupins. Evelyn wondered if she should return later. If her mother would be more receptive if she came without Lily in tow.

She was about to say as much when there was the sound of glass breaking somewhere in the kitchen. Even from so far away, it sounded as if the house itself had cracked in two.

"Bird's probably got into the house," said Lily. "Silly thing."

"That didn't sound like a bird."

"Maybe it's Eddie!" Lily laughed. "Coming home after all this time."

Evelyn looked at Lily and found she could no longer indulge her little sister's naivete, or her denial. Without replying she turned and hobbled back up the path. She heard Lily calling after her:

"Evie? You've not said goodbye to Mama."

And then, when she didn't reply:

"I'm sorry, Mama. Honestly, sometimes you'd think she wasn't brought up properly."

A Burial

She'd gone up to the east wing to fetch Eddie because there was no one else to talk to. She could hear Lily rampaging through one of her piano pieces, and Jamie was out by the flower beds, too busy and too tired for conversation. Everyone else had gone. Guests and staff trickling away over the weeks and months, and the garden looking somehow more overgrown and more withered at the same time. Evelyn was more bored than lonely these days. She'd not been to school since Christmas. She was unsure if it had closed, but at any rate her parents no longer insisted that she and her sister attend, and her few friends had not kept in touch when they left.

Eddie was a good listener, though. There were times when she thought of him as a kind of oracle, sitting on his perch, silently preening himself. Behind his black and unknowable eyes there seemed to be *some primitive intelligence that understood exactly what was happening in her world and in the world at large. That had answers for her, if only Evelyn were able to decipher them.*

When she reached the landing, she heard a tense conversation coming from one of the rooms. Voices were raised more often than not now. The weather was so hot it seemed that everyone, Lily and Jamie included, was permanently on the brink of boiling over.

She came to the door of the east wing sitting room and loitered outside with one ear on her parents. She traced the maze of cracks in one of her father's oil paintings. The portrait was not of their father, but it looked a lot like him. An ancestor, a great-grandfather at least. The heavy, saturnine brow. Colors dim and austere. The hall smelled of furniture polish and mildew and the vegetables that were forever stewing in the kitchen. There was the sound of an orchestra coming from a radio inside the sitting room, only a little louder than the argument it was meant to disguise.

We're not leaving, said Papa. I'm afraid that's the end of it.

Well, yes, actually, that will be the end of it. Because we won't be able to feed our children.

I thought we were self-sufficient? I thought that was the whole point of your hippie commune.

Oh my God.

What?

I cannot believe how much of a snob you still are.

Well. I don't know what to call it.

Firstly, it wasn't a hippie commune. Secondly, you can only have a commune if there are people here to work in it, so no, we are not self-sufficient. There is no one left. Everyone is going. Everyone has gone. Do you want to give Evelyn and Lily a spade each and tell them to start digging?

They were quiet for a while. Evelyn took a gulp of orange squash.

It was so weak it was almost water. She noticed the glass had left a ring-shaped mark on the top of the bookcase, and she scrubbed at it with the corner of her dress.

Her father sighed.

This isn't a forever thing. People will come back. And we still have Jamie.

Jamie is leaving, too.

Since when?

Since this morning. You're not listening to me. Please, please, listen to me. We cannot make this work on our own. There is a reason everyone is going.

I'm sorry. I don't know what to say. We have to stay put. This is my home.

Excuse me, your home?

My family's home.

Her mother flew into a rage.

We are your family! I am! We are! Me, and Evelyn, and Lily. And you're happy for us to stay here and starve just because of your bloody stiff upper lip!

A pause.

I'm not going to give all this up because of a few hot summers.

Oh my God.

I'm sorry. I don't really expect you to understand.

Because I'm a pleb.

Here we go. Of course you were going to say that. No. Because you don't feel the responsibility in the same way I do.

What about the responsibility of keeping our children alive?

Christ, the melodrama.

No, not melodrama. A few hot summers? Do you not see? Everything has changed. We are not living the same lives anymore. None of this matters.

To you, maybe.

No. No! You don't get to accuse me of not caring. I gave up so much to be with you. To come and be in this house. I can't believe, after all this, with everything that's happening, you're still insisting on holding me hostage here.

Evelyn heard her father shifting his weight. Heard her mother's long exhalation. The door seemed to strain against the atmosphere within.

If you want to leave, then leave, said Papa. *I'm not holding you prisoner. But the girls stay here.*

How dare you.

I mean it.

You can't just say that.

Well. Good luck finding a lawyer.

Someone threw something against the wall and there was the sound of shattering glass. Evelyn stood back and felt the banister push into the small of her back. She heard tussling from within, more objects being hurled, a piece of furniture falling. Then a sharp metallic clang and a brief fluttering of wings and then someone crossing the room. Evelyn crouched behind a bookcase on the landing and felt her father's footsteps through the soles of her own feet. The door flew open and shuddered when it struck the wall, and when she peered from her hiding place her father's great shoulders were already disappearing down the hallway.

Evelyn stayed where she was for a long time before going into the room. Her mother was sitting on a couch, still and upright. Her face showed no expression whatsoever.

Careful, there, she said.

There was broken glass on the floor and cushions in disarray. One of them had split and there were feathers rocking in the draft.

The birdcage lay on its side with the bars badly bent, and the budgerigar inside was not moving.

Is he all right? she asked, and her mother just looked at the bird but did not answer her.

Evelyn bent down and righted the cage, and the bird fell onto its sandy floor. Evelyn thought his feet curled slightly. She opened the door and lifted the bird and held him in both hands. He seemed to cool and stiffen even as she cupped him.

Please don't tell her, Mama said, and Evelyn nodded. She waited a minute more, then put the bird gently in the pocket of her pinafore.

Shall I bury him?

Yes. I think you should.

Where?

Her mother took another few moments to collect herself.

Maybe somewhere near the wall? What about behind the beehives?

Evelyn thought that was a good idea.

She avoided her sister all day and held a small ceremony in the evening. Just her and a shoebox and a trowel. The first thing they'd ever buried in their web of special things, and Lily didn't even know about it.

9

Lily continued to chatter as they approached the house. She seemed intent on distracting Evelyn from whatever might be waiting for them within.

"I thought we were meant to be deadheading," she said.

"I think that can wait, in the circumstances."

"What are the circumstances?"

Evelyn did not say.

"It's just a bird, Evie. They get confused by the windows. Don't you remember?"

Evelyn ignored her and went inside.

She was blinded by the gloom at first. Then shapes began to appear: tables and chairs, a red blanket, white ashes, the black, heavy curve of the cooking pot. Farther inside the kitchen, beneath one of the store cupboards, the shards of a broken jar and a slick of honey creeping over the floor.

There was an underwater stillness. No sign of any bird or animal. Their store cupboard was open, and Evelyn was sure she hadn't left it so. She went and looked inside, stepping over the glass and the honey. There had been about a dozen jars in there when she had checked the previous night, but now there seemed fewer. Her blood whined in her ears. There was no bird or rat that could open a cupboard door and carry off a sealed glass jar, she was fairly sure of that.

Lily eventually joined her. She saw the mess on the floor.

"Oh dear," she said.

"There's some honey missing from the shelf, too," said Evelyn.

"How much?"

"Two or three jars, I think."

"How much is left?"

A pointless question, Evelyn thought. "I haven't counted."

Lily's breathing grew quieter. "Look," she said, "it's there." She pointed to the hulk of an old refrigerator at the back of the kitchen.

Evelyn went to fetch the windup lamp. She turned the handle two, three times, and it fizzed into life. She came forward slowly and pointed it at the corner. A pile of dirty rags heaved in the darkness. There was a pair of old leather boots poking out of the bottom, and in the middle of the bundle were five pale fingers, wrapped around a jar of honey. The rags shifted and wheezed as she brought the lamp closer.

"What is it?" said Lily.

Evelyn shook her head. The creature smelled of dust and blood and something else she didn't have a name for. Nothing had come over the wall for a very long time. She and her mother had dealt with unwanted visitors, back then. There were monstrous things that lurked in her memory—hers, not Lily's—but this was not one of them.

"It shouldn't be here," whispered Lily. "We need to get rid of it."

The silence was measured by their frantic breath. Lily came forward holding her shears open in one hand. The tips quivered in the lamplight.

"I'm not sure that's the answer," said Evelyn.

"Give me the lamp," said Lily.

"I don't think—"

"Give me the bloody lamp!"

Evelyn handed it to her and watched as her sister edged toward the rags. When Lily was a few feet away, the creature suddenly twitched, yelped, and flew up into the air. The stench hit Evelyn in waves.

It tried to run away but seemed unsteady, drunken even, weighed down by its huge boots. It staggered around the kitchen and tried to push past Lily and the shears. Lily swiped vaguely, as if she were waving her paintbrush at a canvas. Evelyn felt sorry her. For them both. By luck, rather than by design, the tip of the shears caught the thing on the back of one of its legs. It cried out and fell. The jar tumbled to the floor and smashed in almost exactly the same spot as the other one.

Lily made a strange, uncertain noise of triumph. The rags lay on the floor and sobbed while blood and honey pooled in the cracks between the kitchen tiles.

10

They watched and listened while it squirmed for what seemed like hours. Lily still held the shears at her side. Evelyn tried to take them from her, but her sister's fingers were so hard and cold and tightly clasped they seemed carved into the handle.

"I told you," Evelyn said. "I told you there was something here."

Finally her sister said: "It makes a lot of noise."

The creature smeared itself across the floor until it was curled up in the ashes next to the stove. It made noises that were high-pitched and strangely articulated. Cinders settled on its legs like snowflakes, turning a deep red where they touched the wound in its thigh.

"Is it a man?" Lily said.

Evelyn had not heard the word for so long. Had not spoken it for even longer. She squinted into the shadows. She couldn't really remember what a man looked like.

"I don't know," she said. "I don't think so."

Her head felt hot and swollen and her words sounded distant to her own ears.

"Are you a man?" Lily asked the thing. She held the shears in both hands now, and pointed them at the rags as if she were divining for water. The heap shifted and whimpered. Evelyn put out a hand and gently pushed the shears down.

"Steady on," she said, and this felt like an answer to Lily's question, because a man would not have deserved such consideration.

"It's disgusting," said Lily, her voice breaking slightly, as if she were moments from crying herself. "Get rid of it, Evie. It stinks. It's stinking the whole kitchen up."

"How? Where do we put it?"

"Throw it in the lake."

"We drink from the lake."

"Throw it over the wall, then. Put it on the bonfire. I don't know!"

The rags heaved up again and started crawling toward the kitchen door on all fours. Lily screamed.

"Quickly, Evie, stop it!"

Evelyn could not move quickly. She was too old for any kind of pursuit. The figure slipped between them and scrambled like a dog toward the daylight. When it reached the doorstep it tried to stand on its bad leg, but cried out and collapsed and fell face-first into the gravel.

Evelyn caught up and stood over it. A new and frightening

thing in the bright sunlight, curled and twitching in its rags as if it had just been born. It had a scarf wrapped around its head with gaps for its eyes and nose. Around its shoulders a rag worn like a cape, and beneath that a T-shirt so thin and full of holes it looked like the diaphanous cobwebs that gathered in the high corners of the toolshed. A handful of letters faded almost to invisibility across its chest, which stirred some inexplicable feeling of sadness in Evelyn. Skinny arms wrapped around its stomach, their skin dry and scaly like the feet of a chicken.

Lily came and peered over her shoulder.

"What are you going to do with it?"

"I don't know."

"Let's just get rid of it. Please, Sissie."

Evelyn thought of lugging it to the lakeshore. Or pushing it over the wall. Neither seemed right, and her indecision came not just as a surprise but as an affront, to Mama and everything Mama had taught her. She did not want to destroy the thing, and she could not explain why.

"Let me think."

"There's nothing to think about! Wring its bloody neck!"

"We can put it in the icehouse."

"What? Why?"

"Just while we decide."

"I have decided!"

"Let's all just calm down a minute. Let me think."

Lily was quiet only for a moment. "We're not putting it in the icehouse," she said. "Absolutely not."

"Why not?"

"What if it makes all the meat go rotten?"

"The meat's past going rotten, I think."

"Or it might eat what we've got left."

"Then we'll tie it up. Go and get some twine from the shed. Quickly. Before it tries to make a run for it again."

The thing did not make a run for it, did not move at all, save for a couple of long, shuddering intakes of breath. It seemed very young, very frail. A fledgling fallen from its nest. Evelyn preferred to think about it this way, as something plucked from the air, rather than imagine where it might have come from on its skinny legs.

When Lily returned with the spools of twine, they got on their hands and knees and wound it around the thing's ankles, then around its wrists, hands tied behind its back. The twine was old and dusty, and they had to make several loops before it felt secure. They pulled it tight until the string bit into its skin. The creature continued to sob silently but didn't resist at all.

Evelyn stood up slowly and massaged her knees where the gravel had imprinted itself. She looked at their quarry, then looked at Lily. Her sister was fidgeting with the rings on her fingers.

"What about around its neck?" she said.

"What do you mean?" said Evelyn.

"We should tie something around its neck. Tight, so it can't swallow anything."

"I don't think we need to do that."

"Are you sure?"

Evelyn nodded, though she wasn't sure of anything. Lily flared her nostrils and turned away.

"It's disgusting," she said again.

Evelyn found a large sack that their mother had once used for composting. They rolled the thing inside it and dragged it all the way across the gravel and through the herb garden, one sister at each corner, straining like horses at a plow. They had to rest every ten paces. When they reached the icehouse, Evelyn went inside and shoved the bag up against the rear wall and then stood in the darkness, panting.

"Shouldn't we hang it up?" suggested Lily, loitering at the entrance.

"No need for that, I think," said Evelyn. She felt that the thing had already endured more than was necessary. Lily squinted, unconvinced.

Evelyn left the creature and went to join her sister. They shut the iron gate and Evelyn found a spare piece of wire to bind it shut. They spent a few moments looking through the bars but could no longer see the outline of the sacking.

"What now?" said Lily.

"I don't know," said Evelyn. "We should probably ask Mama."

"You know what Mama would do."

Evelyn nodded. She knew well enough. They were quiet for a long time. She looked back at the garden, and the birds sang and looped overhead as if nothing out of the ordinary had happened.

"Maybe it'll die by itself," said Lily after a while.

"Maybe," said Evelyn.

"If we don't feed it or water it, it'll just curl up and die and that'll be that."

"Yes. I daresay."

"All right then."

Lily seemed more reassured by the idea than Evelyn. She pressed her face up against the bars, though there was nothing to see. Evelyn watched her sister. Her heart still fluttering, hot and thin as a paper lantern.

"One of us should keep an eye on it," said Lily.

"Yes," said Evelyn. "One of us should."

In the end they both stayed. They helped each other to the ground and sat cross-legged outside the gate, listening to the sniffs and rustles of whatever lurked in the gloom. After a while Lily clawed a handful of gravel from the path and began throwing the stones one by one between the bars of the gate. Evelyn caught her hand.

"Don't do that," she said.

"Why not?" said Lily.

"Just don't," said Evelyn.

11

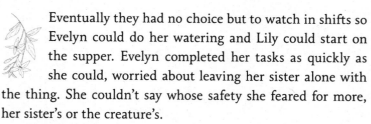Eventually they had no choice but to watch in shifts so Evelyn could do her watering and Lily could start on the supper. Evelyn completed her tasks as quickly as she could, worried about leaving her sister alone with the thing. She couldn't say whose safety she feared for more, her sister's or the creature's.

When Evelyn finally came in for supper, they cleaned the mess that had been left on the kitchen floor and wordlessly chewed their way through a bowl of barley stew. There seemed no way of addressing what had happened. The thing in the ice-house was not just inarticulate but somehow beyond language entirely. When they had finished, Lily let her spoon rattle in the bowl, then said:

"We're all right, aren't we?"

"Yes," said Evelyn.

"If we just leave it, it'll take care of itself."

"Yes, probably."

"It'll just starve."

Evelyn didn't reply to that.

"It won't get out in the meantime, will it?"

"Not likely. Trussed up like a chicken." Evelyn paused. "Speaking of which."

She went out to put the hens into their coops, and by the time she'd got back, her sister was wrapped up in their bed. Their bowls were left unwashed on the kitchen table.

Evelyn got under the blankets with Lily, and they both tossed and turned for a long time. Evelyn was too hot and her sweat felt dirty and viscous on her body. She stuck a leg out to cool herself, then tore off the blankets completely.

She'd thought her sister was asleep, but Lily said, suddenly: "Are you scared?"

Evelyn lay still for a moment. "I don't know," she said. "I don't think so."

"Good," said Lily. "If you're not, then I'm not."

In truth, Evelyn was scared—but not, she thought, for the same reasons as her sister. Lily began breathing heavily, and then snoring, but Evelyn remained alert and wide-eyed. The moon was up and so bright it seemed as though night had not come at all. She could see every flake and crack in the ceiling plaster, every cobweb.

Twice Evelyn thought of getting up and going to the icehouse. She did not understand where the urge came from. Curiosity, perhaps, but there was more to it than that. Each time she imagined opening the gate her heart began to thump, as if she were already guilty of something, just by thinking it. Just being awake so long past their prescribed bedtime was transgression enough. Sometimes she thought she could hear the creature's whimpering, though the icehouse was too far away and the kitchen door was closed. Then she thought she heard Mama reprimanding her. Each voice seemed as real and as unbelievable as the other.

An hour passed in this state of paralysis. Then two. Then, without any warning, her body roused itself, almost without Evelyn's permission, and she slipped out from beneath their blankets and padded silently to the other side of the kitchen. She filled her battered hip flask with water and spooned the remains of the barley stew into her dirty bowl and took one of their remaining jars of honey down from the shelf. These she put in a wicker basket along with her sewing kit and the windup lamp. She listened for Lily's snores, convinced herself they were not feigned, and went out into the garden.

The moon was enough to light her way to the icehouse. The gravel path like a snowfield, the icehouse an igloo. She turned on the lamp when she reached the entrance, unwound the wire, and lifted the gate on its hinges so it would make less noise when she opened it. She went to the back of the icehouse and found the figure lying with its face to the wall, half out of the sack. She placed the lamp on the ground in the center. It lit the place warmly, and along with the basket and the little bowl the icehouse took on the feel of a hermit's cave.

"I'm sorry about Lily," she said.

It didn't move. Only the tiniest shift in its tattered cape suggested it was alive at all.

"I've brought you something."

It seemed to stiffen.

"I don't know if you can understand a word I'm saying."

She bent down and laid a hand on its shoulder, and it flinched but made no attempt to get away. She rolled it over into the lamplight. Its eyes were two oily pools between the folds of its scarf.

"Let's have a look at you, then," she said.

She unwound the fabric from the creature's head, feeling the weight of its skull, and brought the lamp a little closer. A pale and grimy face, flesh that yielded too easily beneath her fingers. Its hair was black—though it might not have been the same color clean—and as stiff as the wires that sprouted in certain corners of the kitchen. It looked like a memory of Lily as a child, coming home after swimming in the lake with weeds in her hair and mud between her fingers and toes.

They looked at each other. The thing blinked slowly. Tears had left pale, meandering riverbeds in the dirt on its cheeks.

Evelyn unscrewed the cap of the hip flask and brought it to the creature's lips, but it strained away and buried its face in the ground. It was still bound at its wrists and ankles, and it curled and uncurled slowly like a worm she'd unearthed.

She pulled the thing back upright and tried again with the flask, but again it twisted its head away.

"There's nothing wrong with it. It's not a trick. Look." She drank from the flask herself. She scooped some of the barley porridge from the bowl with her finger and sucked on it. "See?" she said. "It's rather good."

The thing turned and regarded her warily. Its mouth opened with a dry click and she saw the pink tip of its tongue, lurid in the middle of its pale face. She offered the hip flask for a third time and the creature leaned forward. She upended it, and half of the water dribbled over its chin and down its neck.

"Whoops-a-daisy," she said. "There's a good boy."

She had always known this was what the thing was, though she had never seen one before. Not in this life, at least. Saying the word aloud produced a strange vertiginous feeling. As if she were on the edge of some precipice, and the darkness of the boy's eyes was the abyss below.

He swallowed the water and coughed and then glanced at the bowl of barley.

"You want some?" said Evelyn.

He nodded.

"You can understand what I'm saying, then."

He nodded again.

"Goodie good."

She fed the boy spoonfuls of barley porridge, catching the spillages from his lips and cheeks as if she were feeding a baby, until the bowl was empty. The writing on his T-shirt caught her eye again. A longing for something. Somewhere she had been, once? She fancied she could taste oranges, then shook the memory from her head.

"How is your leg?" she said.

The boy looked down at the tear in his trousers as if noticing it for the first time. The fabric had a dark sheen, but the wound was not bleeding as freely as it had been.

"Come here," said Evelyn. "I'll do my best with it."

He didn't move. She came over and sat beside him. She made him lie down across her lap and unbuttoned his trousers, exposing his skinny thighs. The wound was already infected and the smell was putrid. Evelyn cleaned it as best she could with a damp cloth and found it still opened quite easily, a dark and lipless mouth. If she had left him until morning, then all might well have gone as Lily expected. Evelyn hummed to herself and took the needle and thread and the jar from inside the basket. She unscrewed the lid and stuck a finger into the cool silkiness and set about smearing the honey on his flesh. He turned away.

"It will help with the infection," said Evelyn. "I know you've got a taste for it, but don't go licking it all off again. Are you listening?"

Without waiting for an answer, she wetted the end of the thread and took a few attempts to pass it through the eye. The boy's face was still turned to the wall when the needle went in. He cried out.

"That's enough of that," said Evelyn. "My sister hears you, there'll be hell to pay. For both of us."

She took his scarf and tied it tightly around his mouth, then continued with her work. His skin was sticky and delicate, like the skin on a bowl of soup.

When she had finished, she inspected the stitches in the lamplight. The wound would heal, but the scar would not be a neat one. Twenty years ago—ten, even—she would have made a better job of it. She shrugged and sighed.

"You'll do," she said, and put everything back in the basket. "I'll bring you something else tomorrow night. I'm afraid I'll have to keep you like this until we know you're not going to get up to any more mischief. My sister will come around, I think. Once she's calmed down, we can decide what to do with you." She paused and looked at his filthy and sallow features. "I take it you don't want to go back to where you came from?"

The boy gave no sign that he'd heard her, and Evelyn was glad. She wished she hadn't said anything. The question of where he might have come from was still too large and dark and formless a thing for her to countenance. A door she resolved to keep locked and bolted.

The future, though. She might glance in that direction. The glimmer of something opened up before her when she looked at him. She studied his slender limbs and his unlined face. *By God*, she thought, *he's got years and years in him.*

She closed the gate behind her and came quietly back to the house. In the kitchen Lily was no longer snoring. Evelyn replaced the bowl, the jar, and the flask, and put the sewing kit back in the dresser. She got under the blankets and lay there a while with her eyes open, staring at the ceiling, then at one of her hands, blue with reflected moonlight. The scent of him was still on her, she thought. Something else besides dirt and sweat.

"Where've you been," said Lily.

Evelyn swallowed. "Little girl's room. This bladder of mine. Can't hold more than a thimble these days."

Lily rolled over and breathed heavily through her nose. Perhaps tired. Perhaps annoyed at the interruption. Perhaps disappointed in her sister's talents as a liar.

A Plan

Evelyn left Lily in bed and came downstairs to get a glass of water, the house all echoes and shadows. She took the long way around, as she often did when she found herself sleepless. She looked in at the starlit rooms, stood in the great, dead silence of the library, the ballroom, her father's study. She wandered the landings and the long, paneled galleries that were no darker by night than they were by day.

She found her mother at the table in the kitchen surrounded by books, as she was almost every night now. Working by candlelight, monk-like in her hooded dressing gown. Evelyn was almost at her elbow before her mother noticed she was there.

Hello, Mama, she said.

Her mother looked up. Seemed to take a moment to recognize her.

Hello there, she said. Can't sleep?

She shook her head.

Too hot?

Lily's snoring.

She pulled up a chair at the table and drew one of the books toward her. It was thick and ancient. The page edges were soft and grubby with years of thumbing, the cover loose and joined to the spine by only a few scant threads.

Be a bit careful with that, that was my mother's.

Evelyn opened it and smelled the rich must of the paper. The book was beautiful. Each page detailed the names and appearances of wildflowers, the watercolors still vivid despite the years. Like some illuminated manuscript. Evelyn read the names aloud, syllable by syllable, her finger slowly tracing the letters. Garden lobelia. Goldenrod. Toothwort. Foxglove. Weaselsnout.

They're like magic words, she said.

They are, aren't they? said her mother.

Like a witch's spell.

Nothing wrong with being a bit witchy.

Her mother gently took the book from her and leafed through a few pages, then stopped and slid it back.

Here are the real magic ones, she said. Good for potions and lotions.

The page was covered with drawings of herbs and roots. Feverfew. Milk thistle. St. John's wort.

Lily would like these, Evelyn said. What are you reading about?

Squashes.

Like orange squash?

Her mother smiled and kissed the top of her head and showed her the book she was reading. Pictures of alien fruit and vegetables, all tendrils and swollen protuberances. Underneath her other elbow another book, blank, that she was copying into. The words were arranged in columns in a tiny, deliberate hand.

Can I see? said Evelyn.

Her mother lifted her arm.

What is it?

It's nothing yet.

What's it going to be?

Just making a plan. To keep us all fed and watered.

Are we staying?

For the time being, her mother said. Not forever.

Evelyn thought about forever and found it not unappealing as a prospect. She did not miss anybody, not really. She liked their tiny world. Like fruit left to dry, it had toughened as it had shrunk, and in its toughness Evelyn felt secure. An indestructible nucleus of a family.

Are you sad? said her mother.

No, said Evelyn.

Well. You're being very brave.

I like it here.

Her mother looked at Evelyn as if she didn't quite believe her.

We'll be all right, with a bit of luck, she said. Probably safer staying here for the moment anyway.

We can eat the apples from my tree, said Evelyn.

Oh goodness, said her mother. We'll be gone long before then.

Evelyn tried very hard to hide her disappointment.

That night they stayed awake for hours. Evelyn pored over the pictures of the flowers and plants, tried to commit them to memory, tried to imagine what they might be used for. Her mother kept reading her vegetable books, occasionally writing in her notebook, or underlining something with finality. Eventually Evelyn came and sat beside her and leaned on her shoulder. The smell of her dressing gown, soapy but not exactly clean. They were still there when the kitchen window began to show a faint violet glow. There was a creaking of floorboards overhead, and Mama told Evelyn she should run back to bed. She handed her a book to take with her and then bent back to her work.

12

For the next two days Evelyn went about her tasks and thought of little else besides the boy. Thought of his slender hands and sinewed forearms and imagined how they might handle a spade or a hoe. Imagined them making bread, peeling fruit, whisking an egg. It seemed a heretical thought, and she felt her color rise when Lily passed her in the garden, going to and from the gazebo. Sometimes Evelyn would pass through the orchard and hear her sister at the bars of the boy's prison, throwing pebbles and muttering curses and imprecations that were all but unintelligible. When this happened she would go and stand beside her sister, lead her gently away by the elbow, and Lily would say: "Why is it still alive?" Evelyn just frowned and said she didn't know, and then, come midnight, she was back in front of the boy's sad face offering him scraps of their supper and cleaning his wound.

On the third morning after the boy's arrival, Evelyn turned over and saw that her sister's side of the nest was empty. Her heart clenched. Lily was rarely the first to wake and never the first to rise. By the time Evelyn was on her feet, knees and ankles throbbing with the effort of it, Lily was in the doorway and hanging off the frame.

"It's got out," she said.

"What?"

"It's got out of the icehouse! God knows how."

Evelyn staggered across the kitchen and fumbled her feet into her slippers.

"Did you see where he went?"

"No," said Lily, and then seemed to stop breathing entirely. "He?" she said.

"Yes."

"What do you mean, 'he'? I thought we agreed it wasn't a man. It's not a man, is it, Evie? Tell me it's not a man!"

She sounded terrified. Evelyn was frightened, too, but not for the same reasons as her sister.

"It's not a man. But I was thinking it might be a boy."

"A boy? Like in the book?"

"Yes."

"Why? How?"

"I don't know."

"Evie!"

"Do you want to stand here chatting, or do you want to go and find him?"

She left the kitchen and went out onto the lawn, shielding

her eyes against the bright sun. She scanned the garden and listened, but heard nothing. It was too cruel, to have him delivered to them and then snatched away so quickly. Lily was still trying to talk to her, but she turned away and made for the icehouse.

The gate was wide open, and there were spirals of twine in the center of the floor where the boy had freed himself from his bindings. Also, glinting in the dirt, one of her sewing needles. Evelyn picked up both. The twine was ancient. It would have taken only a few thrusts with the needle before it started to come apart.

"I told you he's not in there."

Lily was behind her, silhouetted in the arch. Evelyn closed one fist around the needle and held out the pieces of string.

"Silly of us to think these would hold, I suppose," she said.

Lily frowned and looked at Evelyn's other hand, dangling by her waist.

"Why don't you go round the back of the house and I'll search here?" said Evelyn.

Lily's head jerked up. "Split up? So he can jump out and deadhead me with the shears? No thank you, Evie."

"I don't think he'll do that."

"You seem very confident all of a sudden."

Evelyn pushed past her and pocketed the needle in her nightdress. "Come on, he can't have gone far."

Lily insisted on holding Evelyn's hand while they wove around the vegetable beds and flower beds and the rows of apple trees. There was no sign of the boy. No footprints in the soil, no broken stems.

They went around to the back of the house. The day was

already very warm. Evelyn was so tired from her midnight meetings with the boy and the hours of worry that came afterward that it felt as if there were condensation on the inside of her skull, on the backs of her eyes.

"A boy," Lily muttered. "Where would a boy have come from?"

Evelyn didn't say anything. She went to the edge of the lake and saw where some of the long grass had been flattened.

"You know what boys turn into, don't you, Sissie?"

Evelyn squinted and tried to discern a trail.

"We should have strangled him while we had the chance."

Evelyn unclasped her sister's hand.

"We're not going to cover much ground joined at the hip like this, are we," she said. "Go round that side and have a look in the grotto."

"What if he comes for me?"

"He was a feeble little thing when we found him. And he hasn't been fed for days."

Lily raised her eyebrows, but Evelyn did not respond to the implication.

They split and skirted the lake on different sides. Evelyn searched among the willows and the pampas and then under the gigantic, leathery leaves of the gunnera. It seemed a likely hiding place for the boy since it was where she and her sister had hidden as children. Under its leaves she'd liked imagining she was tiny, an insect, barely visible, while their mother and father had gone around the lake calling her in for supper.

She was lost in this memory when she heard Lily cry out. Evelyn came to the edge of the water and saw her sister's nightdress drifting ghostlike into the artificial cave at the far end of

the lake. She hitched up her own dress and walked quickly
through the long grass, and by the time she got there the lake-
side was echoing with the sound of a scuffle.

The grotto had once been empty, but since the storm, their
mother had used it as a repository for the garden's old statuary:
stone limbs and heads and torsos, remnants of some ancient
and forgotten pantheon. Young men, bearded men, men on
horseback, men holding invisible swords or bows and arrows,
face down in the soil or peering out of the heap under brows of
thick moss. The boy had crawled up to the top of the pile as if
to claim it as his own. He was high enough that the wet ferns
dangling from the grotto roof brushed against his white forehead. Lily was grasping vaguely at the boy's ankles.

"Get off there! Horrible thing!"

Evelyn met the boy's eyes. "He's all right, Lily," she said.
"Easy does it."

Lily didn't listen to her, and she got her fingers entangled
in the laces of the boy's boots.

"Got you!" she said, as if she had snared a stray pigeon that
had found its way into the house.

"Careful, Lily," said Evelyn.

Lily dragged the boy down. Evelyn watched as his limbs
clattered slackly over the broken stones and onto the floor. Lily
straddled him and beneath the curtains of her hair clasped her
hands around the boy's throat. One of the boy's legs twitched.

"Lily, stop that! Leave him be!"

Evelyn hurried over and attempted to prize her sister's fingers free.

"We've tried leaving him be, haven't we," said Lily. "Hasn't
got us very far, has it?"

"He can't breathe!"

"That's the point, Sissie."

"Lily, if you don't release him this minute, I shan't let you wear the Marigolds."

Lily looked at her, and her fingers loosened. The boy gasped.

"You can't say that," she said. "It's not up to you."

"I mean it. I'll go back to the house right now and I'll cut the fingers off with the shears and then nobody will get to wear them."

"You wouldn't dare!"

"I would."

Lily seemed to consider this for a moment, and then resumed her efforts on the boy's neck.

"I said *stop it*!" Evelyn shoved her sister with her hip.

As soon as she made contact, she realized quite how badly the two of them were put together. Not of an age for scrapping. Lily released the boy and fell sideways, banging her head on the broken elbow of one of the statues. She lay on her back wheezing for a few seconds and then sat up, prodding at her temple, her expression more one of surprise than pain. Her nightdress was smeared with dirt and algae from the floor of the grotto.

Evelyn got down beside the boy and brushed the hair out of his eyes.

"You're all right," she said. "She didn't mean it."

"Yes, I bloody well did!" hissed Lily.

"Let's get you sitting up."

Evelyn raised the boy by his armpits and leaned him against the pile of broken statues. He lay there like a doll, impassive as ever, accustomed to injury and to suffering. Lily watched them with disbelief.

"What's wrong with you, Evie?"

Evelyn didn't answer. She tried to get the boy to stand, but his injured leg buckled beneath him. Lily pointed.

"You stitched him up, didn't you?"

Evelyn pulled the boy's arm over her crooked back, and they hopped and staggered toward the mouth of the cave. Lily began patting her sister's pockets while she was occupied with supporting the boy. She thrust her hand into one, and when she withdrew it she was holding the needle between finger and thumb. She raised it to the light, the thread Evelyn had used still knotted through the eye.

"I knew it! You've gone doolally, Evelyn!"

"He was hurt."

"I know he was hurt, I was the one who hurt him!"

"Well, we didn't want him bleeding everywhere, did we?"

"Didn't we?"

They glared at each other, Evelyn sagging under the burden of the boy, light as he was.

"Have you been feeding him?" Lily said. "You have, haven't you? I'm not stupid, Sissie! Don't think I didn't notice!"

"It was only leftovers."

"Why? What were you thinking?" She paused. "What would Mama say?"

Evelyn felt sick at the suggestion. She did not reply. She had no answers for her sister, or for Mama. Not yet.

"Talk to me, Evie."

"Later," she said, and she hauled the boy out into the sunshine and back toward the house.

13

 Evelyn wrapped the boy in a blanket and went looking for some clean clothes for him. She came back with a pair of old jeans and a jumper that had been her mother's.

"No point you running off now," she said. "Absolutely nothing outside that wall, is there?"

It was the same reassurance she'd always given Lily, but posed to the boy, the question no longer sounded rhetorical. His very presence disproved the theory. He just looked at her.

"Come on," she said. "Skin a rabbit."

He flinched.

"Silly thing."

She raised his arms and peeled off his T-shirt. His chest brittle and pale and ribbed like a fossil. She watched him as he dressed and asked questions that ranged no further than what was in front of them. Would he like more water? Was he tired? Was he cold? She thought of other things but knew they were too large to address right now, too large perhaps to put into any kind of words.

She went and made him a cup of mint tea, but he wouldn't touch it.

Lily eventually returned. She stood on the threshold but came no further.

"What on *earth* are you doing?" she said.

"Well, he's not going back in the icehouse, is he? I'll turn my back for five minutes and you'll be wringing his neck again."

"So what if I do?"

"We need to look after him."

Lily stared at her, her mouth slack with disbelief. "Need to? Excuse me?"

"Please, Lils. Please hear me out." Evelyn got to her feet. Behind her she heard the boy retreating under the blanket.

"He could help us."

"He could kill us," said her sister.

"He won't kill us."

"I have your guarantee, do I?"

"Yes."

Lily scoffed.

"He could help us with the garden," said Evelyn. "He could look after everything when we're gone. The bees, the beds, the orchard. He could look after us, and Mama."

"You need your brains testing, Evelyn."

"Look at him," said Evelyn. "He's not dangerous."

They both turned. The boy had gathered the blanket beneath his chin, and his pale head seemed to float disembodied above it. His cheeks were sunken and his eyes seemed bruised with fatigue. Lily folded her arms and shook her head.

"We don't know where he's been. He's probably poisonous."

"He just needs looking after. A wash. Something to eat."

"Well, apparently you've already seen to that. The little girl's room! I'm not an idiot, Evie."

Evelyn went over to her sister and took her hand, but Lily snatched it back. Evelyn tried again, more gently, and this time Lily didn't move. Evelyn felt her sister's pulse through the thin skin of her wrists.

"We talked about this," she said. "We're getting old, Lily."

They were silent for a long time. Lily examined the fingers on her other hand. Evelyn knew they were sore from what had happened in the grotto.

"What's your point?" she said.

"My point is we can't look after the garden forever. What'll happen when we've gone to be with Mama? Someone needs to carry on with the work. Otherwise what are we doing here? Why are we working at all? The work comes first. The work comes before everything. Mama always said that."

"We won't be with Mama anytime soon."

"But we will. One day. And even before that someone will need to take over. I don't feel on top of things even now. And your joints being what they are . . ."

"I can't help my joints."

"I know that, Lily."

Lily let her arms drop and stamped her feet. "I don't want him here," she said. "I hate him. Look at him. I've got pins and needles all over." She paused. "I can't remember my routine, Evie. I've been trying and trying for the past few days, and I can't remember half of the steps. He's completely thrown me."

"But he's here now."

"Thanks to you! I don't want him getting under our feet. Eating our food. Like having a bloody animal in the house!"

"You always wanted an animal in the house and Mama wouldn't let you."

"Don't *start*, Evie."

Evelyn saw the bruise on her sister's forehead from when she had fallen in the grotto, and she suddenly felt as if there was something alien about her. The boy had made everything seem alien, in fact. The world made new.

"Will you think about it? Please, Lils."

"Think about what?"

"Keeping him."

"Think about it, she says! I haven't been doing anything but that for the last three days!"

She turned away and went past the boy toward the pile of clothes, selected the largest and most elaborate of their mother's ball gowns, and threw it over her head.

"I need to practice," she said, and went out again into the day.

The kitchen was very quiet in her absence. When Evelyn turned back to the boy, it seemed he had been watching them both closely. A long time passed. Birdsong and insects outside, jarring and unreal. Eventually he lowered the blanket from his nose and mouth and he cleared his throat and said:

"I think she's going to kill me."

He spoke quietly and deliberately, as if unused to it. Such a strange voice. Like a woman's in its timbre, but not in its soul. Not at all.

It was some time before Evelyn answered. How long had it been since she'd had a conversation with anyone other than her sister? She felt as if to do so was to offer up some part of herself that she would not recover. To offer up a part of Lily, too, perhaps. She waited and thought. When the words came they were not the words she had expected.

"Don't worry about her," she said. "She's just in a bad mood, that's all. You surprised us. We don't get many surprises here."

And that was the end of it. They looked at each other, and the silence poured back into the spaces around them. She filled a cup with cold tea and gave it to him, and this time he took it. He drew a deep and shivering breath.

"Are you cold?" she asked.

The boy shook his head.

"Do you want something to eat?"

He shook his head again, then lay on the floor and pulled the blanket over his head and curled up like a grub.

She studied the shape of him. Boys did become men, Lily was right about that, but what her sister actually had in mind, she did not know. A cocoon, perhaps. A chrysalis. Poor Lily, so resolutely ignorant. But then how much did Evelyn really understand? Her mother had only given her the scantest information on the ways of men and women before she had sealed her lips against such things, and now Evelyn could not deny a perverse desire to learn firsthand, to feed and water the grub and see what it might grow into.

14

Evelyn and her sister barely spoke for the next few days, and the boy maintained his customary silence. Lily did not acknowledge his presence at all, much less discuss his future with them. She went to practice her dancing, sometimes ventured farther afield to paint some obscure corner of the garden, and only after terse negotiations agreed to perform some of the tasks that Evelyn gave her.

Evelyn spent almost all day in the kitchen, since she still wasn't sure she could leave the boy alone. Nor did she want to ask her sister to look after him. She moved around him, tidying blankets and straightening chairs and wiping surfaces. None of them things that needed doing. She sat at the kitchen table, reading the almanac over and over, and glanced up every time there was a rustle or a sigh from the boy. She offered him water and porridge and was met, always, with only a nod or a shake of the head. Every time Lily came back inside, her gown billowing like a ship's sails, the boy would retreat under his blankets.

At night they tied his hands and feet, at Lily's insistence. Evelyn did not want to—nor did she think it necessary, since she barely slept—but thought she should capitulate to her sister on something at least.

On the third day Evelyn was still sitting with the almanac and ruing the tasks that she had not yet done and that her sister refused to do. She began to wonder if the boy might not be the answer to their problems after all, but simply yet another task, one that exceeded all others. She sometimes thought of him as some filthy rag that had become caught in the delicate mechanism of the garden, one that she might never pull free.

In the evening Lily came back to make their supper. She took a seat at the kitchen table and began massaging her bare toes.

"My feet are killing me," she said.

It was the first thing Lily had said in a long while. In the spirit of reconciliation Evelyn came over and bent to take hold of her sister's foot, but Lily slapped her hand away.

"I need my shoes. I wouldn't have this problem if you'd just let me go into the house and get them."

Evelyn looked at her. Her sister talked about her dancing shoes all the time, but she'd never suggested actually retrieving them. In truth, Evelyn didn't like her mentioning them at all. Every time she did, Evelyn inevitably pictured where the shoes were—the room, the carpet, the toys—and it was becoming harder for her mind to draw a curtain across the whole scene.

"That's enough of that, Lily. I know you're joking."

"I don't know if I am."

"We're not having this conversation," she said. "Give it a rest. I mean it."

Lily continued rubbing at the knuckles of her toes, then her ankle. She pointed at the boy.

"What's he been doing, then?"

Her sister had not even mentioned the boy since she'd stormed out of the kitchen a few days before, and Evelyn was glad for the change of subject.

"Nothing. He's just been sitting there."

"Has he said anything?"

"Not really."

"Well. How exciting. Thank goodness we have him to help out."

Lily levered herself out of the chair and went over to where the boy had concealed himself. She whipped away the blanket, and he squirmed as if exposed to a bright light.

"Let's see you, then."

"Let him rest, Lily," Evelyn said quietly.

"Rest? He's been resting ever since he got here. I thought he was meant to be chipping in. That was the whole point? Horrid little thing."

By now the boy had his hands over his face. Lily went to the umbrella stand and fetched her walking stick. She came back and used it to prize his arms apart, then his legs, until he was lying spread-eagled on the floor and Evelyn was paralyzed by visions of her sister slowly, deliberately, crushing him like a beetle.

Lily poked at the tear in his trousers and the wound beneath it.

"You made a dog's dinner of that stitching," she said.

"It's cold in the icehouse," said Evelyn. "And dark."

Lily made a noise that was half a sniff and half a laugh.

"Should have asked me," she said.

She paced around the boy in a slow circle, pinning his hands and feet to the floor with her stick as she passed. He moaned quietly as she applied pressure.

"No wonder we didn't hear him creeping around," she said. "Look how skinny he is." She pointed the stick in his face. "Just because you're sickly doesn't mean you can sit around all day convalescing. You think I'm going to push you around in a wheelchair while you take the air, you've got another think coming! Had enough of that for one lifetime. You'll have to pull your weight."

The boy turned his head to one side.

"I can," he said. "I will."

Lily did not seem to hear him. She looked at Evelyn and then peered at the boy's face. She gently maneuvered his head with her stick until their eyes met. Her mood then seemed to change very suddenly.

"Horrid little thing," she repeated, and went over to the stove. The boy quickly reassembled his blanket fort, and the three of them were quiet again as the day began to darken.

When supper was ready, Lily brought over two bowls of barley. There was no bowl for the boy, as usual. Lily blew on hers and ate some and gestured outside the window. She said with her mouth full:

"This needs some meat in it."

Evelyn looked at her. "I haven't had time to get any. You're welcome to get it yourself."

Lily shook her head. She never got the meat herself. It was up to Evelyn to brave the cold shadows of the icehouse, and always had been.

Evelyn got up and scraped the dregs of the pan onto a plate—there were only two bowls, since Lily had started using Mama's as a plant pot—and brought it back to the table. She looked over at the boy and patted the chair beside her.

"What are you doing?" said Lily.

"Maybe he wants to join us."

"At the table?"

"Yes."

Lily shook her head again and blew hard on her next spoonful. The boy watched them from his den, wide-eyed. Evelyn looked at him.

"Only if you want to," she said.

After a while he crawled over to the table and took a seat, the first time he had done so since his arrival. Lily edged away a little. He looked down at the plate, sniffed at the spoon, then put it in his mouth.

Lily continued to eat noisily. Evelyn watched her and wondered, briefly, how she must seem to the boy. Her jewelry, her faded silks, the tangle of her hair dipping into her bowl. As strange a creature as he had appeared to them.

Lily raised her voice but didn't look up from her supper. "How was the apple pie?" she said.

The boy stopped chewing.

"Good, was it?"

The boy nodded.

"Are you going to say thank you?"

She waited.

"No, thought not."

The boy set down his spoon and slithered back to his bedding.

A Meal

Suppertime was intolerable. Their father insisted that they continue to eat at the table, as a family. As they and their forebears had always done. *I think we should maintain certain standards,* he often said, and it was meant both as a joke and not. They had not had any visitors for months now. It seemed to take all the energy out of their parents to confront the same three faces every evening, to hear the same remarks, the same rebukes, the same silences.

Lily had started trying to cook and one night made an attempt at a crumble with the first of the apples, though they were still tiny and painfully sour. There was no fresh butter for the topping, so Lily had made it using an ancient packet of crackers that she obliterated with a rolling pin.

Well, I think this looks jolly good, said their father. He smiled at Lily, but his eyes had a permanent look of sadness about them.

He tucked in with the serving spoon and filled their bowls. Their mother was scribbling something in a notepad and did not respond when Evelyn put a portion in front of her.

What do you call a homeless snail? said Lily.

I don't know, Lily-bear, said their father. What do you call a homeless snail?

A slug.

Yes, of course, a slug, said their father, but he didn't laugh.

Their mother looked up suddenly.

Any luck getting chickens? she said.

No, said their father.

Have you tried?

I have tried. I think we may have to cast the net a little wider.

Her mother put down the notepad and pulled her bowl toward her.

The shells will be good for getting rid of the slugs.

She tasted a little of Lily's crumble and frowned.

Gosh, she said. This tastes very sweet, Lils.

I like it sweet, said Lily.

How much sugar did you put in?

She shrugged.

Mama got up and went to the store cupboard and took down the packet of sugar. It rattled hollowly when she shook it.

Well, that's that, then, their mother said, and crushed the paper bag in both hands and left the kitchen without finishing her dessert.

The rest of them ate in silence. When Evelyn asked if she could get down from the table, her father suggested they go out and have a swim for an hour or so. A swim and a wash, since they were rationing what came out of the taps now. The girls did as bidden, but even with all the splashing and whooping they could hear the raised voices once more in the main house. Every time Lily's name came up, Evelyn playfully dunked her little sister under the water so she would not hear what followed. It happened so many times and for so long that Lily started to get suspicious, and then angry, and she escaped Evelyn's clutches and paddled to the bank.

Much later, Evelyn went looking for her mother and found her watching television in one of the sitting rooms. They had not watched any television for a very long time or listened to the radio. The electricity was rationed, too, but Evelyn suspected that nobody wanted to see what was being broadcast anyway.

She crept in silently but did not go and sit next to her mother. Instead she watched over the arm of the sofa. The TV's sound was turned down, and she could hear her mother breathing as if she had recently finished some exercise. The screen showed a red map, the shade deepening in the south, so deep in places it looked almost black. In the past, she remembered, there had been a person in front of the map to explain the colors and the numbers, to give an outlook for the days to come, but either there was nobody left to do this or the television company wasn't willing to put somebody through the misery of it.

There followed some pictures of a city in a desert, and Evelyn thought of her books on the Egyptians, and found herself intrigued, excited even. There were people moving about in the desert, too. They looked as if they had been raised from the sand, fashioned from it, and they trudged about with only their eyes showing that there was any kind of a soul beneath the crust of their skin.

Her mother noticed she was watching and quickly turned the television off. She held out her hand and wordlessly pulled her daughter to her chest and held her tightly.

Where's your sister? she said.

I don't know, said Evelyn.

Is she all right?

I think so.

Did she hear?

Evelyn shrugged.

Her mother squeezed her again and then got up and went purposefully out of the room.

That night Evelyn went along the landing and found her parents holding each other on the bed wearing all their clothes. The bed was shuddering, and she had no idea whether they were laughing or crying, but whichever it was, she did not want to interrupt and she passed by the open door and went to the bathroom without putting on the light.

15

In the early hours of the morning Evelyn turned over and saw the boy, motionless, eyes half open. She sat up too quickly and wrenched something in her back and cried out. Beside her Lily's head rustled in its nest of hair.

"What is it?" she said.

"Nothing. I forgot he was here."

When Evelyn stood, the pain was excruciating. Somewhere next to her spine her muscles had turned hard and unyielding, clenched like a fist. They pulled her whole body sideways, and she bent like a crone.

"Well, that's all I need," she muttered, and shuffled over to make up the fire.

Lily slowly roused herself.

"Is he dead?" she said, standing over the boy.

Everything apart from his mouth was wrapped tightly in his blanket—Lily's blanket—and his chest was barely moving. He looked as if he were bound in readiness for a burial or a pyre. Lily nudged him with her foot and he sighed.

"Not dead," she said.

Once the fire was lit, they had tea and ate some dry crackers. The boy sat up with his hands still bound and watched them carefully. Some of the panic had gone from his eyes.

"You'll have to do some work today," Evelyn said to him, "now my back's like it is."

She untied the string at his wrists and ankles, and he rubbed his grazes with a fingertip. Lily bit noisily into another cracker and said nothing.

"How is your leg?" Evelyn asked. "Can you stand up?"

He got to his knees, then to his feet, and stood a little lopsided in Evelyn's shirt and her mother's trousers. He slowly shifted his weight to his bad leg. He winced, then took a few faltering steps and steadied himself on the table.

"It's all right," he said very quietly.

"The thing speaks!" said Lily.

That was enough to make him sit down again.

"Perhaps he could help me with the bees," said Evelyn.

"Perhaps he could make me another apple pie," said Lily.

"He could," said Evelyn, though she knew her sister was being sarcastic. "Do you know about bees?" she said, turning to the boy.

He shook his head.

"Do you know what I mean? When I say 'bees'?"

He shook his head again.

"Buzz buzz," said Evelyn, and swirled her finger in the air.

He made a small O with his mouth that suggested recognition, but otherwise said nothing.

"Come with me. I'll show you."

IT WAS BRIGHT and humid in the garden, though they'd had no rainfall, and the air was like syrup. Everything seemed to have grown six inches overnight. Such a joy, such a marvel, on days like this. Enough to make Evelyn's eyes brim. Enough to make her feel twenty, thirty years younger, while she stood on there on the doorstep, massaging the warmth and the sweetness into her muscles.

She and the boy went at a snail's pace across the lawn, through the vegetable patches and the orchard and over the small bridge that crossed the remains of a stream. She thought she felt the boy relax, too, but might have imagined it. His gaze snagged on certain flowers as they went. She told him the names, and he nodded but did not reply. In one of the beds on the far side of the orchard was a flourishing tree peony, and he stopped beside it and sniffed the air. He did not move for some time.

"Very nice smell that, isn't it? You can stick your nose in if you like."

The boy looked at her as if she might be trying to trick him. She showed him it was safe, and he buried his face in one of the flowers. When he stepped back, he was wearing a look of complete astonishment and there was pollen clinging to the tip of his nose. He muttered something.

"What's that?" said Evelyn,

"I love it," he said.

The word was such a surprise. She smiled.

"Yes," she said. "So do I."

He had sniffed another half dozen of the flowers before Evelyn chivvied him along. When they reached the beehives, she rested on a tree stump and he stood crookedly on his good leg.

"You've seen these, I take it?" she asked.

He nodded again.

"I noticed one of them had moved. Were you looking inside?"

He shook his head.

"Then why did you move it?"

He looked around the clearing, over to the lilac and the newly mended wall, back along the tunnel of honeysuckle that led to the lawn.

"I didn't mean to."

"What happened?"

"I was running."

"Running?"

"I didn't see it. I ran into it."

"I see. Why were you running?"

He just shook his head. Evelyn did not press him, surprised he'd said as much as he had. They listened to the bees working.

"Did you knock over the wall, too?" she said after a while.

"I'm sorry," he said. "I had to climb over."

Evelyn paused.

"It's all right," she said. "We fixed it."

"I was so hungry."

"So I gathered," she said. "A whole apple pie!"

"I thought I was dying. It was such a long way."

Evelyn stopped smiling. What was such a long way? She found herself suddenly face-to-face with the question that had been in her head ever since she had first visited him in the icehouse. It was perhaps the biggest question of all. An immense, fearful question that could no longer be ignored.

"Where did you come from?"

He sat on the ground and tore a clump of dandelions but said nothing.

"Are there other boys and girls like you?" she asked.

He nodded.

"Where?"

He gestured vaguely with one arm. "Back in the other place."

His words felt like something unearthed. Artifacts she'd disturbed without meaning to. Evelyn decided she wouldn't ask any more questions. Her thoughts strayed beyond the garden and gave her that familiar and horrifying sense of vertigo. She'd probed too much and now she wondered whether rebuilding the wall had achieved anything, whether any battle to keep the garden sacrosanct was to be fought in her head, and Lily's head, and nowhere else.

Evelyn tried to haul her thoughts back from the precipice.

"You don't want to go back to the other boys and girls?" she asked.

The boy shook his head.

"Then why did you try to run away the other day?"

"I wasn't running away."

"You were hiding in the grotto."

"I don't know what that is."

"By the lake."

"I just wanted to have a look. I've never seen anywhere like this. It's so . . . I don't know how to say it."

Evelyn studied him. He looked scolded. Guilty of something, beyond breaking the wall and stealing their honey.

"Do you want me to go back?" he asked.

Evelyn regarded him as he stood lopsided, hand on his wounded thigh.

"You can stay," she said. "But you have to work. We all have to work. We're like the bees."

He nodded. "I can work."

"Good."

"You don't need to tie me up anymore."

"Are you sure?"

"I'm not going anywhere."

She sat for a moment. She pictured the almanac, the tasks still outstanding.

"We should collect some honey," she said. "You can make up for the jar you broke."

"All right."

"Second one along. Next to the one you bumped into."

He limped over to the hive, leaned against it, and immediately snatched his hand back when the bees began to crawl over his fingers.

"It's all right," said Evelyn. "They're a friendly lot. I used to have a smoker to calm them, but they're used to me now. They might give you a few stings. Nothing life-threatening."

He looked at the hive doubtfully.

"Take off the lid," said Evelyn.

The boy tentatively embraced the hive. His arms were amazingly long. He could reach all the way around it. He lifted the top section with ease and held it aloft while the bees drifted around his neck and face.

"You can put it down," said Evelyn. He practically threw it to the ground and began waving his hands around and shielding his eyes. "Stop flapping! Then they really will sting you."

He flapped anyway. Evelyn rocked forward on the tree stump, thinking she might go and help, but then her back spasmed and she closed her eyes and stayed where she was. The boy was making sounds that were almost inaudible, as though he was trying to reason with the bees in their own secret language.

"Calm down," said Evelyn. "Look inside. Carefully. You'll see ten frames. Ten bits of wood."

The boy shielded his eyes and squinted as though facing a bright light.

"You see them?"

"Yes," he said.

"Good. Lift them out, slowly, one at a time, and let me look at them."

He faltered for a moment, choosing the best place to hold the frame. He dipped his hand in and out, in and out, then finally lifted one. Evelyn assessed it from where she was sitting. Only half of the cells on the frame were sealed.

"Next one," she said. They went through another four before they found one that the bees had completed. It was slick and golden, honey spooling from one corner onto the edge of the hive. "Bring that one here," said Evelyn.

The boy did as he was told. He came over blinking and spluttering, still wafting his hand in front of his face. He gave the frame to Evelyn and she held it in her lap. She couldn't resist tasting the honey with a finger. Delicious beyond words. So intensely sweet it somehow made her feel younger than she was, a real-life elixir. Some of the bees had come with the frame, reluctant to abandon their finished work. Evelyn cast her eyes over the neat geometry of the cells and watched their busy, furred bodies nudging gently up against one another.

The thought of the "other place" came back to her, of other boys and girls. She imagined hundreds of them emerging from a hive as big as the house, crawling from cell to cell. Flying in a swarm to investigate her and Lily's garden. Sent by a queen, perhaps, to collect what was needed for their colony.

At some point Evelyn looked up and realized the boy was screaming and had no idea how long he had been screaming for.

16

When they got back to the house, Lily was standing in the doorway wearing their mother's plum-colored track-suit and a pair of kitten heels. She was holding a bundle of the boy's old clothes, his boots perched on top. She looked at the boy, who was still sobbing and sniffing, and after a moment or two said to Evelyn:

"I'm going to burn all these."

"Why?" said Evelyn.

"Because they're disgusting."

She threw them on the gravel and went back inside.

They went in after her, and Evelyn sat the boy down at the kitchen table. She poured him a cup of water. Their jug was nearly empty. He took two slow swallows and then held the cup against his swollen lip.

"He was stung inside his mouth," Evelyn said when Lily did not ask.

The boy moaned.

"Oh, for crying out loud," said Lily. "I never kicked up this much fuss. You see, Evie? He's no use at all."

"I think it was the surprise more than anything," said Evelyn. "I don't think he knows anything about bees."

"I don't think he knows anything about anything," said Lily.

Evelyn thought again about what the boy had told her. She thought she might not mention it at all. It would not be the first thing she had hidden from her sister, but perhaps, in light of the boy's arrival, there was no longer reason or compassion in trying to conceal such things. She cleared her throat.

"He said something."

"Yes?"

"He said that there are others."

Lily took out a large tin mixing bowl and started adding flour and water. She put on a good show of being unconcerned.

"And you believed him, did you?" she said. "More fool you."

"I don't know if I believe him or not," said Evelyn.

Lily worked the mixture for some time before she spoke again: "Why would you say that?"

"Say what?"

Lily looked up, her fingers still submerged in floury sludge. "Even if you believed him, why would you tell me that? Are you trying to scare me?"

"No, I'm not trying to scare you."

"Like Mama all over again. We agreed there's nothing out there, didn't we?" She paused and then said, again: "We *agreed*."

She shook her head and began working the dough harder, the bowl skittering about under the force of her hands. Evelyn said nothing. The remark stung. So many years gently probing and extracting each individual terror their mother had left imprinted on her sister. All undone now.

"Well, I suppose it's obvious, isn't it," said Lily.

"What is?"

"That there must be others. He didn't sprout out of the flower beds, did he?"

"No," said Evelyn, though she would happily have believed that fiction.

"Maybe they'll come looking for him," Lily said.

"Yes," said Evelyn. "I wondered about that."

"Well. You should have wondered about that when you decided to keep him, shouldn't you?"

"If we'd let him go, he might have gone and told them about us anyway."

"Nonsense. We should have left him to shrivel up and die, and that would've been the end of it."

There was another long pause, and Evelyn could see Lily's jaw working as hard as her fingers, as if she were molding a question behind her lips.

"What did he say, then?" she said. "About the others?"

"Nothing."

"Did you not ask him?"

"No. Why would I want to know?"

"Why would you not? Seems you and Mama were both wrong to blazes."

"Wrong how?"

"Well, it's not monsters out there, but it's not nothing either. Is it? So what is it then? More horrid little boys?"

The bowl was silent beneath her hands, and she seemed to expect a straightforward answer.

"I didn't ask him," said Evelyn. "He doesn't want to talk about it anyway. So that's the end of that."

A bank of clouds passed in front of the sun, or perhaps it was just the mood in the kitchen, but the world turned momentarily gray. Evelyn could see that Lily was still thinking about what she had said. She had always had a more vivid and searching imagination than Evelyn and could not keep it confined to the inside of her head. That was another reason she and Mama had argued so much. So many questions that their mother had been unable, or unwilling, to answer.

What if someone or something did come looking for him? What kind of someone or something would that be?

Lily began kneading again but abruptly swore and pushed the bowl away. She flexed her fingers.

"These bloody things won't do what I tell them to," she said.

She came back to the table and sat beside Evelyn in the half-light. The cloud persisted in its long eclipse. She seemed to have left her questions and worries and the whole topic of the boy's provenance behind with the bowl. Abandoned, but to be returned to.

"How is your back?" she asked.

"I'll live."

"And the garden?"

"Getting away from me a little. I've not had time, what with looking after him."

The boy coughed. They both seemed to have forgotten he was there, nursing his sore lip. He said something that neither of them could hear clearly.

"What's that?" said Lily.

"I'm sorry," he said.

Straightaway he lifted the cup to drink, as if to hide behind it. Evelyn and Lily looked at him, and then at each other. Evelyn wondered—and she guessed her sister was also wondering—whether he was apologizing for what had happened, or for something that might happen in the days to come.

A Dance

Lily put on a performance in the upstairs drawing room for the rest of the family. She'd had only a handful of ballet lessons before her teacher had left, but it seemed her heart was set on a life on the stage, and perhaps to her this still seemed a possibility. She had also decided at some point that it was her job to keep everyone's spirits up, and Evelyn was glad of it, since she was no performer herself.

It was winter, but the night was very warm and all the windows were open. Her father was sitting on the sill of the oriel window with his eyes closed. The moon fell across the fields outside their shrunken world, the ragged grass already brittle and bleached. There had been no sheep or cattle to crop it for a very long time. Within the garden wall the orchard was taller than Evelyn now, and this year's fruit very nearly edible straight from the tree.

Lily had put two standing lamps on either side of the rug in the center of the room, the shades angled to flood the floor with light. She was hiding behind a screen that wobbled slightly as she readied herself. Evelyn sat on a sofa with her mother. The rug that was to be Lily's stage depicted a hunting scene, a stag bounding through voluptuous greenery pursued by hounds and men with horns and bows and arrows. On the walls of the drawing room were portraits of men from a similar time, in similar dress, who Lily counted as the larger portion of her audience.

Ready, Papa, said Lily.

He didn't move for a few moments, and then very quietly he stood up and came and sat on the opposite end of the sofa to their mother.

Right then, Lily-bear. Away you go.

There was the crackle of a record player and the strings of an orchestra burst into life, and before Lily even came out, their mother gasped. She put her fingers to her lips. Lily emerged from behind the screen wearing her swimming costume and a long, knitted scarf and began a series of leaps and pirouettes that Evelyn could see tired her out very quickly. Halfway through the routine she sat in an armchair to catch her breath and grinned at her audience. Evelyn laughed and looked at her father. He was smiling faintly. She looked at her mother. Her hand was still in front her mouth and Evelyn could not read her expression.

The orchestra began anew and Lily roused herself from the armchair.

Your outfit was never as good as that, Evelyn's father said.

It was a moment before Evelyn realized he was talking to her mother.

You saw Mama dance?

Lots of times.

Evelyn knew Mama had been a dancer, though she'd mentioned it only a few times, and when she did, it was as if she were speaking of her dim and distant childhood.

Her mother watched Lily for a minute.

He met me at the stage door, she said, and there was an almost imperceptible roll of the eyes.

You should have seen the bouquet I got for her.

It was ridiculous. He could barely fit into my dressing room with it. Not that he should have been in my dressing room at all.

Evelyn kept watching her mother, trying to decipher whether she was speaking in anger or fondness or some mixture of the two.

He came to see me three times in the same run at the Palladium.

What's a palladium?

It's a big theater, her mother said. Did we never take you?

Evelyn shook her head.

Oh, it was gorgeous, Evelyn. All the carvings on the boxes, and the ceiling. All the gold leaf. It was like Versailles. Wasn't it?

Her father nodded, and his gaze seemed to light on something far, far beyond their drawing room.

What's verse eye? said Evelyn, but Lily shouted:

You're not watching!

They dutifully stopped their conversation and continued to watch her unruly performance. Another minute or two passed. Evelyn looked at her mother again. She was blinking hard.

Can you still dance?

I don't know. I haven't tried.

Why did you stop?

I married your father, didn't I?

You could have carried on.

Well. Life got in the way.

Evelyn looked at her mother a little longer and then went back to watching Lily, who was spinning furiously from one corner of the rug to the other. Her sister had just centered herself beneath the chandelier and was tentatively raising herself onto her tiptoes when the power went for the last time and darkness seemed to flood through the open windows. All four of them sat in complete silence as the last echoes of the orchestra drifted from the house and away over the barren pastures.

17

Days passed and Evelyn wondered whether she would ever be able to stand up straight again. She felt her head bowing her spine like a bud on a stem. She found herself constantly looking at the floor, wondering if this was the beginning of her last, slow descent back to the earth she had sprung from.

The boy was put to work in her stead. Every morning she talked him through the tasks in the almanac and sent him on his way with Lily as his grudging chaperone. Evelyn heard them together while she sat outside the kitchen door mending their clothes. Lily had started speaking to the boy in the same way she spoke to the slugs and the pigeons, with a kind of resigned exasperation. She would hiss and suck her teeth when he did something wrong and then give her instructions again, slowly and carefully, as if he were entirely brainless. The boy would reply with one or two words, his voice youthful and bleating.

He worked hard, as he had promised. He dug over the winter beds in an afternoon, where it would have taken Evelyn and her sister several days. He trimmed the hawthorn. He cut back the ivy that was creeping into the toolshed and prying the roof from the walls. He dredged the stream that led from the lake and cleaned the rusted sluice gate. Every morning a bucket of fresh water appeared on the kitchen doorstep; sometimes there were three or four eggs in a box beside it. In the afternoons he would come back and lie on the lawn for an hour or two while Lily practiced her routine, and Evelyn would quiz him on the garden and his morning's labors but nothing else beyond that. The larger questions, about him, about the outside, lay submerged like a dark reef, and she did all she could to steer clear of them.

One afternoon she looked up to see him standing in the middle of the lawn, turning on the spot and shielding his eyes with his hand.

"What are you looking for?" Evelyn asked.

He stopped spinning and came over to her chair, a deep scowl on his face. "How did you do it?"

"Do what?"

"Make this."

"The garden?"

He nodded. She set her sewing to one side. Lily's sequined dress, which she had split again while practicing.

"We didn't make it. Our mother did. We're just looking after it."

"She said there was a storm at the beginning."

"Lily did?"

129

He nodded again. He had never once used either of their names.

"Oh, yes," said Evelyn. "The really big one. We had to dig it all out by hand. Mama and Papa and me and Lily. Dust and sand a couple of feet thick in places. It got everywhere, on your skin, in your hair. You couldn't tell us apart from the statues in the garden." She paused. "Sometimes I can't believe we really did it. Sometimes I think I dreamed it."

"She says it might happen again."

Evelyn felt her temper flare. No doubt the boy was a more receptive audience to her sister's pronouncements and predictions.

"Lily says lots of things. To get a reaction, mostly. We've only known three or four storms since we've been here. The last time we had one was . . . oh, donkey's years back."

"Donkey's?"

They looked at each other. Evelyn herself didn't understand the phrase. It was just one that her mother had used.

"It was a very long time ago. And even then we only got a little dusting. It was very far away, but we could still see it. Went right up into the sky. Lightning and all sorts."

The boy looked up as if some vestige of the storm still hung there.

"Why don't you go in the rest of the house?" he said.

Evelyn blinked. Thrown from one unwanted memory to another. "You're full of questions, aren't you."

"It's so big, but you only use the kitchen."

Evelyn thought back to Lily's game of hide-and-seek and wondered if it had been the boy she'd seen in the window. And if it had, what he might have seen, too. She glanced back at the house. Locked doors, closed curtains. Dark landings, perhaps a little daylight from a broken shutter creeping along the floor-boards, the shelves. That rug. That vase.

"We don't go in there because it's dangerous," she said. "Don't even think about it. For your own good."

"Dangerous how?"

"It's full of men's things."

"Men's things?"

"And worse. Mold and poison in the air. Electrical residue. Makes your hair and teeth fall out just like that." She snapped her fingers at him and realized in that instant that she was not speaking in her own voice. A mother's warning. She took a couple of breaths and added, "You steer well clear. Do you understand?"

He nodded. He looked scolded.

"Now. Let me get on."

The boy wandered back to the lawn. Evelyn took up her sister's dress again but could not concentrate.

Not long afterward, Lily came back from her practice. She was buoyant, humming a tune to herself and conducting some tiny, imagined orchestra with one finger. She stood in front of Evelyn's deck chair and cast her in shade.

"I remembered it," she said.

"Remembered what?"

"All the steps!"

"Oh. Goodie good. See, you don't need your shoes after all."

Lily didn't reply to that. She took a few deep breaths.

"I want to play cards tonight," she announced.

Evelyn looked up. She let the dress fall in her lap and wondered, suddenly, if her sister had been talking to the boy about the house, as well as about the garden and the storm and everything else.

"If you want," she said.

"No need to look quite so worried, Sissie. You might actually win something if the beast of burden is playing."

"The what?"

"The beast of burden." She nodded at the boy. "That's what I call him."

"That's not very nice."

"He likes it. Don't you?" she called over to where he was sprawled on the lawn. He sat up but didn't say anything.

"Not even listening," said Lily. "Not a thought between his ears. What have you been talking about anyway?"

"This and that," said Evelyn. She paused. "I wish you hadn't mentioned the storm to him."

"He knows what a storm is, Evie. He's seen worse things than we have."

"I don't want to know what he's seen. I'm sure he doesn't want to be reminded." She paused. "And don't talk about Mama, or the house. Please."

They both looked at him. When Lily spoke again, it was loud enough for him to hear.

"If you say so. Haven't got time to make polite conversation with him anyway. I spend all my time telling him what to do, a hundred times over." She looked back at Evelyn and shielded her eyes against the sun. "So. Cards tonight?"

"Yes. Why not."

"Good. And a snifter of potato wine." She nodded in agreement with herself and called over to the boy: "Right, come on, you horrible thing. We still haven't burned your filthy clothes. Have you washed at all since you got here? If you've given me lice and I have to cut my hair, I shall throttle you."

18

Lily returned in the evening wearing oven gloves and a bandanna and smelling of woodsmoke. The boy came back a little later holding his old boots. He put them in a neat pair by the kitchen door. Evelyn frowned when she saw them.

"You're keeping them?" she said.

"I thought it was a shame to get rid of them," said Lily.

"Why?"

Lily shrugged. "I don't know. I just liked them."

She came in and took off her gloves and mask and started heating a pan of soup.

They played their card game after their supper. There were twenty-five cards in their mother's deck, soft and grubby and thumbed to disintegration. The set had three angular, sad-looking queens and one king whose mustache matched the contours of a supercilious smile. Lily called them the family cards. The queens were the sisters and their mother, and she said the king looked like their father. "Who's got Papa?" she used to wonder out loud once the cards had been dealt, and their mother would get angry and the game would be over.

The boy had played cards before but did not know any of the games that Evelyn and Lily knew. They'd had to invent their own to suit their butchered deck. Evelyn sat with her cup of cloudy potato wine, drank it down to its sweet floury dregs, and watched as Lily impatiently tried to explain the rules to the boy. Evelyn found it very funny. The wine warmed and loosened her, and soon she was laughing aloud, all of her light and drunk and billowing like a sheet on a line. She helped herself to another cup.

Lily and the boy kept drinking, too. He winced and spluttered at every mouthful but always went back for more. While they were still arranging their hands, Evelyn saw Lily show the boy her cards and give an almost imperceptible wink. The boy very nearly smiled.

"What are you doing?" said Evelyn.

"Nothing," said Lily.

Evelyn frowned and put down her first card.

She was the best player among them and she won the first two hands. Then followed a run of bad luck and she lost the third and the fourth, and continued losing, until it became clear that the other two had formed some unspoken alliance that perhaps even they weren't aware of. In the final round the boy produced "Papa" from his sheaf of cards and slapped it on the tabletop, leaving Evelyn with nothing. Lily clapped in triumph, though the victory wasn't hers.

"He got you, Evie!" she crowed. "Not as stupid as he looks, is he?"

The boy scooped all of Evelyn's cards from the middle of the table and added them to his own. Evelyn shook her head.

"That's not fair," she said. "You can't team up."

"Says who?" said Lily.

"We've never played it like that."

Lily laughed. "Are you joking?" she said. "You used to do it with Mama all the time!"

"Do what?"

"Gang up on me."

"No we didn't!"

"You have a very selective memory sometimes, Evie," Lily said, and laughed shortly, but Evelyn couldn't work out how serious the remark was meant to be.

Lily drained her glass and dealt the cards again. As soon as she had finished, Evelyn leaned over and peered at the boy's cards and started helping him to arrange his next hand.

"Don't!" cried Lily. "She's trying to trick you!"

"I would never do such a thing," said Evelyn.

She took her chair round to their side of the table and started swapping cards in and out, laughing at her own brazenness. Lily started laughing, too, screeching in delight and disbelief. The boy sat between them, unsure if he was the butt of the joke or not. Lily bent a card between thumb and forefinger and fired it in front of his nose at Evelyn. Evelyn caught it and threw it back. Lily slipped a thin arm between the boy and the back of his chair and poked Evelyn in the ribs. Evelyn started to squirm.

"Stop! Don't!" Her eyes were watering. "My back!"

"Should have thought of that before you started cheating."

"Ouch! I mean it!"

The boy slipped out from between them. They fought for another few minutes, jabbing and scratching with a kind of fearful hilarity, the scrap forever threatening to turn into something more violent than good fun. Eventually Evelyn grasped her sister's wrists and held them firm and there was a pause in hostilities. Her back throbbed dully beneath the wine, but there was a kind of pleasure in each spasm. Evelyn kept a hold of Lily's thin arms and looked around. The boy wasn't at the table.

"Oh. Where's he gone?"

Evelyn got up, staggered, slumped back into the chair. She squinted against the brightness of the lamp and saw that the boy was at the far end of the kitchen, where the other door had once been.

"What are you doing all the way over there?" she said. She heard the slur in her words and felt faintly embarrassed.

"Do you think we frightened him?" said Lily.

"Silly thing," said Evelyn. "We're not really fighting."

"Aren't we?" said Lily. "I was." She gave another grin that Evelyn could not read.

"Come back here," she called to the boy. He was looking at the wardrobe that covered the doorway to the rest of the house. Evelyn felt very sober very quickly. "Come on, we were only playing. Nothing for you to see there. Quickly now, back you come."

The air in the kitchen seemed suddenly thick with their breath. A winey miasma between them and the boy. When he turned around, there was a faint scowl on his face. He came back to the table and filled their glasses with wine again.

"That's enough for me," said Evelyn.

"Boo!" said Lily. "Fill me up. Yes, please, right to the top. Thank you very much." She drank it down in one go. "Pour yourself one while you're at it." He did.

Evelyn said, "It's bedtime, both of you," but neither seemed to hear her.

"I know what you're thinking," Lily said to the boy. She pointed a finger at him and then leaned over the table and prodded the boy's nose.

"Lily, leave him."

"You're thinking about what's behind that door, aren't you? Nosy little thing! Well, we've got questions, too, you know. So how about a deal." She gave a slow, drunken wink. "We'll tell you what's inside the house if you'll tell us what's outside the wall."

"That's enough, Lily!"

Both the boy and Lily jumped.

"I don't want to talk about it," said Evelyn. She looked at the boy. "Neither does he."

"Ah, he doesn't mind. Do you? What's in that big old head of yours?"

She rapped on his skull with one swollen knuckle, but the boy just closed his eyes and shook his head.

"You see? He doesn't want to talk," said Evelyn. "Now. Bedtime. What would Mama say if she knew we were up so late?"

She went and settled into their nest, but her sister continued watching the boy with a new intensity. Over the course of many days, suspicion had turned to fascination, without Evelyn realizing it. And was there a closeness, too? It had seemed so from the way they'd played cards. Evelyn felt something cold in her belly that she dared not call jealousy.

The boy looked into his lap and examined his fingers as if he didn't recognize them. Lily sniffed and poured them both another cup of potato wine, but he didn't drink his.

"Well, this is dull," she said, wiping her mouth with the back of her hand.

Evelyn rolled over in her blankets. She no longer billowed. She was on the other side of drunkenness now, damp and cold and sluggish and dizzy. Her sister sat and hummed to herself, sometimes posing questions to the boy, to Evelyn, to the darkness. She never got a reply, but there was time. Evelyn closed her eyes and forced herself to sleep, knowing that her sister was strong, and that the boy was weak, and her questions would find answers soon enough.

19

Dead gray light of dawn. Lily had pulled the blanket over both of their heads and was whispering straight into Evelyn's ear, the way she used to when they were children and she had a secret to reveal. Something she'd spied. Something she'd overheard.

"He's all right really, isn't he," she said.

"Yes, he's all right," said Evelyn. Her throat was very dry and her head was spinning.

"Definitely not a monster."

"No."

"I'm glad we kept him."

"Yes. So am I."

The smell of wine on Lily's breath had the sweetness of rotting vegetation and Evelyn turned her head in the opposite direction. She tried to sleep. Lily kicked at their blankets and let them settle before speaking again.

"I'm sorry I made such a fuss when we found him. Gosh, what a palaver!"

"It doesn't matter, Lily."

"It was a surprise, though. Wasn't it?"

"Yes."

"We've not really had any surprises, have we? Not since Mama went. Day after day after day. Always the same."

"That's why we've done so well."

"I suppose." She paused. "How many days do you think we've been here, Evie? In total."

"I don't know," Evelyn said. "There's no point in counting, is there."

"No, I suppose not. I wonder how many days we've got left."

"There's no point in thinking about that either."

"Which of us do you think will go first?"

"Lily, stop it."

There was another pause, longer this time, and Evelyn thought Lily had fallen asleep. Then she spoke again.

"I can't bear to think of you here on your own. I hope we go at exactly the same time."

"So do I."

"Think of that! Both arriving to see Mama at exactly the same time. I wonder if she'll be happy to see me."

Evelyn reached over and took her sister's warm and clammy hand in hers. "She'll be happy to see both of us," she said.

"I'm not sure about that, but there we go," said Lily. "Do you think Papa will be there, too?"

"I have no idea," she said, and that was the truth. She didn't know where Papa was, not in this world or the next.

There was silence again, and then she heard Lily's lips opening and closing in the darkness, as she searched for her next words.

"He wasn't so bad either. Not as bad as Mama used to say."

"Of course he was, Lily. He left us, didn't he? Just like Mama said he would."

"I know . . ."

"He never did a lick of work. Just marched around like he owned the place, guzzling what he wanted until we had nothing left. And then off he went. Because that's what men do." Evelyn corrected herself. "That's what men did."

"But the boy's *like* a man, and he's all right, isn't he? Maybe Mama was wrong about Papa. Maybe she was wrong about all sorts of things."

The blanket was up against Evelyn's face, and her skin was damp with her own breath. She felt suffocated all of a sudden and threw off the covers.

"No, Lily. She can't have been wrong, because we're still here and nobody else is!"

"The boy's here."

Evelyn didn't have an answer for that.

After a few moments Lily said: "Sometimes I think I can remember things about Papa."

"You shouldn't."

"Nice things, I mean. Like his big coat. And his big boots."

Evelyn pictured the boy's boots by the door, rescued from the bonfire just that afternoon. She knew why Lily had kept them—the memory had come to Evelyn, too. Their father's boots, caked in mud, festering in the footwell of their car, a pair of grubby socks packed inside. She thought of a walk they had been on, hardly any distance at all, probably, although she remembered it as some great expedition. She was on her father's shoulders for most of it, fingers interlaced in his thick black hair. They'd seen a pheasant. And a deer. Had they seen one, or had they just hoped to see one?

"Stop it, Lily," she said, the vision evaporating.

"Stop what?"

"You're doing it again. Trying to remember things. It won't do you any good. Won't do either of us any good."

"Maybe I want to remember some things."

"Well, I don't. Keep it to yourself."

Evelyn was speaking louder than she'd intended. She stopped and listened for the boy. She could not hear him.

Lily swallowed noisily and then they were quiet again. Evelyn pulled the blanket back over her head and turned from her sister in the dark. The colors and shapes of dreams were beginning to congregate around her when Lily spoke up again.

"Probably won't happen, will it. What are the chances."

"Of what?"

"Both of us going at the same time. We couldn't even make it happen. There would always be one of us left behind, even if it was only for a few seconds. I think those seconds would be worse than anything. I think they'd feel much longer than a few seconds. I wouldn't want you to have to go through that. I wouldn't want anyone to."

Lily sighed.

"I hope you go first," she said. She kissed Evelyn's temple and rolled over and went back to sleep.

EVELYN REMAINED AWAKE for some time, thinking on all that her sister had said. It had always troubled her when Lily questioned Mama. But it was true, the boy was not a monster. Hadn't she known that the moment she laid eyes on him? Hadn't she been the one to stay her sister's hand? He was meek and he was helpful and they both enjoyed his company. But no, she thought, that was no reason to question anything her mother had told them. It was men she had spoken of, not boys. The boy was something else altogether from the likes of Papa. She would have to curb their curiosity, though. The boy's and her sister's.

Evelyn was feeling a good deal calmer—hopeful even—when she heard the latch on the kitchen door. She lay very still as a strip of gray light appeared and disappeared. She heard his feet over the tiles. He was trying to tread quietly, but it still sounded as if someone had let a wild animal into the house. The air moved as he did and she caught a scent that was wholly new and that inexplicably made her feel like crying.

For as long as she and her sister had been talking, the boy had not been in the kitchen at all. At liberty in the garden, and perhaps elsewhere. She listened as he made his little camp under the table, and then turned over, trembling, as if she were the one who had been caught doing something she shouldn't.

20

The light coming through the kitchen window was very pale and Evelyn's first thought was that snow had fallen, though it had been a lifetime since she'd seen any. There seemed an ashen patina on everything, and she worried, briefly, if a storm had passed through in the night. Or was about to descend on them in the days to come. Just the thought of it made Evelyn tired. What a cruelty it would be, for the garden to go under when she and the boy were just getting on top of things.

The thought of the boy brought with it the dim memory of early morning. She was not sure if she had dreamed it—his skulking return from some unknown errand. She sat up and looked around for him. He was not in the kitchen. She got up and opened the back door, and there was no bucket on the doorstep, no eggs. It was midmorning by now, the day overcast and the sun bright white where it broke through the clouds.

Evelyn took a stick that was leaning in the corner by the door and went on a lap of the house's exterior. She called out to him as she walked along the gravel path, but the boy did not come.

She rarely took in the full extent of the house, and when she did, it always seemed so much larger than she expected. There were always more windows and doors, more nooks and corners in the complex geometry of its circumference. Something haphazard about the way it had been built, with rooms and annexes and whole wings added by successive generations, seemingly on a whim. All contributions to Evelyn and Lily's vast and desolate inheritance.

She rounded the east wing and passed the servants' quarters, looking for ways into the house she might have missed or which might have appeared recently. She came to what had once been the main entrance. On either side were stately columns that had once sprouted acanthus leaves, and on top rested a pediment, like the atrium to some ancient temple. All concealed and crumbling now. She probed feebly with her stick but could not reach the doors. Thick weeds had made a barricade around the house as high as Evelyn's shoulder, and beyond that was the web of ivy and clematis, the branches strong and clutching and bone-hard. Only a very few places where the brickwork still showed through, pale pink like exposed skin. The foliage went all the way to the roof and softened the edges and angles of the house, so that from a distance it looked as if the whole place had been draped in a thick green dust sheet.

Something came to her. She'd posed for a photograph here. Lots of people had. The facade of the house bright and clean, the smell of hot stone in the sun, as if the whole thing had been freshly hewn that morning. A party? A wedding? But whose? It couldn't have been her parents', not if she was there to witness it.

She coughed and spat as if to dislodge the recollection. She didn't understand why such visions had started to arise in her so readily, after all this time.

She rounded the sunroom at the western end of the house, the glass panes all replaced with a mixture of chipboard and chicken wire so it admitted no sun whatsoever. Where there had once been French windows, their mother had nailed two wooden doors removed from the interior of the house, horizontally, one on top of the other. In front of these Evelyn found the grass and weeds were flattened. It looked as if some vagrant had spent the night on the doorstep.

She came to the edge of the undergrowth and prodded at the broken stems. Her heart suspended and still in the cavern of her chest. She raised the stick and rapped on the door with its curved handle.

"Nobody home?"

Lily came around the corner, piling her hair up on her head. She looked gray and bleary-eyed but was grinning nonetheless. She was still wearing their mother's tracksuit but was barefoot and hobbling, her skin white and veined like quartz.

Evelyn felt guilty for some reason, though of the three of them she had the least cause.

"No," she said. "I suppose I'll have to call back later."

There was a pause in which one of them might have laughed, but neither did.

"What are you doing, poking around here?"

Evelyn didn't dare voice her suspicions out loud. On the evidence of the card game, and the conversation they'd had in the early hours, she wasn't even sure who Lily would side with if Evelyn were to accuse the boy of any transgression.

"I think this is where the animals are getting into the house."

Lily shrugged and said: "I'm sure they're getting in everywhere."

"Maybe we could find some time to firm up some of these boards," said Evelyn, and she knocked again on the barricade to the sunroom. Lily laughed and then started coughing.

"You're joking," she said. "Yes, why not, we're only twiddling our thumbs around here, aren't we."

"I mean it," said Evelyn. "I don't think I like the idea of things just coming and going. We don't know what they're picking up from inside."

Lily seemed to wince with her whole body. "Can't we just have a break today?"

"A break?"

"I've got a splitting headache."

"That's your own fault. Come on. No time like the present."

Lily sighed. "Let me ask the beast of burden. He'll know his way around a hammer."

"We can do it ourselves, I think. He's got enough on his plate."

"Don't be silly, Evie, he'll do it in half the time and you know it. Where's he got to, anyway?"

Instead of turning to look at the wilds of the back garden, Lily looked up at the house. Evelyn's head throbbed hot and cold. Was her sister hiding something? No. She was mischievous but not outright deceitful. But then, Evelyn knew from her own experience, it was quite possible for them to keep secrets from each other.

"I don't know," she said. "I haven't seen him all morning."

"We should have him tethered," said Lily, turning back. "Stop him wandering off like this. Come on, then. Shall we go and find him?"

Lily held out her hand expectantly, but Evelyn did not take it. An uncomfortable moment passed.

"You can go," Evelyn said. "I'm going to stay up here and do a bit of sewing. My back is still not right."

"Oh," said Lily. She let her hand fall. "Well. If you like."

"Bring him straight back, please."

"As you wish."

Lily glanced up at the house again and then wandered off in the direction of the lake, hollering for the boy as if he were a lost dog.

Evelyn waited until she could no longer see or hear her sister and then tapped again on the higher of the two wooden doors. Then she pushed on the lower one, and it rocked slightly beneath her stick. She looked for the nails that attached it to the frame of the sunroom and found them lacking in all but one of the corners. She stuck her walking stick in between the door and the frame and levered it gently. The last of the nails gave up and the door fell into the weeds.

She looked behind her and listened. At first all she could hear was the sound of her own blood throbbing in her ears. Then a distant echo of Lily, still calling for the boy. Then her mother's scolding voice, accompanied by a hot flush that reached her fingers and toes.

"Well, you would do something about it, wouldn't you?" she said. "We can't just have him coming and going willy-nilly."

She listened again for Mama, but there was no reply. She got down on her hands and knees.

"Evelyn, you are a stupid girl," she said.

The frame of the French windows was completely broken, and Evelyn found smears and handprints on the dirty tiles within. The boy had been here. Squirming through the hole like it was a cat flap. Through the gap she saw the dim shapes of things. A carpet of dead flies that shifted in the draft. The bleached legs of a wicker chair. A wineglass.

Evelyn's heart hurt. She shut her eyes and looked away. The smell came to her, the same one she had noticed when the boy had returned that dawn. Dust and rot and beneath it something spiced, barely there at all. Tobacco, was it? She had forgotten her father had smoked. It got into everything. Evelyn put a hand over her nose and mouth. The scent made her sick and drew her in at the same time. It made her want to crawl on her belly like a worm, into the rank and comforting darkness of the sunroom and then on into the rest of the house, the sitting room, the drawing room, and what came next, the playroom? No, no, no, it did not exist; none of those rooms had ever existed.

She heard Lily's voice again, lower this time, as if leaving space for another to talk. She was about to stand when she risked another glimpse inside and saw a shapeless bag on the tiles just inside the door. It was notable only for the fact that it stirred no memory in her at all. The canvas was stained, and there was a loop at the top and two straps that were badly frayed. The object seemed wholly alien to her and the family and the house. Evelyn looked around for her sister and the boy. When she saw no sign of either, her arm snaked through the frame almost against her wishes and she wrestled the bag out through the hole.

Evelyn replaced the door and stood cradling the bag for a

moment. Then she took it to the toolshed and tucked it under a workbench, but did not have time to search its contents. She hurried back to the kitchen and found her sewing kit, and when Lily came around the side of the house, the boy in tow, Evelyn was sitting in a deck chair with Mama's ball gown in her lap.

"Found him!" Lily cried.

Evelyn was still out of breath and struggling to conceal it.

"Jolly good," she said, but did not look up. She did not want to lay eyes on the boy.

"Gosh, Sissie, look at your knees!"

Evelyn looked. Her nightdress was tented between her bony legs, and the material was dark with dirt and grass stains.

"Spot of weeding, that's all," she said.

"I thought you were sewing?"

"I am. Now."

She covered her knees with the ball gown and started to thread the needle.

"You know that can wait," said Lily. "I think we're all feeling like death warmed up today."

"If I don't mend this now, you'll be complaining about it later."

Lily didn't say anything.

"Where was he, then?" Evelyn said.

"He was in that far corner. Behind the pampas. Sitting on the wall like a garden gnome!"

Evelyn pricked herself with the needle. She hissed and sucked on her finger. It was covered in dust from the floor of the sunroom. She raised her head and addressed herself to Lily alone.

"What was he doing on the wall?"

"Not a lot, by the looks of things."

Evelyn finally looked at the boy. Pale and contrite as ever. Perhaps this explained why he was so sickly. Perhaps he had caught something from going inside the house.

"Don't climb on the wall. You've already broken it once."

He looked at his feet. "Sorry," he said.

"And you need the glasses, too. You don't want to go blind, do you?"

"To be fair to him," said Lily, "he came all this way without them. Walked for miles and miles. Maybe you don't need sunglasses after all? Another thing Mama got wrong! I'm starting to think she didn't have a clue what she was talking about."

"And you'd know better, would you?" snapped Evelyn.

"Calm down, Sissie."

"I've had enough of you talking about Mama like that. And I'm sure she's had enough, too! Sometimes, Lily, I don't think you understand the first thing about what she did for us. The rules are there for a reason. We wear the glasses for a reason. We stay out of the house for a reason. Can you not grasp that?"

Lily seemed to be on the cusp of an apology, but then she glanced at the boy and gave a faint smile. As if they were guilty siblings, standing before a parent. The boy kicked at the gravel with his old boots.

"Well," said Lily eventually, "you obviously got out of bed on the wrong side this morning. I feel god-awful, too, Sissie, but I'm not taking it out on you. Come on, beast of burden, we've got logs to split."

"I told you we need to fix the sunroom."

"And I told you it can wait. If we're doing anything today, we're collecting firewood. Would you rather be warm tonight or keep a few squirrels out of the house?"

Lily didn't wait for an answer and led the boy away. Evelyn

watched them go. There was an impertinence in the way Lily had spoken to her that was new and unsettling. At the corner of the house the boy stopped and glanced back, but Lily clicked her fingers at him and the pair disappeared from view. Evelyn started over on her sewing, and as she plunged the needle into the fabric she found herself reminded of sewing the boy's wound, the soft white thigh, the bright red smear of his blood.

A Test

She was standing with Mama on top of the grotto, examining a cut on her finger she'd received wrestling with some brambles. Her mother was beside her, looking out over the lake. Lily was sitting slightly farther away with her legs dangling over the grotto's edge. She had discovered a recorder in one of the toy chests and had been playing it ceaselessly and tunelessly for days.

I'm fairly sure there's a spring under here, their mother said. So with any luck it won't dry up. There'll be rainwater coming from somewhere or other. Don't you think?

She had her map of the estate under one arm. She unfurled it and studied it for a moment and then gazed back toward the house.

With a bit of work we might be able to dig some channels all the way to the vegetable plots so we don't have to carry so much water.

Irrigation, that's called. What do you say to a bit more digging, girls?

There was a pause, and the pampas grass rattled and hissed in the hot breeze.

Yes, Mama, said Evelyn.

Lily lowered the recorder from her lips.

Is Jamie going to come back?

Evelyn tried to remember when it was that he had left. She honestly could not remember how many years it had been. Two or three? The last face she'd seen that didn't belong to her family. His plaid shirt still hung from a nail in the toolshed.

No, said Mama. I shouldn't think so.

Can we go swimming?

No, Lily. Not right now.

They made their way back to the house, Mama unspooling a ball of string and fixing it with small stakes into the ground to mark the path of the proposed stream. Along the way she tested Evelyn and her sister on the names of the plants and flowers. Evelyn knew them all.

This one?

Chaffweed.

And that?

That's sowbread.

I like the dinosaur plant, said Lily.

It's called gunnera, said their mother.

It's got leaves like dinosaur skin.

Yes. It does.

They came around the front of the house, their mother still tracing a straight line with the string. Inside the toolshed their father was sawing something, and Evelyn thought she could smell cigarette smoke. They went past the open door, and a little farther on the string ran out. Their mother stuck the final stake in the earth and said:

Here, look at this.

Evelyn and Lily crouched down beside her. She took a little of the soil between her thumb and forefinger and sprinkled it onto the backs of their hands.

This is loam, she said. Feel how light and sandy that is.

Is that good? asked Evelyn.

For most things, yes.

Lily started playing her recorder again.

Come on, Lily, pay attention. She turned back to Evelyn. We could maybe plant a little bit of wheat here. Not a whole field of it. Enough to make a bit of bread. Not just wheat, actually. All kinds of cereals.

Breakfast cereals?

Mama smiled. Yes, we can have them for breakfast. But it's maybe not what you have in mind. Not the sugary stuff that you remember.

Lily was playing a single high note very loudly.

Lily! Mama shouted.

She snatched the recorder from her and Lily began to cry. Mama closed her eyes and took several long breaths.

I need you to listen, Lils.

There was a clang from inside the toolshed and their father stepped out into the heat of the day. He had a newly grown beard, and his thinning hair was stuck to his forehead with sweat. Lily ran to him and clutched at his legs. Clouds of sawdust escaped his trousers where she held him.

You could go a little easier on her, he said.

She needs to listen, said Mama. If we're staying here, then we all need to listen and learn, or we're going to die.

For God's sake, you don't need to say it like that!

I do. It's time somebody was honest around here.

Not around the girls.

I'm sorry, am I the only one living in the real world, here? Am I the only one who wants to try and make this work? I didn't even want to stay in the first place. Or have you forgotten that? You wanted to stay. So we stayed. On the assumption that we were all going to pitch in. But if any of you don't want to do that, then you can go north with everyone else and live in the car.

Lily blubbed something from behind her father's legs.

What's that, Lily-bear?

I don't want to.

Don't want to what?

I don't want to stay.

It's not too shabby, is it?

I miss . . .

Lily gasped between sobs.

I miss . . .

But she got no further than that.

Their mother and father looked at each other for a long time. Their father aged and disheveled under his beard. Their mother panting, as if struggling to master something inside her. She brushed a strand of hair out of her eyes and turned to Evelyn.

Well? she said.

Evelyn stood perfectly still. Pinned to the earth by her mother's look.

What? she said.

Come on, said Mama. If everyone's taking sides.

Evelyn did not reply. Her mother swore and then kicked the stake out of the ground in a spray of dry soil and walked away toward the house. Lily ran in the opposite direction. Their father went lumbering after her but could not keep up. From where she stood, Evelyn watched the members of her family take their slow and separate paths through the parched greenery, and began to wonder how much of the burden would fall on her—had already fallen on her—to keep them and the garden together.

21

Lily and the boy did not return at lunchtime. Evelyn made herself a salad but did not feel hungry in the slightest and left the leaves untouched in the bottom of the bowl.

She took herself off to the burn to consider what should be done. About the boy, about Lily. There was the bag she'd found, too. She'd hidden it under the workbench in the long wooden box they used for the croquet mallets. She could not bring herself to open it. She'd had enough revelations for the day, and who was to say the bag's contents wouldn't be as unsettling, or as poisonous, as the inside of the house.

The burn was her mother's favorite place in the garden, and a good spot for thinking. Evelyn had never been sure why it was called that. Her father's word for it. The way he said the word gave it two complete syllables. The stream emptied from the lake, black and silken in the shade of the trees, and ran over rocks and roots all the way to the wall, where it disappeared under a small arch into the beyond. Sometimes it dried up, only to return with one of the obliterating downpours that visited them very occasionally. The water in the lake rose and fell but never disappeared. Their mother had said it was fed by a spring, and if the spring survived, then it must have been raining somewhere. Some other lush and verdant place that Evelyn preferred not to think about.

She sat on the bank among the flowers. Campion, brunnera, buttercups, wild garlic. The grass was cool under her palms and her thighs. She saw wagtails and thrushes dipping in the stream, a storm of gnats boiling in a shaft of sunlight. There was a knotted rope swing hanging over one of the pools, from before.

Evelyn closed her eyes and breathed in the sweet-savory smell of the garlic and heard wild laughter. She thought it was the sound of Lily on the swing, and the memory came to her with more force than any before it. It seemed to replace every other thought and sensation with an intensity like the smell of her father's tobacco.

She should never have looked in the sunroom. It had made a breach not just in the sanctity of the house but also in herself, and now everything she wished to forget would come in a torrent and she would have nothing with which to shore up her being. She made fists of the garlic leaves on either side of her.

She heard Lily's laugh again, and it was joined by another and the rustle of leaves. She opened her eyes and looked downstream and saw her sister and the boy tramping toward her. The boy held their wood axe over one shoulder and was helping Lily through the undergrowth. There was a slight smile on his lips. The expression made him look different, older.

A smile, after everything he had done!

They saw her and stopped laughing, and Evelyn felt a cold flush at the base of her skull.

"Would you believe it," said Lily. "She's actually having a rest for once."

"I think I've earned it," Evelyn said flatly.

Evelyn looked at the boy, and the boy stopped smiling and looked at his feet again.

"You won't believe this," said Lily, and ruffled his hair. "Those poplars that have been lying there for years? Sawed and split, the lot of them! You can't stop him when his blood's up."

Evelyn watched them. Thick as thieves. She doubted Lily would even care if she told her what she knew about the boy's activities.

"What were you laughing about?" Evelyn asked.

"Oh, nothing. Just a silly joke."

Evelyn found their faces closed and uncommunicative. The boy leaned into Lily and raised a hand to her ear in a whisper. Lily nodded and smiled.

"Go on, then," she said.

The boy glanced at Evelyn and then went off on his own, up the burn, back to the house.

"What was all that about?" said Evelyn.

"I can't tell you."

"Lily."

"He's going to give you a surprise."

"He's already given me one surprise this morning."

"What do you mean by that?"

Evelyn watched the boy's willowy silhouette loping along

the path. A purpose all his own. She was struck suddenly by how little she actually knew about him. Not his name, nor his age. She couldn't even guess it, when years meant nothing to her anymore. Ten years old? Twenty? If she had to answer, she would have said he was somewhere between the two. She wondered if that meant he was actually closer to being a man than she'd first suspected. Hadn't Lily said so under the covers? Why had she not found that more alarming at the time?

Evelyn waited until he was out of sight and then took her sister's hand.

"He's been going in the house," she said.

Lily blinked a couple of times. "Has he?"

"Yes. I'm sure of it. He's been going through the sunroom. Where I was looking this morning."

"How are you so sure?"

Evelyn paused. "I just am," she said.

Lily smiled.

"What?" said Evelyn. "This is not funny, Lily!"

"You had a peek, didn't you?"

"No."

"You did! You disobeyed Mama. Well, hurrah for that! A teenage rebellion at the ripe old age of . . . whatever you are."

Evelyn gripped her sister's wrist more tightly and Lily grimaced.

"Ouch! Go easy!"

"What do we do? We can't just have him going in and out of the house as he pleases!"

"Can't we?"

"Excuse me?"

"It doesn't really matter, does it? He can do what he wants. If he wants to risk life and limb, that's up to him."

"It's not just that it's dangerous. There are other things in there."

"Like what?"

"You know what I mean!"

"I don't, actually. Unless you mean monsters, but I think I'm a little old to be falling for that again."

"I'm talking about the things from before. All of those things that Mama kept us safe from. Men's things."

"As far as I remember, she never actually said what those things were," Lily said.

"Yes, and thank God she didn't! I don't want to know anything about them."

"You don't have to. You're not the one going into the house, are you?" Lily shrugged. "Doesn't make any difference if he goes wandering round up there. Means nothing to him. They're Mama's rules, not his."

Evelyn let go of her sister's arm and stared at her in disbelief. "Why are you being like this?"

"What am I being like?"

"Bloody-minded."

"I'm being the opposite of bloody-minded. You're the one who's incapable of thinking about things differently."

Evelyn was lost for words. The nonchalance in the way Lily spoke. She wondered if her sister was still slightly drunk from the night before. Or perhaps she had always felt this way? The vagueness of their mother's threats had made a blank space of the inside of the house, and only now was Evelyn realizing that she and her sister saw that blankness quite differently. It excited Lily. It terrified Evelyn.

"You knew he'd been in the house, anyway," Lily went on.

"Didn't you see him up there in the window days ago? When we were playing the game?"

"Yes, exactly!"

"Then why are you flying off the handle now?"

Evelyn took several breaths to steady herself. She thought to tell her sister about the bag, too, but Lily began picking her way through the garlic and the nettles back toward the path.

"Don't just walk away from me, Lily."

Lily shook her head but kept on walking.

"Honestly, Evie," she said, "sometimes you sound so much like her, it's frightening."

22

Evelyn got to her knees in the dirt and the sawdust on the toolshed floor and unrolled the top of the boy's rucksack. It had perhaps been full of provisions when he set out from wherever he'd come from, but now it contained only a few items. She handled them with a mixture of wariness and deep reverence. A pair of woolen gloves, most of the fingers worn through. A lamp that did not work. A pad of paper with only a few sheets left in it, and those already scribbled upon. She caressed the surface of each one and felt the deep etchings of a pencil. The lines were wobbling and scattershot, but not, she thought, without meaning. On one of the sheets, among the lines, were bunched squares and triangles like a child's building blocks. A house, perhaps, but not their house. It was not swathed in ivy and the roof was angular and the walls did not bow and swell. A few of the lines the boy had drawn curled around it. A map, was it?

She studied it for some time and then heard her mother's voice again and worried that these, too, were men's things, and were therefore imparting something forbidden and perhaps toxic to her soul. She quickly closed the pad and put it face down on the floor.

She carefully arranged the items in front of her. She knew her sister would wonder at them, would covet them. Mama, on the other hand, would have thrown the rucksack and everything in it onto the bonfire. Evelyn did not want to do that. Not yet, anyway. Another act of disobedience. Perhaps Lily was right about her long-arrested rebellion.

She lifted the bag and turned it upside down, but it still felt heavy. She groped inside and found a zipped pocket that contained a plastic lozenge a little smaller than her hand, with a small glass window and twelve rubber buttons arranged in a grid. Some of them were numbered. Hadn't she and Lily had one of these? A toy, bright red and yellow. She remembered going into different rooms, the thing pressed coldly to her cheek. Lily's high voice coming through the static. *Come in! Come in! Is anybody there?*

Evelyn stared at the telephone through rising nausea. She pressed all the buttons, but nothing happened. She pressed the little transparent square, and nothing appeared there either. She tried the buttons again, then held the mouthpiece to her lips and waited a long time before finding the courage to whisper.

"Hello?"

The telephone was dead. It seemed inoperable, but what did she know about such things? What if the boy had been using it, night after night? Who on earth was there to talk to?

Lily called to her from the kitchen and her heart flailed.

She put the telephone in the pocket of her nightdress and bundled everything else back into the rucksack and stuffed the rucksack into the croquet box. She got up and dusted her knees and looked along the rows of sharp tools hanging from the wall of the shed—axes and hacksaws and pruning knives. Studied their blades.

"Steady on, Evie," she said aloud. "We won't be needing those yet."

HER SISTER WAS waiting for her on the lawn.

"Close your eyes," Lily said.

"Why?" said Evelyn.

"Don't come any closer! Just close your eyes."

"I'm not in the mood, Lily. I need to talk to you."

"Stop being such a sourpuss and do it!"

Evelyn closed her eyes. All she could picture was the contents of the bag.

"Ready? I promise you'll feel better afterward. We have a surprise for you."

Lily took her by the elbow and led her over the gravel and up onto the step. Evelyn had an unpleasant memory of helping their mama around the garden, just before the end, before she'd capitulated to the wheelchair. Mama had spat at her, told her she didn't need help, that she wasn't a child.

Evelyn stepped into the coolness of the kitchen and smelled woodsmoke and garlic and a sweetness she hadn't expected. She heard the slight wheeze of the boy and felt fearful all of a sudden.

"All right," said Lily. "You can open them."

Evelyn opened her eyes. The kitchen was festooned with flowers. They were tied into bouquets and arranged in cups and vases, on the table, on the work surface, on the windowsill, around their bedding. Hundreds of varieties, almost every kind the garden had to offer.

"Gosh," said Evelyn.

"They're for you," said the boy.

"For me?"

"To say thank you. And sorry. And . . ."

He fidgeted with the waistband of his too-large trousers. When she looked at him now, all she could think about was him creeping through the house, seeing things, touching things. And perhaps broadcasting everything he was seeing and doing on his old telephone. She felt its leaden weight in her front pocket.

"Well, you could show a little more enthusiasm," said Lily when Evelyn had been silent for a long while. "Aren't they gorgeous?"

Evelyn nodded. "Yes. They are. Very pretty."

"He's a good boy really."

Lily gave her sister a meaningful look. As if this made up for everything. For breaking the most sacred of all Mama's rules.

"Do you like them?" the boy asked.

"Very much," said Evelyn. She picked a stem out of the vase on the table and looked at its ragged white end and felt it already going limp in the warmth of her hand.

THEY PLAYED CARDS again that night. Evelyn won a few games, but she knew it was because they were letting her. She looked around at the boy's handiwork as if in admiration, but the only thing she thought was that all the flowers would be dead in a few days, and there would be bare patches in the flower beds that none but she would notice.

She still had not found an opportunity to tell her sister about what she had discovered, and by now had stopped looking for one. The longer they played, the more it seemed clear that Lily would only become overexcited by the bag and the telephone. She would probably give the boy another pat on the head for bringing them into the garden. It was in both of their interests, thought Evelyn, to keep the items to herself.

"Gosh," said Lily when Evelyn had won her third game, "what a drubbing. Have you been practicing without us?"

Evelyn held the stack of all twenty-five cards. She straightened their edges.

"Seems it's my lucky day," she said.

"One more? What about you, beast of burden?"

The boy waited for Evelyn to reply.

"I'm going to bed," she said.

"Then let's all go to bed," said Lily.

Evelyn got up and said nothing. She wanted to sleep by herself tonight. She went over to their bedding and started arranging the blankets.

"Oh, good heavens!" Lily said. "We've never read him the book!"

"I don't think we should read him the book. It'll just confuse him."

"It'll be fun, Sissie. He'll like it."

"He won't understand it. We don't even bloody understand it."

Lily made a face. She led the boy from the table over to their bedclothes, lowered herself, then felt beneath her pillow for the book. She looked up and patted the floor. The boy sat cross-legged and floppy beside her.

Lily peeled open the first of the dry, curling pages and traced it with a dirty fingernail.

"What are you doing?" said Evelyn.

"What?"

"That's not where we'd got to."

"We may as well start over. For the boy."

Evelyn folded her arms.

"Come on, Evie, sit down with us," said Lily.

Evelyn didn't. She went over to the dresser and opened the drawer. She pretended to read the almanac with one hand, and in the other she held the boy's telephone, turning it over and over in the warm depths of her pocket.

"Suit yourself," said Lily. "Right. Everybody ready, then?" She cleared her throat.

"*There is no one left,*" she began.

Evelyn noticed the boy was listening very attentively. There was a sadness in his young face and for a few moments her anger at him subsided, and flared, and subsided again.

Lily went on. "*When Mary Lennox was sent to Misselthwaite Manor to live with her uncle, everybody said she was the most disagreeable-looking child ever seen . . .*"

Evelyn listened until the end of the first chapter. Almost against her will the book brought her some solace, the story so familiar and so utterly remote. The bittersweet remembrance of something they had never even had. She did not know what the boy thought about it. She did not know what the boy thought about anything.

"There," said Lily. "What did you think of that?"

"It was good," said the boy.

"See!" said Lily, though she didn't turn around to address Evelyn. "I told you he'd like it."

"Fine," said Evelyn. "But that's all. Bedtime now."

"Have you seen one of these before?" Lily asked the boy.

"Yes," he said.

"They have books where you came from?"

He nodded.

"We've got more in the house," said Lily. "Mama wouldn't let us read them, though."

He looked at his lap and scratched his thigh with one finger.

"What else do they have?" asked Lily. "In the other place."

Evelyn gripped the telephone tighter but did not say anything. Perhaps she would hear the answers this time. Perhaps she wanted to.

The boy shrugged. "Lots of things."

"Like what?"

"I don't know. Lots."

"Things we don't have here?"

"Yes."

"Electric things?"

"Yes."

"Do you have a car?"

"I don't. Some of the men do."

"The men . . ." Lily repeated, almost in a whisper. She waved the book in front of his nose. "You must know all sorts of things. I bet you understand this better than we do."

She began scanning the first pages again. Evelyn came over from the dresser and seized the book from her sister's hand. She tossed the pages across the room and one of them detached completely, making chaotic somersaults in the air. Lily watched her in disbelief.

"What was that for?"

"You know what it was for. What did I tell you earlier?"

"That was about the house."

"It's the same thing! Give me strength, Lily!"

Lily crawled on all fours to retrieve the book and tried to slot the loose page back among the others.

"You've ruined it," she said.

"Good." Evelyn fetched the almanac from the dresser and threw it down in front of the boy. "There," she said. "If it's a good book you're after."

It landed face up between them. *Lunchtime. Bathtime. Bedtime.* Evelyn gathered her blanket in her arms and went farther into the darkness and remade her bed. She did not want to see either of their expressions; she saw them anyway when she closed her eyes.

THOUGHTS OF THE sunroom came to her again and again as she tried to settle that night, though she'd hardly seen anything at all. A few dim outlines, but all the more menacing for their lack of substance. Thoughts of men and cars and electric things. The telephone, too. It was still in the pocket of her nightdress, and sometimes she rolled on it and had to stop herself from crying out when it dug into her hip.

When she fell asleep, she dreamed more black dreams. Some presence hefting itself about in the rest of the house. Man or animal or some other more malevolent thing. Doors slamming, though she didn't know if they were slamming open or closed. She was young in the dream and moved about with ease. She tried to get outside, and when she finally found the way through, she saw that the garden was in full bloom but littered with boxes. The boxes were oblong in shape and made of a wood so dark and polished it might have been granite. She knew that the boxes contained bodies. They were beyond number. She realized there was a garden party taking place, and the guests wafted happily through the grounds, laughing and talking and resting their drinks on the boxes' lids. When Evelyn approached one of them, there was a knocking from inside. She didn't know if this meant she should open the box or keep it closed. Anxiety turned to dread, a great black lurch, and suddenly she was awake again and staring at the ceiling.

She listened for a moment. The boy and her sister were still whispering together in the darkness, and her heartbeat doubled. She did not listen any harder, for fear of understanding them.

"Stop chattering and go to sleep," Evelyn said into her pillow.

They were quiet for a few minutes but then the whispering started again. Evelyn took the pillow from under her head and covered her ears, with each breath more certain that the boy was no less dangerous than a man—perhaps more so, since his dissimulation had fooled even Evelyn—and that he and all he had touched would need to be excised like the rot from an apple.

A Lesson

She woke up one morning with blood on her bedclothes. Two perfectly round spots on the sheets, one orbiting the other. A third on her nightdress. She stared into her lap and felt more curious than scared. Lily found her like that when she woke a few minutes later. She leaned over between their beds and looked herself.

What happened? she said.

I don't know, said Evelyn.

Does it hurt?

Evelyn shifted where she sat.

I don't think so, she said.

She went down into the kitchen without getting dressed. Her mother was washing muddy roots in the sink, and when she saw what had happened she let them drop into the brown water. She seemed not worried but sad. It was as if something she had foreseen and hoped to avoid had at last come upon the household, something she had not told either of her daughters about.

What is it? Evelyn asked.

It's nothing to worry about, love. It'll stop soon.

But why's it happening?

It just means you're getting older. It happens to all of us.

Will it happen to me? said Lily.

Yes, said their mother. If you ever decide to grow up.

That was the only explanation she ever gave them. She took Evelyn to her bedroom and showed her how she could keep from ruining her clothes.

Evelyn did not feel like she was getting older. Only a few days earlier Lily had informed her that it was Evelyn's twelfth or perhaps thirteenth birthday, and Evelyn had not believed her. Lily had given her three boiled sweets she had found in the car glove box and a card with a pop-up snail that she'd made herself.

Evelyn went about her tasks in the garden as usual. She liked being busy; or rather, hated being idle and the thoughts that accompanied idleness. She enjoyed the work more than usual that day, feeling stronger and more accomplished in the secret knowledge that she was now unequivocally a young woman. She made a point of tending to her apple tree to mark the occasion. It had grown as strong as she and was heavy with blossom.

At midday Mama found her and said it was time she learned what to do with the beehives. It was as if she, too, wished to acknowledge her daughter's womanhood, though not explicitly. When they made their way back to the house, her father was sitting in a deck chair on the gravel. He was shirtless and his eyes were closed. Next to the feet of the chair was something reddish in a squat glass tumbler. He and Mama did not speak, but there was little of note about that. Their father was silent most of the time now, though he wore the look of someone subjected to loud noises nobody else could hear.

The hives were seething that day. The bees' droning was so deep it felt as if they had found their way through Evelyn's ears and into her skull. She wanted to run away at first, but her mother held her hand tightly and maneuvered her in front of the hive as if she were some kind of votive offering. She removed one of the frames and showed it to Evelyn.

Can you see the queen? she said. The big one? There. She's in charge. She's the one that lays the eggs. And she encourages all the other bees to do their jobs, too. All these workers, they're all lady bees. They're the ones who build the hive and go looking for food and look after the little bees. And they're all working together. You see? No one's complaining that they've got too much work to do. You don't get one bee trying to take more than she needs from the other bees. Everyone just does their bit.

She examined the frame and didn't speak for a while.

What about the boy bees? Evelyn asked.

The males? Well. There aren't very many of them. That's one there. She pointed with her little finger. They stay in the hive for a while and they eat and eat, and then they leave the hive and have their wicked way with some other bees from another colony. All right for some, isn't it?

Evelyn noticed her mother was looking past her ear toward Papa. He picked up his glass and drained the whole thing and then started to splutter. When she turned back, her mother was smiling, and the smile turned into a laugh, and then she couldn't stop laughing and soon there were tears in her eyes.

What? Evelyn asked. What's so funny?

But her mother wouldn't say.

23

The next morning the sisters rose without speaking while the boy remained encamped under the kitchen table. Evelyn put on her old plaid shirt and jeans and went to let the chickens out. Lily came past her a few minutes later on her way to the gazebo, one of their mother's woven shopping bags under her arm. Evelyn watched her go as the hens gathered around her.

"Keep an eye on that one," she said to the cockerel.

The cockerel looked at Evelyn and shivered, and a thin cloud of dust rose from its plumage. She looked at the other chickens, and they, too, seemed coated in something like fine flour. Sawdust from the coops, she assumed. The chickens were older, too—wasn't everybody?—and less able to preen them- selves. Yes, that was it. Any other conclusion was not worth entertaining. And yet hadn't the rest of the garden also seemed a little dull, a little faded, in recent days?

She collected the eggs and went back inside. In the kitchen the boy was going around his flower arrangements, swapping blooms in and out and lifting their drooping heads. They were already looking withered, and not even a day had passed.

"They'll fade more quickly if you keep touching them like that," Evelyn said.

He drew his hand back. "What's happening to them?"

How could he not know?

"They die when you break the stems," she said.

"They die?"

"Eventually."

"She didn't tell me."

They were silent for a moment, and Evelyn realized that they were alone for the first time in days.

"So. She put you up to this, did she? A team effort."

"Oh no. It was my idea. But she showed me where to find the ones you liked."

"That was kind of her."

"Do you have a favorite?"

Evelyn looked around the kitchen. He'd collected half of the garden. She loved them all—grieved for them all now. On the windowsill was a teapot crammed with thick spears that glowed purple and orange against the sunlight. She went over and examined them. Lupins, snapdragons. A familiar bouquet.

"Where did you get these?" she asked, though she knew the answer.

"Out there." He made a vague gesture.

"Where, exactly?"

"By the big rock."

"Did she tell you that you could pick these?"

"I don't know. I don't remember."

Evelyn put on her slippers and took her stick and opened the back door. She walked as fast as she could, faster than she could. She felt her hips grinding. She took the well-worn route past the toolshed and out toward their patch of wheat, knowing that the boy was still behind her but not speaking, or perhaps speaking very quietly, and she came to the spot that marked her mama's grave and found the rock bare and the flowers gone and the whole plot flattened by the boy's huge feet.

She got on her hands and knees and put her forehead to the warm earth.

"I'm sorry," she said. "I'm so sorry, Mama." Over and over.

After a while she was aware of the boy standing silently beside her. He tried to put a hand on her shoulder, but she snarled and he backed away. He did not try again and went back to the house. Evelyn remained there, prostrate, for some time.

When she finally came back to the kitchen, the boy was standing on the doorstep wringing his hands. She ignored the ache in her heart and in her knees and marched toward him as if she were twenty years younger. Straighter than she had been in days. Her hand was raised before she even reached him, and he cowered slightly but did not move, as if already resigned to punishment.

"You stupid creature!"

She kept her hand raised but did not move any farther, struck by a vision of her mother, in the same position, silhouetted against the sky.

"You can't just go around doing what you like. Chopping flowers off left, right, and center. Do you have any idea what Mama will say?"

She felt a throbbing in her arm and began to lower it.

"Ruined. All ruined. After everything I did for you. After I fed you, and clothed you, and stitched you back up, this is what you do."

He tried to get past her, but she reached out and without thinking grabbed the thigh that Lily had cut with the shears. She squeezed the muscle between her thumb and her fingers, and he cried out.

"I know where you've been going at night, too. I know about the house. You're probably wondering where your bag is, aren't you? And your telephone."

The whites showed all the way around his eyes.

"What's it for? Who have you been talking to?"

"No one!"

"You're a liar!"

She squeezed his leg a little tighter and he gritted his teeth.

"Tell me. Show me how it works."

He was about to speak when Lily came around the corner of the house.

"Sissie, stop it!"

Lily pulled her away and Evelyn let go of the boy's thigh. She looked at her sister and then at her hand, as if it had behaved of its own accord.

"What's all this about?" Lily said.

Evelyn wanted to tell her about the telephone, but still she could not find the words.

"The flowers, Lily," she said in the end, her voice not half as loud as it had been. "He took them from Mama."

"He wasn't to know, was he? It's not his fault." Lily touched his thigh lightly with her fingertips. "How could you be so beastly?"

"He needs to learn."

"Oh, for goodness' sake, Evie."

"I mean it. If he's going to stay, he needs to follow the rules."

"They'll grow back."

"It's not just about the flowers. I told you. He's been going into the house."

"And I told you I don't see what the problem is."

"From now on I want him where I can see him."

Lily narrowed her eyes and a hint of a smile appeared on her face. "Oh. I see."

Evelyn frowned. "You see what?"

"I see what this is about."

"It's about making sure he doesn't ruin everything we've done."

"I don't think it's about that at all. I think it's about you. I think you're jealous."

"*Jealous?*"

"You're jealous because he's changed his mind. Because he likes me more than you."

Evelyn wanted to slap her sister, too, but was forestalled by something. By the thought that there was some truth in what Lily had said. Not so much that she was no longer the boy's favorite, but that she was no longer Lily's. That they were no longer each other's favorite.

While she groped for words, Lily took the boy by the arm and led him back into the kitchen. Evelyn was about to follow them but stopped when she heard their feet on the tiles. The boy's boots thumped heavily, but Lily's steps were almost soundless. Evelyn looked down at her sister's feet. She was wearing silk pumps that Evelyn had never seen before, the toe round and padded, two broad ribbons crossed over the top of her foot. They were slightly too big for her. The flowers, the house, the telephone, all quite left Evelyn's mind.

"Lily," she said quietly. "Where did you get those shoes?"

Lily ignored her and helped the boy into a chair. She fussed around him, examining his thigh, stroking his hair, offering him water.

"Was that what you were carrying to the gazebo?"

Her sister still didn't reply.

"I know they're not yours because yours would be too small now. So they must be Mama's."

Lily finally stood up. She looked at the pumps and raised one foot and then the other. The satin was wrinkled and grimy and of no color whatsoever.

"Yes," she said, "I suppose they must be."

"He got them for you, didn't he? You sent him into the house to find them."

Lily looked at the boy and then back at her sister and laughed. "Oh, for crying out loud, Evelyn."

"He got them from upstairs, didn't he?"

"If you insist."

"Where else would they have come from?"

"Maybe I found them," Lily said.

"You found them."

"They were lying in the grass by the wall. You must have buried them, and something must have dug them up."

"I didn't bury them," Evelyn said. "I'd remember that."

"Oh, yes, Sissie, because your memory is so infallible!"

Evelyn came forward and pointed a quivering finger at her sister's face. "You've been telling him to go into the house to fetch things for you, haven't you? What else did he get for you? Books? Clothes? Papa's gun?"

"Papa didn't have a gun. You're being hysterical."

Evelyn's head swam, and she found herself clinging to the back of a chair.

"After all this time! After everything Mama said! How could you be so idiotic?"

"You looked in the house, too, didn't you? I know you did. Snooping around the sunroom."

"Snooping! I did no such thing."

"Of course you did. But then it's fine when you do it, isn't it? I was always the one Mama took it out on."

"Yes. And frankly I'm starting to understand why."

Lily gave Evelyn a look that was almost like pity. "Take a deep breath, Sissie. It's just a pair of shoes."

"It's not *just* a pair of shoes, and you know it! You're trying to get something back, Lily, something else, and you know you can't. And you know you shouldn't. Mama said so. Where will it end? Are you just going to empty the house of all our old things? Why don't we just open the place up and go back to sleeping in our old bedroom?"

And then she pictured it, suddenly, their little twin beds, the shaft of yellow sun from the skylight, a conference of stuffed animals between them. She closed her eyes and clapped a hand over her mouth.

Lily put a hand on her shoulder, but Evelyn shrugged it off.

"I think you need a rest," Lily said. "I found the shoes. Are you listening? There's no conspiracy here. It was a bit of good luck. I've not been sending him into the house to do anything." She paused. "But it's nice to hear you trust me as much as ever."

Evelyn felt exhausted. Perhaps she had been mistaken after all. Had she buried the shoes? She honestly had no memory of it. But they had buried so many things over the years.

"There's something else," she said, feeling the weight of the telephone in her pocket.

"There's always something else!" cried Lily. "For goodness' sake, Evelyn, please let it go. You're like a dog with a bloody bone." She turned to the boy and brushed the fringe from his eyes. "Come on, you'll live. Still plenty for us to be getting on with."

The boy looked at Evelyn and seemed to be on the verge of speaking, but he closed his mouth and pushed back his chair. Then the pair of them went arm in arm out into the garden, Lily padding soundlessly in her new shoes. The more Evelyn looked at them, the surer she was. She had never buried them. She should trust her instincts, she thought, and her instincts told her that Lily was mischievous and covetous and a bad liar; that perhaps, at long last, her sister deserved some sort of punishment for her wayward behavior.

24

Evelyn sat at the table with the boy's telephone and probed its buttons but could not make it speak. If she could make it speak, then her sister might understand. She might convince her of the danger the boy posed. To the garden, to both of them. She turned the scratched plastic over and over until her palms and fingers grew sweaty and she dropped it onto the wooden tabletop. It clattered heavily and the noise echoed around the kitchen and produced a feeling of such intense panic that Evelyn went back to their blankets and hid it in her nightdress again.

Lily and the boy came back briefly. Lily swapped her shoes for boots and rummaged in the dresser while the boy waited at the door.

"He's finished all his jobs, so we're going to do some painting," she said. "Feel free to join us once you've had enough of your tantrum."

Then they left her alone again.

Evelyn had one final fumble with the telephone and in her frustration pressed all the buttons at once as if she were attempting to crush the whole thing with her bare hands. The transparent window in one half of the phone turned from gray to a kind of phosphorescent green. Evelyn dropped it and watched it glowing. Another unwanted memory arose from that turquoise light: the smell of chlorine, humidity, her small toes on the edge of a tiled pool. She closed her eyes again.

The telephone made a noise, and when she opened her eyes, there were words across the screen: *Have you found them?*

Evelyn stared at the letters for a long time, as if each one needed careful deciphering. When the message was clear, she made an almost inaudible moan.

The boy was not alone. He was a forerunner of some kind, a herald of something more terrible. She thought of the scraps of paper in his bag, the picture of the house, the lines that led to and from and around it. Of course it was a map. Drawn by someone who had perhaps heard of the house but never seen it. Or, stranger still, by someone who had seen the house before its dilapidation. But who had sent him? And why? Perhaps Lily already knew.

Liars, Evelyn thought, the pair of them.

She wrapped the telephone in a handkerchief and then again in one of her mama's work shirts. She had no idea how the thing worked but thought of it as a kind of conduit for all the poison that lay beyond the garden. What if someone was listening to her even now?

Decisiveness was all. She had vacillated ever since the boy

had arrived. She took the bundle under one arm and marched out to the back of the house and threw the telephone, shirt and all, into the shallows of the lake. It floated there for a few seconds and then was swallowed by the marshy water. She went back to the toolshed and took the boy's rucksack from the croquet box and did the same with this, poking it under the weeds with the longest rake she could find. She stood at the lake's edge for a few minutes, then headed off toward the bottom of the lawn.

LILY WAS SITTING on her stool beside the remains of the old greenhouse, its glass panes long since shattered. Her paints were beside her on one of the greenhouse shelves, which she could reach through the empty frame. The only colors that Lily had left were reds and oranges and obscure shades of brown. All the green had been used up long ago, and the blues and yellows shortly after that. She'd tried making her own pigments from the flowers in the garden but without much success.

The boy was sitting on the grass in front of a rowan tree, his good leg bent, his bad leg extended. Evelyn waited behind one of the rhododendron bushes, then crept in among its branches and crouched there, smothered by the flowers' heavy scent, pricked and skewered in her back and thighs. She could see the edges of her sister's painting. It was of the boy. Lily *was* his favorite, surely. Evelyn never painted pictures of him. Next to the stool Lily had three more sheets of paper that she had painted over countless times because there were no more in the house. They were stiff and ridged like corrugated iron.

"Such lovely long legs on you," Lily said.

The boy waggled one foot, embarrassed.

She'd filled an empty can with water and she washed her brush in it. Evelyn looked at the design. A bleached picture of a pineapple, yellow rings at its base. She fancied she could taste the can's contents, fleetingly. Something else the boy had scavenged? They had not eaten tinned food since the days before Papa left them. He was the one who had found the tins, she remembered. It was one of the few useful things her father had done.

Lily loaded the brush with paint and scraped it across the board again. The bristles were worn down to stubble.

"I suppose you wouldn't have got this far with stumpy little legs, would you?"

The boy shrugged.

"You're very lucky, you know. That Mama isn't here anymore. She'd have had your guts for garters as soon as she laid eyes on you. I mean, I know *I* nearly had your guts for garters, but that was just because you surprised us."

He leaned forward and examined something on his knee.

"Hold still," she said. "I can't paint you if you keep shuffling about like that."

"I think your sister wants me to leave," the boy said.

"Oh, nonsense."

"I think she hates me."

"She doesn't hate you. She might hate me, of course. That's a possibility. She only seems to like me when I do what she says."

"Would she make us leave?"

"I don't think so, no." She paused. "Although maybe it wouldn't be such a bad thing if she did."

Evelyn wrapped her arms around herself, unable to believe what she was hearing. Unwilling to believe it.

"What do you mean?" said the boy.

"Oh, I don't know," said Lily. "Sometimes I think it would be nice to talk to somebody else. I didn't even realize how much I needed it until you arrived. You know, I think that's why I was such a terror when I first saw you. I don't think it was surprise at all. I think it was the opposite. Because I knew there was someone else out there, someone normal, whatever Evelyn or Mama used to say. Talking to me like I was a congenital idiot. Of course there was someone else. I thought about it all the time." She paused. "God, yes. A chat and a cup of tea with someone other than my sister. Imagine that."

Evelyn could not imagine it. Was this the truth, then? That Lily had been crawling the walls all this time, her heart set on abandoning Evelyn, and Mama, and the garden, at the first opportunity? In trying to protect her little sister from everything outside, had Evelyn only fostered in her a greater thirst for it? She felt like sobbing.

"The place you came from," said Lily. "Could we get there?"

Evelyn did not know who, exactly, she meant by "we."

The boy shook his head. "I don't want to go back there."

"It doesn't sound so bad. From what you said?"

"It's not bad. But there are better places. Better people." The boy paused for a moment and stroked his arm as if to soothe himself. "I don't want to leave this place," he said. "It's perfect."

Lily laughed. "You should tell my sister that," she said. "I'm sure she'd appreciate it."

"She wouldn't want to go, would she."

"Evelyn? God, no."

"Would you leave her?"

"No, of course not. I don't think so. Though she can be

hard work. Such a stickler. Half the time it's no different from living with Mama." She pointed her brush at him. "I didn't even realize that until you got here."

She went back to mixing her paints and the boy sat thinking.

"There might be another way," he said.

"Another way to what?"

"If you want company."

"Go on."

"I could bring someone here."

Lily's brush hung poised above her board for a moment. The silence roared in Evelyn's ears. She saw bright spots floating before her eyes. The world overexposed. She held her breath and waited for what her sister might say next.

"Oh gosh," said Lily. "Well, I don't know about that. Evelyn certainly wouldn't have it."

"That's what I thought."

"Who is this someone?"

"Just a friend."

Lily continued to paint without speaking, occasionally holding out her brush to gauge the boy's proportions. Eventually she said:

"I suppose I might be able to bring Evelyn around."

"Really?"

Lily put the wet brush to her lips, then laughed.

"No. Not really. I don't know what I'm saying, she wouldn't consider it for a moment. You were a surprise. But throwing open the gates and inviting people in? Can you imagine her face? No. She'd throw a wobbly if we even tried to mention it. Then she really might force us to leave. She'd invoke Mama. Conjure her spirit to hound us from the garden." She paused and her smile disappeared. "Yes, Mama wouldn't be happy at all."

Lily glanced down at her painting.

"This one isn't very good. Sorry. I think we should start again."

She picked up another piece of paper.

"You talk about her a lot," said the boy.

"Who?"

"Your mama."

"Not much else to talk about round here."

"What was she like?"

Lily set down her brush and looked at him. He seemed to hang on her reply, and fear it, too. He had never mentioned any parents of his own. Perhaps, Evelyn thought, he hoped Lily's answer might fill a space somewhere in himself.

"Well," said Lily. "That depends on which Mama you're talking about. No one's just one thing, are they? She changed a great deal. Of course she changed. Living somewhere like this."

She paused again.

"She was fierce," she continued. "She cared fiercely. And she was angry. But there were plenty of things to be angry about."

"Like what?"

"You've seen what it's like outside, haven't you? No one's patting themselves on the back about that."

Evelyn did not want to hear any more. They had exchanged so much, the boy and her sister, and this was only one conversation. Who knew what else had passed between them? Lily's world was a greater world, now, and Evelyn knew it. Perhaps it always had been that way. Populated with visions and memories and even hopes for the future. Lily pictured something where Evelyn saw only a featureless gray expanse. Her own world had never been larger than that slim corridor of green between the house and the wall, between the days before and the days to come. But it was too late to imagine anything different now. The admission that there was somewhere else, somewhere better perhaps, was not liberating but crushing. The shame of it. The waste, the waste.

Evelyn extricated herself from her hiding place and went back down the path, through the tunnel of hydrangeas and rhododendrons. She felt things unraveling. Perhaps this was how it ended, just as Mama had said. Again that needling regret that she had stayed her sister's hand in the first place, that she had not finished the job herself when the boy was in her lap, limp and weak like an injured bird.

There would be no one else admitted to the garden. She was resolved on that. If others came, she would not welcome them in as Lily intended. She would welcome them as their mother had done. And she certainly would not allow herself to go with them.

She was halfway to the house when she suddenly felt so light-headed with rage and worry that she had to stop and steady herself. She stood with her head bowed and thought she should go back to them. Let them know she had heard every treacherous word. Send them packing to this other place, if that was what Lily really wanted. She looked down at the lawn and saw her own footprints coming toward her from the bushes. She bent over and placed all five fingers in the grass and found a layer of dust a quarter of an inch thick at its roots.

She stood up and looked around the rest of the garden. She remembered only one other time when the leaves had taken on this silvered look. When the air was always hazy, regardless of the weather. She knew what it meant, and the thought of it seemed to smother any urge to confront her sister or the boy. She drifted back to the house, noting with a strange disinterest the tiny eruptions that accompanied each step.

An Accident

Evelyn came out of the back door of the house and found a
bare patch of gravel where the car had been. A large rectan-
gular island in a sea of dust. She didn't know where the
car had gone, or who had taken it. She didn't think it ran
anymore.

The house was empty apart from Lily and herself. Lily was still
asleep, and walking the long halls and landings had the muted feeling of a dream. Twilight all the time now, no matter what the hour
of day. She walked out of the kitchen door and deliberately didn't
wear shoes so that the gravel would hurt the soles of her feet and
prove that she was, in fact, awake. The garden was in gorgeous full
bloom, despite everything. She walked to the bottom of the grounds
and found her mother at the gate, standing in the middle of the driveway. The gates were open. She cut a defiant and forlorn silhouette.

Evelyn stood beside her mother and looked down the unpaved road to where it curved out of sight. It was as pitted and cratered as the surface of the moon.

I thought the car was broken, she said.

So did I, said Mama.

A long time passed.

Go and get your sister, said Mama. Time we should be getting on with things.

They spent the day drawing water from the lake. They were still nowhere near finishing the channels that their mother had proposed for the front garden. Endless purgatorial hours back and forth with buckets and tubs, their mother saying nothing apart from an occasional muttering under her breath that was new and frightening. Lily squatted in the reeds, showing her sister handfuls of frog spawn. Everywhere the warm and fetid stink of the lake's edge.

They were inside eating supper when they heard the rattle of the car's engine and the crunch of gravel under its tires. Their mother leaped up, knocking her plate to the floor. By the time Evelyn was outside, the boot of the car was open and her parents seemed to be struggling with each other. Evelyn went to the rear window of the car and put her face to the glass. It was loaded with tins of fruit and vegetables, ham and corned beef, beans and marrowfat peas, several drums of water, some white unlabeled boxes that Evelyn presumed were first aid supplies but that Lily continued to maintain, for months afterward, were doughnuts or cream cakes or some other treat.

You left us, their mother said. You left us, you fucking bastard.

He struggled as she gripped his wrists and brought his face an inch or two from hers. For a few seconds it was impossible to tell whether they were kissing passionately or trying to claw each other's eyes out.

In the middle of the night Evelyn was woken by the engine

starting again. She sat up in bed and heard the car laboring over the gravel. It choked and stopped. The driver restarted it and then revved it again and pressed the accelerator down fully. Evelyn's heart roared at the sound. There was a spray of stones and an impact that she felt in the very roots of the house. Lily sat up next to her. The darkness itself seemed to vibrate.

What was that? Lily said.

Evelyn told her to stay in bed and went out onto the landing. A commotion in the kitchen. Before she reached the bottom of the staircase, her mother swept past her into the hall. She didn't even see Evelyn. She was wearing her nightdress, and it was smudged and bloodied. There was a deep cut on her forehead that looked black and almost oily, and she was holding her elbow to her chest as if she had broken or dislocated something. Evelyn's father was not far behind her, following dumbly, one arm half outstretched in an ambiguous gesture—Evelyn didn't know if he was offering help or asking for it.

He seemed a wraith these days. So thin. She remembered only vaguely the brassy and booming voice he had once had, and could not square it with the man who now haunted the landings.

Perhaps you'll decide to stay put now, said Mama.

Evelyn waited for them to pass. She went down the hall and out of the kitchen, and there on the right-hand side of the house was the car, its front crumpled like a paper bag, the windscreen shattered from where it had been driven into the corner of the exterior wall of the playroom. There was smoke coming from under the wrecked bonnet but no flames that she could see. The food was still packed on the backseat, and it seemed undamaged.

Her mother appeared.

Come away, she said. Come away, Evie. It was just an accident.

One of her arms was dangling uselessly at her side.

Evelyn went back upstairs to bed. There were footsteps all over the house, up and down stairs, but no talking. Eventually the house was silent again. When Evelyn told her sister what had happened, Lily was quiet for a while, almost long enough for Evelyn to fall asleep, but then she got up and went downstairs and came back with a tin of pineapple rings she'd snatched through one of the car's broken windows. Evelyn watched as Lily tried to open it with a screwdriver. She succeeded only in puncturing a hole in the outside of the tin, but that was good enough for both of them, and they spent the rest of the night passing the tin between them and supping on the syrup that squirted out.

The next morning their mother's arm was in a makeshift sling, though she still had one free hand with which to padlock the gates of the estate and throw the key far, far into the middle of the lake.

25

In the gloom of the kitchen Evelyn made tea and drank it without tasting it. When she looked down into her cup, the surface of the water was speckled with the detritus that had fallen from her hair. She thought and thought about everything she had heard by the greenhouse, about the state of the garden, about the dust that even now clung to the fingers of one hand.

Lily and the boy arrived an hour later, Lily still chatting quite happily. She went and arranged the boy's portraits on the dresser and then came and sat down beside him, opposite Evelyn.

"We've decided to forgive you," said Lily.

Evelyn didn't reply. Lily waited for a moment and then

shrugged. She got up and silently fetched one of the blue-and-white china teacups, its rim serrated with years of chips, and poured herself some tea. Lily took a sip.

"Is there anything you'd like to say, Sissie," she said, "now you've had time to reflect?"

Evelyn stared at her through the steam. "There's a storm on the way," she said.

Lily raised her eyebrows, drank again, and passed the cup to the boy. "What makes you think that?"

"Haven't you noticed?"

"I can't say I have."

"I suppose not. I suppose you've had lots of other things to think about."

Her sister sighed. "I thought you might have calmed down by now, Evelyn. But I'm not sure I appreciate your tone."

Evelyn got up and went to the kitchen window with her tea. She surveyed the lawn, imagined them having to dig the whole garden up again. Then imagined having to do it by herself and felt so unutterably lonely that she didn't know where to look.

She heard Lily push her chair back and walk over to her. She touched her gently on the arm and Evelyn flinched.

"I don't think we need to worry. The garden can cope with a bit of a dusting. When has it not?"

Lily's eyes were gray and clear and seemed full of optimism.

"Easy for you to say," said Evelyn. "You won't even be here."

"Won't I?" Lily smiled. "I thought I had another few years in me. Do you know something I don't?"

"I know what you've been talking about with him."

"This again . . ."

"I heard you, Lily. Just now. By the greenhouse. And no,

there's no way we are allowing anyone else in here. And yes, I will lose my temper if you try to convince me otherwise."

The boy looked between the two of them.

"You were eavesdropping?"

"Thank God I was. The things you were plotting."

"Well. You know how Mama felt about that. That's another one of her rules you've broken."

"Don't talk to me about what Mama would and would not want."

"You're a hypocrite, Evelyn, do you know that?"

Evelyn could feel tears coming again, but an echo of her mother's voice was enough to make her swallow them.

"Am I such bad company, Lily?" she said. "Am I so intolerable?"

"You can be a perfect sod, yes. But that has nothing to do with it."

"You said you wanted to leave."

"I don't want to leave you, Sissie. Of course I don't." Lily paused. "But there are other people. Out there. Don't you think it would be nice to see somebody else? To talk to somebody else? You're always saying that we won't be around forever. Don't you think it would be good for us? After the way Mama went?"

Evelyn threw her cup to the floor, and it shattered. A piece of it skittered across the tiles and came to rest next to the boy's boot. He lowered his eyes. Lily placed her own cup on the table but didn't say anything.

"I've asked you to stop talking about Mama like that," said Evelyn.

"I'm only saying what we both know."

"What you know and what I know are two very different

things, sister dearest. I have not had the luxury of ignorance. If you'd seen the things I've seen, you would not be quite so quick to jump ship. I can promise you that."

Lily rolled her eyes. "Back to monsters, is it?"

"You don't know the half of it."

"I know the whole of it, actually. Because he's told me. Tell her."

She looked at the boy as if expecting him to explain himself to Evelyn, but he said nothing. He picked up the fragment of the teacup and put it on the table, where it sat, rocking back and forth.

"We're not having any more visitors," Evelyn said. "I don't care who they are. And they won't find us anyway because your telephone is at the bottom of the lake." The boy frowned. "And your bag and your gloves and your silly little drawings."

She could see the boy's shoulders rising and falling with his breath. He seemed stirred for the first time since he'd been in the garden. An uncharacteristic color in his cheeks.

"In the lake?" he said. "Why?"

"Why do you think? Inviting all your friends here without permission!"

"Telephone?" said Lily. "What telephone?"

"Don't pretend you didn't know."

"I don't know anything about it."

"Well. Shoe's on the other foot now. Horrible thing when people keep secrets from you, isn't it?"

"You sound like a bloody child, Sissie." She paused. "Does it work?"

"You see!" cried Evelyn, though her triumph could not have been emptier. "That's why I didn't tell you! You'd let the world and his wife know we were here!"

"Did you use it?" the boy said.

"Of course not."

"But did you turn it on?"

"Yes. I'm not a complete idiot. I read the message. Whoever it was from."

"And you threw it in the water?"

"Yes. Thank God I did."

They held each other's stare for a moment.

"No one is coming here," Evelyn said, "so if you really can't stand me, then you need to think long and hard and make your choice. You both stay, or you both go. I don't care which it is."

It was well into the afternoon, now, and Evelyn realized she had not dressed herself. Could she not even achieve that much, these days? She changed into her jeans and shirt and pulled the belt roughly around her waist, tightened it until it hurt, pricked on by her slovenliness. She was suddenly desperate to be digging and pruning and watering. To set the tone for the days to come. No more interruptions, no more indulgence of Lily's or the boy's foibles. They would not leave. They could not. They would stay and they would work, and if a storm came, they would dig everything out, and the garden would go on as it had always done.

She fetched a broom to sweep up the remaining fragments of china and pushed them into a small mound by the doorstep.

"I don't think it's as simple as that," the boy said.

Evelyn had a memory of the shock she'd felt when he'd first spoken in the silence of their kitchen. There was assurance in the way he spoke now, a tone that seemed an affront to her decisiveness and angered her afresh.

"Do you not?" she said.

"I don't think we can be sure that no one's coming."

"I have made sure," said Evelyn, but her voice faltered slightly.

"No," said the boy. "If you turned the phone on, then they'll know where I am."

"They?"

"And if they know where I am, they'll come and get me. They'll probably come and get you, too."

"Who?"

"The others."

"What others?"

The boy didn't answer. He simply heaved a great sigh, then laid his head upon the table, ear to the wood, as if listening for someone's approach.

26

Evelyn went alone to the toolshed and began carrying armfuls of their implements back to the kitchen. Stakes, spades, forks, a pitchfork, a scythe. Their mother's sickle was still sharp enough to fell a sapling in one go.

When she came back with the first lot of tools, Lily was with the boy by the dresser, comparing the merits of the various paintings she had made of him. Evelyn dumped the tools on the table, and Lily watched her but said nothing.

"I'll do everything myself then, shall I?" Evelyn said. "As per usual."

"What exactly are we meant to be doing?"

"Getting ready."

"I think this is all a bit much, Sissie."

"Obviously you do," said Evelyn. "You'd rather welcome them in and give them supper and a hot bath."

"You haven't heard him talk about them. They're not monsters, they're just people."

"You mean men."

"And women."

"Well, I trust him about as far as I can throw him. Men, monsters. Same difference."

"They won't hurt you," the boy said, though he seemed unsure.

Evelyn squinted at him.

"They will want to look in the house, though. And they'll probably want to take you back with them," he said. "They'll want to take all of us back."

He and Lily exchanged a glance. Evelyn seemed not to recognize either of them. Their faces had changed. As if they had been impostors all along.

"They'll do no such thing," said Evelyn, shooing them away from the dresser. She opened the drawer where they kept the almanac, but it was not there. She reached farther in and groped about but found only splinters. She slammed the drawer shut again.

"You," she said, pointing at her sister.

"What now?"

"You've taken the almanac."

"Of course I haven't. Why would I need to take it when I've got you to tell me exactly what to do all the time? Why on earth do you need it now, anyway?"

"I want to look at the map. I want to see where we can improve the wall. And we need to think about the storm. What we can cover, what we can save."

"I don't know where it is. You're the only one who uses it."

Evelyn looked at her askance and went rooting around the kitchen. She went from the table to their bedding, looking under the pillows and blankets and then opening all the kitchen cupboards.

"Well, it's hardly going to be in there, is it," said Lily.

Evelyn ignored her. She came back to where the boy was sitting at the table. He was examining the tools, one by one.

"Did you take it?" she said.

"No," he said.

"Stand up."

He stood up. She looked under where he had been sitting.

"Turn around."

He turned around. She patted the sides of his trousers and ran her hands over his shirt, front and back.

"Has to be someone else's fault, doesn't it?" Lily said. "We've not touched your bloody almanac, Evie."

"I think you're lying."

"I'm not."

"You were lying about your ballet shoes. You were lying about sending him into the house. I'm sick of you keeping things from me."

"That makes two of us, doesn't it?"

Evelyn looked at her and then in the drawer again, as if by some miracle the almanac might have materialized there. She felt as if she was going mad. She had felt it all day. She looked in the smaller drawers where she kept the sunglasses and where Lily stored their mother's jewelry.

"Well, here's the silver lining," said Lily. "If you've gone doolally, then you're off the hook. His lot aren't going to want to take a madwoman back with them, are they? I'll go with them and you can stay here as long as you like. You and Mama, alone at last."

Evelyn spat on the floor. Lily raised her eyebrows. They both looked at the little spot of saliva fizzing on the tiles, and then Evelyn turned and went out into the garden, freighted with rage and embarrassment and a bottomless, black fear.

SHE STAYED OUT all evening. She made two laps of the entire garden to check the integrity of the wall and after each one she returned to the lawn and stood listening—for the others, for the storm—but the only sound was the wind in the dry and graying leaves.

There was a faint glow from the windup lamp in the kitchen, but she felt no inclination to go inside and get warm. Perhaps Lily and the boy were playing cards and getting drunk. Perhaps they were discussing their new life together, somewhere in the new garden, with other women and other men. With the boy's "friend." From time to time Evelyn would open her mouth wide, so wide her jaw hurt, and breathe in as much of the night air as she could. When she exhaled, the world seemed clearer, and she thought: let them go, Lily and the boy, let them bugger off, so she could finally enjoy the garden in peace. It wasn't as if Lily did any work anymore, and she didn't know the almanac the way Evelyn knew it. Evelyn would be quite able to look after the place on her own. Yes, quite capable of enduring without her sister getting under her feet and spoiling everything.

Moonlit and silent, she searched for special things that she could plant around the house to keep them safe. She found one of the cockerel's tail feathers; a broken, empty egg from a blackbird's nest; a stone with rings like the cross section of a tree trunk. She buried them to the south, east, and west. For the second night in a row she did not sleep, and as she wandered back to the house under a lightening sky, the garden throbbed and slanted around her. The wind had not abated, and her hair was desiccated with the dust it held.

Inside, the other two were asleep. Evelyn looked again for the almanac. She was sure that Lily or the boy had lost it, or more likely hidden it on purpose. Another trick on her sister's part. Another game. As everything was. Stupid girl.

By the dresser she came face-to-face with the boy in Lily's paintings. The work was good. Her sister had captured the peculiar mixture of lightness and sadness in his face. In all four of the pictures he was looking down at the ground or away to something out of the frame. Lost in thought or possibly ashamed of something. Well, so he should be, Evelyn thought. In one of the paintings he was propping himself up on one arm, and the line of his elbow seemed a little off. It wasn't like Lily to leave mistakes in her paintings. She had nothing but time to correct them.

Evelyn looked closer. There was a second line beneath the line of his arm. This was not unusual since Lily had painted over these four pieces of paper hundreds of times, giving them the appearance of some primitive palimpsest. But the line beneath the boy was thin and precise, like a hairline fracture in the paper. And now that she thought about it, the paper did not seem as thick or dog-eared as Lily's usual canvases. Evelyn took it from the shelf and carried it out into the thin light of the dawn. The edge and corner of a vegetable bed beneath the brushwork. A handwritten letter *e*, twice, where the paint was thinnest.

All her work, all Mama's work, obliterated.

Evelyn staggered a few feet onto the gravel. She was already delirious with lack of sleep. She tasted a saltiness at the back of her mouth, and for a moment she thought she was going to be sick, but she hadn't eaten for almost a full day so she just spat and swallowed and spat again, the paper still clenched in her fingers.

After a minute or two she went back and collected all four of the paintings. She put them back in the drawer of the dresser where they belonged. As if that went some way to correcting the fault.

She fetched a cup of water from their kitchen, found herself scooping the dregs from the plastic bucket. The boy hadn't collected any fresh water for days. Hadn't done anything at all. The chicken eggs were no doubt piling up in the coops. She stood and drank, watching the pair of them asleep under the table, under the pile of tools and blades that Evelyn had gathered for the siege that might or might not be coming.

Evelyn set down the cup and picked up the pair of shears. She got down on her knees next to Lily and the boy, opened the handles, and held the blades above her sister's neck. She waited, and she wondered, listening to the maddening sound of Lily's snoring.

A Visitor

Days before the storm descended upon them, they saw men at the gates. Three of them, all caked in white dust as if a new triptych of statues had been suddenly erected there.

We're not going to let them in, are we? Evelyn said.

No, said Mama. She was standing waist-deep in the wheat they had planted. Evelyn was chewing one of the stalks.

What should I do?

Where's your sister?

I don't know.

For Christ's sake. Go and find her and go inside.

Evelyn looked at the gate. The three stone men had not moved. The ground they stood on shimmered in the heat and they seemed to phase in and out of existence. One of them was calling weakly through the bars.

Evie!

Shall I tell Papa?

Her mother did not answer.

Lily was in the first place Evelyn looked, far away from anyone, crouched under the broad, thick leaves of her dinosaur plant. She was reading her book and wearing earmuffs despite the sweltering heat. When she looked up, Evelyn saw she had smeared mud under her eyes like war paint.

Mama wants us to go inside the house, Evelyn said.

Lily shrugged to suggest that she couldn't hear and then went back to her book.

Lily?

She shifted the earmuffs away from one ear.

What?

Mama said we have to go inside.

Why?

Evelyn could not say, and for a long time afterward she wondered why. Perhaps she had not wanted to excite her sister, or perhaps she had foreseen the entire episode play out exactly as her mother had said it would. Or perhaps hope was too cruel a thing to burden Lily with.

It's lunchtime, Evelyn said.

I'm reading.

You're not meant to be reading.

I don't care.

Come on, we should get some lunch.

I don't want to. I'm tired.

But Mama said so.

Why don't you have a thought of your own one day, Evie?

She replaced the earmuffs. Evelyn could hear voices from around the front of the house. Lily rocked back and forth, oblivious. Evelyn tried to grab her sister's hand and pull her up, but Lily wrenched her arm free—each as strong as the other now, all sinew and sunburn. Evelyn did not move for a few moments and then heard her mother scream.

Stay there, she said, though Lily couldn't hear her or her mother, and was intent on staying anyway.

She ran around to the front of the house and up the driveway and saw Mama at the gate. It was still locked, but one of the men had put his hands through and had pinned her arms to her sides. What had they offered, Evelyn thought, that her mother should have gone so close to them? Another now had Mama's neck in the crook of his elbow so her face was in profile, pressed hard against the iron bars while the rest of her body squirmed. He was making some strange rasping sound of hilarity, laughing or crying. The third was pacing from one side of the gate to the other, looking for a likely place to climb.

Evelyn went straight to the front door and into the hall. She called for her father, but he was lurking somewhere in the upper echelons of the house, as he had been for months, and she knew he would not answer. Her mother had imagined and described this scene to her and Lily many times, but as usual it was only Evelyn who had paid her any heed. She went down into the coolness of the cellar as instructed, found the cabinet in the dark, took their father's shotgun and a handful of shells.

When she emerged from the house, the heat was so intense it seemed to have silenced everything in the garden, save for the rough and erratic scraping of her mother's shoes in the gravel. She was no longer screaming because one of the men held a huge and dirt-caked hand over her mouth. Evelyn snapped the breech and loaded two shells as she walked, then raised the shotgun at the men. The steel of the barrel was freezing in her palm.

The third man had found his way over the gate, but when he saw Evelyn coming, he backed up and stood shoulder to shoulder with Mama, as if they were friends, a couple even. Evelyn approached. There were shadows on the man's face despite the noon sun directly overhead. He seemed unimaginably old. He smiled and showed her gums that were blueish and toothless.

Now then, what's all this? he said.

Evelyn had never pulled the trigger before because her mother had wanted to conserve what little ammunition they had. You have to get close, really close, her mother had said, so Evelyn got close.

One of Mama's eyes was swollen, and there was a dark red trickle coming from between the fingers of the hand that held her to the bars. Evelyn looked from man to man, each of them a pale and bloodless scarecrow, all driftwood and rags. Their eyes were bulbous and opaque. Not really men at all; some creature of a different order, raised from a barren earth.

This isn't how you usually treat your guests, is it? the man beside Mama said, but before he had even finished speaking, Evelyn had nudged the barrel up against his leg and pulled the trigger. The sound was strangely dull. She was thrown backward, and the thigh of the man's jeans exploded as if he contained nothing but air. He fell to the floor but didn't cry out. As if the effort was already beyond him.

The wilder of the other two men screamed and made an attempt to climb the gate himself, strange, dry gulping noises issuing from his mouth. His tongue hung like a dog's and was the color of lead. Evelyn got to her feet again and came as close as she dared and fired the second shell into his belly. A pink, hot cloud, and then she felt herself suddenly sodden, and could hardly blink for the blood that sluiced into her eyes and over her lips. The rank taste of sulfur and iron.

She wiped her face and tried to load another two shells, but her fingers were slick with blood and she dropped them in the dust. By the time the breech was closed again, the third man had let go of Mama and was limping into the desert he had sprung from. Evelyn fired through the bars twice but only made a spray of dust each time, and soon the man was out of range, then out of sight.

The first man was wheezing a few feet from her and Mama. He rolled onto one side and fumbled in the dirt as if he had dropped something. Evelyn glimpsed the pattern on his shirt and thought she recognized it, but she wasn't sure, and besides, it was too late for that. Mama got to her feet and went stumbling back to the edge of the lawn. When she returned, she was holding the sickle she'd been using to collect their meager wheat harvest. She stood over the man and looked down. Neither spoke. Evelyn watched, as if her mother were demonstrating some new task from the almanac. As if she were pruning or deadheading an unruly plant.

Her mother slumped down against the gates, and Evelyn went and held her. They sat in silence and the blood dripped from their chins until it thickened and then dried and then started to stink in the heat. Their clothes were heavy with it and creaked when they moved.

When she went to get Lily, Evelyn found her asleep in the grotto, using the book as her pillow. Evelyn and Mama washed in the lake and were clean in time for dinner, their skin pink as if they'd just caught the sun. Lily poked sullenly at her stewed apple and they told her none of what had happened, because there was no way of telling her, even if they'd wanted to.

27

Lily was the first to notice something was amiss when she woke. She sat up and banged her head on the underside of the table, then crawled out, her face creased with pain.

"Looks very clean in here," she said. "Have you been tidying for our visitors?"

Evelyn sat quite calmly in her wicker chair and tugged at a hangnail. She had not slept at all and felt strangely cleansed by fatigue.

Lily looked askance at her and went over to where she had once shared her bed with Evelyn.

"Where are all my clothes?"

"Packed," said Evelyn. "His, too."

"Packed?"

"I think it's time you left."

Lily went looking around the kitchen and then opened the kitchen door, and there, standing on the gravel, were two hessian sacks containing all their clothing and a few meager provisions. Evelyn watched her sister poking around in each one, pulling out dresses, dungarees, her ball gown, her sun hat, one pair of sunglasses. Lily looked up, speechless. She slid her arm farther down into the sack and froze. Evelyn knew what she had found and felt some satisfaction as Lily stood up and produced a ballet pump, cut neatly in half with the garden shears.

"You're a sod," said Lily. "A perfect sod."

"There's food and water for a few days."

"You've lost it. You've finally lost your mind."

"I found the almanac."

Lily dropped the severed shoe into the top of the open bag. "You did, did you?"

"Enough of it, anyway. I think you've made it perfectly clear what you think of me, and Mama, and the garden."

"Don't get all sanctimonious on me now. You hardly ever look at it these days. You said yourself it was all out of kilter. I'm sorry, but I didn't think we needed it." She pointed past her sister to where the boy was stirring, woken by their raised voices. "We've got him now. He knows this whole place like the back of his hand."

"The house as well?"

"I've said I'm sorry," said Lily, dismissing the question. "Yes. I should have asked you. But I only needed a few pages, and you were in such a foul mood. You're always in a foul mood."

"Of course, why shouldn't everyone spend their days like you, Sissie? Dancing and painting and playing like a bloody five-year-old."

Lily seemed stung by "Sissie." Evelyn never used the term, and when she did, she felt as if she was reclaiming something.

The boy came to the kitchen door and slipped outside. He stared at the bags.

"All right," said Lily. "You've made your point."

"I don't have a point," said Evelyn. "I want you both to leave."

Lily looked at her for a long time, then gave a laugh that sounded frail and not far from tears.

"You're serious."

"I am."

"You can't make us."

"I can if I have to. I thought you wanted to leave anyway? Go and meet his friend. What was it? A chat and cup of tea with someone other than your dreadful sister? Well, your wish has been granted."

Evelyn felt as if someone else were saying the words. That she had crossed over a line into some unknown territory, and there was no going back, because she was too proud, too stubborn, too much her mother's daughter.

"I'm not going anywhere," said Lily.

"It's all right," said the boy.

"It's not all right!"

"We'll go."

Lily looked aghast at him and then at Evelyn. "Traitors! Both of you!"

"If your sister doesn't want us here, then we should leave," said the boy. "We'll be OK."

"Where will we go?"

"We can try and find my friend. I'd rather not be here when the others come, anyway. I don't want to go back."

Evelyn felt a renewed surge of terror at the idea of anyone

arriving while she was alone in the garden. But she would not go back on her decision. Besides, if the boy was gone, they might not come at all. And if there was a storm, they might not even reach the garden in the first place.

She was aware that she was trembling and that her face was bloodless, so she made a good show of straightening her back and jutting her chin at them both.

"I have work to do," she said. "Don't take anything else from the stores. I've counted it all."

She left them and set about the watering and tried to think of nothing else besides the tasks that were before her. She ignored the dust that furred the leaves of the tomato plants. Ignored the tip of the boy's rucksack, just visible above the surface of the lake where the reeds had buoyed it up. Ignored the terse conversation between the boy and her sister, Lily's voice high and frantic. She clung to the work. Each moment, each act, a tiny piece of dry land. To step off it into the thoughts that swirled about was to instantly drown.

While she was checking the beehives, the boy materialized beside one of the apple trees.

"I think we will be leaving soon. I took a tarpaulin from the shed. We'll need to shelter somewhere. I hope that's all right."

She looked at him through the black haze of the bees. She could barely hear him. She nodded and turned back to the hive.

"I'll try to look after your sister," he said.

She pretended she hadn't heard him.

"I think I know where I'm going."

She studied one of the frames and remembered something her mother had said. Yes, she thought, just like the drones. Eats and eats and fattens himself up, then on to another colony without doing a lick of work.

He had worked, though. He could have worked for years to come.

"I'm sorry," he said, and waited a while for her to turn around again. By the time she did, he was gone.

WHEN EVELYN RETURNED to the house at midday, the two hessian bags were no longer there and there was no sign of her sister or the boy. A crushing silence all through the garden and the birdsong somehow harsh and grating.

She'd had thoughts for years, decades, maybe her entire life, about Lily dying. Not just thoughts but wishes. Coming from a desire that her sister would leave her alone for once, would stop her joking and her complaining, would stop always seeking to be the center of attention. She had wished for her own death, too, so that Lily could see how much she missed her older sister, how much she needed her. But it was always a child's version of death, not an adult's. The kind of death one returned from, with lessons learned and differences patched up. She knew now that it was this kind of death she had wished for the boy and her sister, though she worried she had sentenced them to something far worse.

28

 After lunch Evelyn went to the doorstep and looked out into the garden. The dust in the air had turned the sun to pewter, though she still couldn't hear the storm it-self. She wondered if Lily would be back before it came. Or if she would be somewhere else entirely.

She decided she would pickle some vegetables. She'd been meaning to for days. She pushed the pile of tools up to one end of the table, then fetched three of their pickling jars from the back of the kitchen. The vinegar in them was cloudy, years old. She set about mindlessly chopping onions, beetroot, and cu-cumbers and filling the jars. When each one was full, she held it to the light and inspected it, the contents pale and fleshy, pushed up against the glass like parts of a small body. She stowed the jars in the larder, then came back to the table.

She missed her sister with her whole heart. Hated her no less for that.

Evelyn looked for another task to keep her from thinking about what might happen or had already happened. In truth she had no idea what lay beyond the wall, not now. There had been monsters once, but that was so long ago. Since then, she had spent day after day after day trying to reassure her sister that no, there were no such things, and Mama's stories had been no more than stories, even when she knew the truth of them.

So many years of divided loyalties. So many years trying to be a good sister and a good daughter, and failing at both because one forbade the other.

She tried to make some dough. Never too late to learn, and she would have to now. It had always been Lily's job in the past, as Evelyn had lacked some intrinsic gift for baking that apparently couldn't be explained. Lily told her she "thought about it too much."

"Perfect job for you, Lils," Evelyn said out loud. "One that requires little to no thinking."

Her words seemed to make it only inches from her mouth before the silence of the room swallowed them and the tide of sorrow rose in her so quickly she worried she might pass out.

She mixed cupfuls of flour and water and added some of Lily's starter, a pot of sour sludge that she had been cultivating for decades. The mixture was sticky and cloying between her fingers. She added more flour. Kneaded and pounded until her knuckles struck the tabletop and the skin on them became sore and scuffed. The gardening tools shuddered at the other end of the table. However she adjusted the recipe, the dough was either too wet or too dry, and soon it had grown larger than the bowl itself and become quite unmanageable.

She left the mess on the table and went out into the day. She walked without seeing or hearing until she arrived at Mama's grave, though that had never been her conscious intention.

She stood in front of the stone. The flowers had not yet been replanted and the earth was still barren. Her whole body felt transparent in the heat.

"She's gone," Evelyn said.

The grave was as silent as the rest of the garden.

"Lily's gone. She went with the boy. Thank goodness."

Such an intense throbbing in her head. Evelyn could not hear herself, much less her mother.

"I'm sorry I let him come in at all, Mama. I'm so sorry. But it's fixed now. He's gone, and she's gone, and it's all better. Just me and you."

Again she felt the urge to weep, but she knew that her mother would not approve, and the effort of repressing her tears gave way to a kind of cramp in the muscles around her mouth.

"We'll be fine," she said. "I'm the only one who knows what to do anyway. I don't even think I'll need to cook. I don't mind eating things raw. And, gosh, how nice to have a bit of peace and quiet, after all this time. I feel like I'm waking up from a bad dream." She paused. "I should have done it a long time ago. I should have listened to you. You wouldn't have stood for it. You never *did* stand for it. I was too soft. But it'll be better from now on."

She waited. Mama still had no reply for her.

"Why are you being like this?" said Evelyn. "Is it because of the flowers? The boy took the flowers. Lily let him. It's not my fault."

The was a gust of wind, and Evelyn blinked the dust out of her eyes.

"It's not my *fault*, Mama!" she cried. "None of this is my fault!"

She turned and left the graveside, walked all through the front garden and then the back, calling Lily's name over and over and hearing only her own voice echoing back from the battlements of the house. Lily could not have gone. Why would she go? She never did anything that Evelyn told her to do, so why start now? She must be hiding. That was it. They both were. Just a game. Lily was too old to climb over the wall anyway. There was no way she could have left.

By evening Evelyn's throat was hoarse and neither had made an appearance.

"Yes, yes," she muttered to herself, "very funny, Lily. Very funny."

She dragged herself to the gazebo and sat there as it grew dark. A sky the color of a faded rose, and Lily somewhere out there under it. There were still sequins wedged in the cracks between the boards. Evelyn could not bear to see them, so she left the bench and went over to the edge of the little island and put her feet in the water. There was scum on the surface of the lake that had not been there before.

The stars came out. Her feet went numb. Evelyn wanted the storm to come quickly, wanted Lily's monstrous eel to come from the depths so she could present herself to it as a willing sacrifice. She didn't know how long she stayed there, but eventually the thought came to her like a struck bell, *Yes, I will*, and she slipped from the shore and lowered herself completely into the black water, her nightdress ballooning around her, her skull deliciously cold.

29

She felt a tug at the back of her dress and jerked up like a marionette. She opened her eyes under the water and found it white with bubbles. Someone dragged her to the surface, where all was noise and movement, thrashing and gasping. It sounded like somebody else was drowning besides her. A long arm tightened around her waist and bore her up, towing her like some outlandish piece of flotsam toward the shore where the windup lamp was on its side in the grass. She felt the soft mud beneath her feet, but she couldn't stand. Couldn't or wouldn't. She pitched over onto the grass and lay there, looking up at the night sky, her arms wrapped around herself as if to hold her bones together.

The boy stood over her with the lamp. He was panting.

"What are you trying to do?" he said.

She didn't answer.

"Both of you. I don't know what you're trying to do."

She rolled onto her side.

"Your sister is inside. The bees bit her."

Evelyn looked back at the lake. The waves they had made were still nudging the dust and debris back toward the shore, and a few yards out was a circle of clear water, as if she had fallen through a hole in thin ice.

She seemed to lie there for hours. Her flesh and her clothes congealed like sodden tissue paper.

"What do I do?" he said. "She's finding it hard to breathe."

The first thing Evelyn thought to say was:

"She shouldn't have been by the beehives anyway."

The boy crouched beside her. "She wasn't by the hives. It was outside."

This made no sense to her.

"They bit her," the boy said again.

"They stung her," said Evelyn. "Bees don't bite."

"They got her on the neck and on her face."

"There aren't any bees outside. Where was she hiding?"

"She wasn't hiding. There were bees in the trunk of a tree. Outside the wall."

Evelyn sat up so her face was level with his. A thin film of dust covered his cheeks, as if he had applied some of Mama's makeup. She tried to ascertain if this was another lie. Another trap. There were no bees, or trees, or anything else outside the wall. Evelyn would always tell herself that.

The kitchen appeared to be empty when she got back. The boy was trying to start the fire but didn't know how. Her failed attempt at dough was still on the table, and there was flour all over the place. Only after a moment did Evelyn notice the blankets in their sleeping place were shaking.

She got down on the floor and crawled underneath them. Her sister's breath was quick and shallow. She was wearing their mother's dressing gown, the hood pulled up. She turned and held Evelyn around the waist despite her wet clothes and pushed her face up against her breastbone. Evelyn could feel the swollen welts against her cold skin.

Eventually Lily spoke.

"You're soaked."

"I went for a swim."

"In your clothes? That wasn't very clever, was it."

"No. It wasn't. Very silly of me."

They spoke flatly and quietly. As if rehearsing lines from a play they had tired of.

"They stung me all over, Evie. Oh, my word, listen to me wheezing."

"You'll be all right."

"What did Mama give me last time?"

"I don't remember."

"It was garlic and something."

"Yes, garlic and something."

"You don't remember what the something was."

"No."

"I think we have garlic, though. Don't we?"

"I think we do."

Evelyn knew they had some in the hamper because she had made an inventory the previous night, but she made no move to fetch it.

"I'm sorry, Sissie."

"I'm sorry, too."

"You must really hate me."

"Of course I don't hate you."

"I don't hate you either."

They lay in each other's arms. Evelyn had no idea whether either of them was telling the truth anymore.

"Were you hiding by the hives? It was a very good hiding place. I looked and looked all day and didn't find you. I suppose I didn't look very hard around the hives because I know how much you hate them."

"I wasn't hiding, Evie. We left. Like you told us to."

Evelyn felt a flush of shame. Her plunge into the lake had been a kind of savage baptism from which she had emerged anew. A different Evelyn had ordered them from the garden. Had packed their bags and destroyed her sister's shoes.

"Did you really leave?"

"Had to get a bit of leg up from the boy. Very unsightly."

If it was meant as a joke, it fell flat. Evelyn lay and thought. It still didn't make any sense to her.

"I don't understand," she said. "Why would the bees be out there?"

"There *are* things out there, Evie. I mean, we hardly went any distance. But I saw things. What were those bushes that Mama made tea out of? Spiky leaves and the big, tall flowers."

"Acanthus."

"I think I saw one of those."

"You should have taken some leaves for your allergy."

"Well. I wasn't to know."

Evelyn was quiet. The bees must have had some reason to venture beyond the wall. And she had always thought of herself and the bees as kindred spirits. She looked into the red darkness of her own eyelids and tried to picture the outside again. She tried to imagine leaving, but the vision would not come. It was all blank, all hopeless. Perhaps the lake had not really changed her at all.

"You don't really want to leave here, do you?" Evelyn asked.

The pause seemed far too long.

"No."

"Are you sure?"

"I think so. I just thought . . ."

Evelyn tensed. "Thought what?"

"I just keep thinking. We have been here such a long time. Day after day after day. So many days."

"I thought we weren't counting."

Lily rolled over and felt among the blankets for something. Then she stood up and took the lamp and went to the rear of the kitchen, where the great black wardrobe stood squarely in front of the door to the hallway.

"What are you doing?" said Evelyn.

She heard her sister open the door to the wardrobe, a door she had always been sure was locked. Lily slowly lowered herself onto the wooden floor and sat down inside it, her throat creaking and whistling.

"What is this?"

Evelyn crawled over to the wardrobe on her hands and knees. Past the boy, perched by the stove like a watchful bird. When she got there she could see the interior of the wardrobe lit by the lamp. The dark wood was not smooth but etched with hundreds, thousands, of tiny horizontal and vertical lines.

"That's us," said Lily.

"Us?"

"Every day we've been here. Since the storm." She patted

the wooden base. "I hid in here when I didn't want to be around any of you. Mama didn't know I had the key. Imagine."

Evelyn gazed and said nothing. The tally started at the top of the wardrobe's rear panel and the marks got progressively smaller, as if Lily had only anticipated a count of few hundred days to begin with. Now there were marks on the sides and the inside of the doors. Some almost too small to see. Others much larger and more violently gouged. Evelyn rested a fingertip on one of these, at the top of the wardrobe. She looked down at Lily.

"That was the day Papa left us," said Lily.

Evelyn pointed to another at the very bottom, on the same panel.

"Mama," said Lily.

"How many?" Evelyn asked.

"Oh gosh." Lily frowned like she was thinking, but Evelyn suspected she knew the number exactly. "There's about ten thousand on the sides. And about ten thousand on the back. And a few on the doors. And now I'm running out of space."

They both sat in silence. Evelyn looked at the darkly crusted mess of her sister's hair and then at the quivering gray centers of her eyes. She had been counting. All this time, it had been Lily, not Evelyn, who had kept the greater of their secrets.

Evelyn ran her fingers over the tallies again, as if they were an ancient inscription to be deciphered. But she could make no sense of it at all. As far as she was concerned, there was only the day, the one that she lived in, and the tasks that were assigned to it. She did not think about yesterday, or tomorrow. And all the while her sister had been thinking of the time yawning behind her, and time shrinking ahead of her. It was Lily who had really seen her future in the boy, not Evelyn. Evelyn had kept him for quite the opposite reason. To keep things exactly as they were. Well, that had not exactly worked out, had it, she thought bleakly.

"I don't want to leave, Sissie."

"Good."

"Not anymore."

Evelyn was very still.

"For the longest time it was all I thought about. I knew there must be somewhere else. And Mama must have known. We could have had lives, Sissie. Like in the book. We could have had children."

"We've got the boy."

"That's not the same. And I know you know that."

She pressed her face against Evelyn's chest, and Evelyn felt her matted, sticky hair beneath her chin. On the reverse of the wardrobe's open door was a mirror. Spotless, unlike the mirrors in the car, or the surface of the lake. She saw her reflection more clearly than she had in decades. Her lips blue from the cold and her face so deeply ridged she looked mummified. She stared and stared.

Lily sat up and saw the expression on her sister's face and turned to look in the mirror herself.

"Oh, Sissie," said Lily. "Look at me. I've swelled up like a party balloon."

Evelyn blinked. "Like a what?"

"A party balloon."

And there it was again. The space between them. Evelyn didn't know what she meant. She heard the words and thought she could picture something, but what she pictured seemed so odd that it couldn't have been real. Lily obviously knew what she meant when she said it. She remembered such things well enough. Her head was full of them, and Evelyn knew for certain, then, that even before the boy arrived, she and her sister had lived in completely different worlds, and the idea that they could know and understand even the smallest part of each other was a wishful illusion.

30

The days went on, but they were different days now. There was the sense that something had already ended and there was to be no reclaiming what had gone before. No amount of careful scrubbing and sewing would revive the almanac. Lily's swelling eventually went down of its own accord, but the red lumps remained as testament to their madness. Evelyn felt constantly cold and damp no matter how long she sat next to the stove, only flushing with heat when she recalled what her sister had done. She thought often about what Lily had said; thought just as often about the silence and darkness beneath the lake, with a kind of longing she wouldn't admit to herself. She went on with her tasks, as she remembered them, but took little pleasure in the work, pottering mechanically about the beds. She sewed her sister's ballet pumps back together, but they seemed somehow more pitiable for being mended.

Lily attempted to build bridges in the only way she knew how. One morning she came into the kitchen wearing the butchered ballet shoes and the Marigolds and her favorite ball gown. She made an announcement:

"I'm ready," she said.

Evelyn was pickling again. She tightened the lid on a jar of beetroot, her fingers smeared in juice the color of blood.

"For what?" Evelyn said.

"To perform."

"The routine?"

"That's right. I think I've cracked it."

Evelyn could not believe it. How long had it been since her sister had begun her practice, had banished Evelyn from the gazebo for so many hours a day? She had given up all hope of seeing the thing.

She was surprised to find herself smiling. Her cheeks were stiff and unaccustomed to it. Perhaps reparations could yet be made.

"Well. I never thought the day would come. Goodie good. Give me a moment to finish up here."

"Wear something nice, please," said Lily, and went shimmering out of the door.

Evelyn stacked the jars in the store cupboard, then washed her hands and went to their pile of clothes. She picked out one of their mother's tartan skirts and a floral blouse and silk scarf. Dared to feel a little excited.

She rounded the car and took the path along the edge of the lake to where her sister was waiting in the gazebo. She had turned some of their old clothes into bunting—faded T-shirts and skirts from when they were very little—and hung it around the posts. She had made a kind of theatrical curtain out of some of their blankets and was pattering about behind it. The boy was standing a little to one side and seemed not entirely sure of his role in the performance. He was wearing a man's suit, much too big for him. Lily must have had him fetch it, but Evelyn was not as stung by the transgression as she'd expected, and chose not to mention it.

"Shall I sit?" she asked loudly.

"Yes, yes, sit, sit," said Lily from behind the curtain.

Evelyn swept her skirt underneath her and sat. The ground was gritty. She placed a palm in the grass, and it came back gray with dust. She wiped it on her leg and tried not to think about it.

"Ready?" called Lily.

"As I'll ever be," said Evelyn.

The boy stepped forward and pulled the curtain to one side. Lily was in the center of the gazebo, *en pointe*. The sinews in her calves stood out, bound in ribbons. Her hair was artfully plaited and coiled and had been pulled back so tightly around her face that she looked several years younger.

Evelyn gasped.

Her sister had painted a backdrop for the performance on four wooden boards that looked very similar to the ones Mama had used to seal up the house. Evelyn wondered if Lily had found a store of leftovers. Or had pried them free herself. Or had got the boy to do it. More astonishing than the boards themselves were the things Lily had painted upon them. Windows and curtains and baroque chandeliers. Evelyn knew these were paintings of the rooms in the house. Knew, without even having to think, that they were perfect likenesses, because the boy no doubt had described them to her in detail. The rooms were not empty either. There were people relaxing in them, smiling, playing. A woman, a man, two girls. Eddie was in his cage on top of a bookcase. Lily began to hum her own accompaniment. She had once had a machine that played music, Evelyn seemed to remember, but there was nothing on hand for this performance. Lily lowered herself onto the flats of her feet and very slowly raised her arms, and then one leg, until it was parallel to the floor. Evelyn still had a hand to her mouth. She watched her sister working through each movement that she had learned when she was younger than the boy, even. Watched her pale and trembling body tracing arc after gentle arc. Such grace in it, and such sadness.

She danced around the painted boards and at times interacted with the figures she had sketched there. She had conjured these from her own memory, not the boy's. The faces were masklike and frightening thanks to Lily's broad brushstrokes and limited palette. She pirouetted from one to the next and seemed to have silent conversations with each of them. She planted a kiss on her father's cheek. She imitated a bird in flight in front of Eddie's cage.

Each act recalling a loss that Evelyn had barely felt, if she had felt it at all, until the full weight of her sister's grief was upon her.

She watched through tearful eyes and could not look away. She did not know how long the performance had been going on for, but it seemed to be reaching a climax when something caught her eye. Something growing in the gaps between the scenery.

"Lily, stop," she said, getting to her feet.

Lily continued to dance, a scowl on her face.

"Lily, please. You have to stop."

"No," said Lily, but then she stopped anyway. There was sweat on her forehead. "Why? What are you doing? I've barely got going!"

"Look."

Finally Lily turned.

The storm was coming. The thunderhead was colossal. It reared like a wave across the horizon, already seemingly overhead, though it must have been hundreds of miles away. It surged darkly, a yellow tinge to each new erupting cloud, as if they were watching the blooming of some immense brassica. The light all around them yellow, too, and sickly. There were threads of lightning at its center, blueish and delicate among the columns and billows of dust, like the veins on the backs of Lily's legs. The wind was already high and grasped at the tops of the trees, but the rest of the garden was still strangely quiet.

"We should go in," Evelyn said. "We have to get things ready."

"But my routine . . ."

Lily pursed her lips and seemed on the brink of arguing, but then her whole face fell slack.

"There will be time for the routine," said Evelyn. "Afterward."

She came up onto the stage and took her sister by the elbow, and they started back toward the house, the boy following behind them.

A Storm

They sat on either side of their mother and listened to the wind trying to force its way through the shutters. The flames of the candles slanting and righting themselves with each new draft. Like someone was coming and going, opening and shutting doors, though everything was locked and sealed. The dust sounded like water cascading from the roof and mocked their thirst. Evelyn shifted her weight one way and then the other because the sofa was broken and a spring had forced its way up through the upholstery. Lily was perched on the sofa's arm, braiding her hair. It was long enough now that she could tuck it into her waistband.

How long do you think it will last? she asked.

I don't know, said Mama.

Will the garden be OK? Evelyn asked.

I don't know, said Mama again. If it isn't, we'll just start again. Nothing else we can do, is there?

The storm went on. Great, yawning periods of silence between the three of them.

I'm bored, said Lily.

Their mother slapped her. Evelyn watched and waited for Lily to retaliate, but she didn't. Nobody spoke for a minute or two.

Give me strength, Lily, said Mama. Bored, are you? Would you rather be out there?

That's not what I meant.

Would you rather be outside with that lot, tearing each other limb from limb? You wouldn't last five minutes. How many disgusting things do you think I've chased from our door while you've been napping or swimming or dancing around like a floozy?

What's a floozy?

Are you listening to me, Lily? They'll eat our food and sleep in our beds and have their wicked way with you as soon as they see you. They'll suck the marrow from your bones given half the chance. Evelyn, knock some sense into your sister, for God's sake!

Mama looked at Evelyn as though she was expecting her to recount what had happened at the gates. Evelyn could barely recount the horror of it to herself, let alone to her little sister. She pictured the bloodied T-shirt and shorts that she had scrubbed and scrubbed but been unable to get clean. In the end she had buried the clothes by the wall without Lily's knowledge, standing over the hole as if attending her own funeral.

Tell her, said Mama.

Evelyn didn't say a word. She wondered why their mother wouldn't tell Lily herself. She suspected that beneath the irritation and the resentment, she was just as protective of Lily as Evelyn was. Perhaps even more so.

Mama shook her head and chewed her lip. Then she got up and left the room, taking one of the candles with her. The sisters sat in silence for a moment or two, the storm shivering through the walls of the house.

What did she mean by that? Lily asked.

By what?

What were you supposed to tell me?

I don't know.

About the men outside?

I don't know, Lils. You know how confused she is.

I don't think she's confused about how much she hates me.

Stop it. She doesn't hate you. She's just worried about you.

I wish Papa would come down sometimes. At least he was on my side.

I'm on your side, Lils.

Lily looked at her with huge and shining eyes. Evelyn hugged her. Outside the room the landing creaked, and Evelyn looked over her sister's shoulder. In the doorway the shadow of their father shifted and withdrew. As if one of the monsters was already in the house.

31

Lily and the boy watched the storm while Evelyn was busy taking an inventory of the food stores. Lily clicked her tongue and sighed.

"It's not so big, this one," she said, face to the glass.

The boy did not reply.

"It'll be over before we know it."

The boy came over and stood awkwardly behind Evelyn for a moment. She waited for him to speak.

"What can I do?" he said.

He'd been at great pains to be helpful ever since he'd dragged Evelyn from the lake, and despite her lingering suspicions Evelyn found it hard to remain ill-disposed toward him.

"Well," she said. "Let's see, shall we?"

She got up and joined Lily by the window. The storm was

well upon them now, and the sky was dark and fulminous. Sometimes a cloud of dust rolled past the window that obliterated the garden completely, and each time Evelyn wondered if the cloud would move on, or if she had seen the last of the lawn and the pond and the flower beds.

"We should cover what we can of the beds," she said.

"Is there any point?" said Lily.

"What do you mean?" said Evelyn. "Of course there's a point." But she could not elaborate beyond that.

Lily didn't reply but went to the door and put a coat on over her dress and changed her ballet shoes for Wellingtons.

The wind outside was not yet so fierce that they couldn't walk, but all three of them were forced to stoop and cover their noses and mouths with scarves. Evelyn suggested they wear the sunglasses, too, and was surprised when her sister agreed.

They staggered to the toolshed, which offered them some shelter. Motes of dust tumbled in neat lines between the gaps in the roof.

"These are what we need," said Evelyn, pointing to the colossal rolls of canvas that had been stored in the rafters for decades.

The boy hauled them down onto the dry earth. Lily tried to lift the end of one of them, but it was too heavy. The boy took the whole thing by himself, lugging it as if it contained a body.

"Vegetable beds first," shouted Evelyn over the wind. She wasn't sure if the boy had heard her, but he went in the right direction anyway.

When they reached the winter beds, she helped the boy stake out the canvas over the soil. The furrows he had dug not so long ago now looked as if they were filled with ash. Evelyn managed to make one corner secure, but it seemed to take hours, and by the time she had secured the stake in the ground, the boy had gone back to the toolshed with Lily to fetch another roll.

They covered the vegetable patches and the herb garden and one corner of the wheat field, where the soil was best. They covered their mama's grave. Evelyn watched the boy struggle with the sheet as it bucked and writhed in the gale. When she looked up, her sister was staring into nothingness. What if Lily was right? What if there was no point? How many more years did she and Lily have, even if they survived this storm, even if they weren't discovered by the others? And then another, inevitable thought: Had there *ever* been any point? *We could have had lives*, Lily had said. The words came back to her, over and over. Had this not been a worthwhile life?

Evelyn found herself fighting a desperate, scrappy fight against the conclusion that no, it had not. That there was nothing intrinsically good or bad in the garden but only what she and her mother had projected onto it; that they had been trying to preserve not the garden but themselves, and their own internal worlds, and that was an impossibility. She was overtaken by a fatigue so bottomless and terrifying she thought she would never manage the thirty paces back to the house.

The boy tugged at her arm several times. She couldn't hear him over the wind.

"The chickens," he shouted.

They herded their three hens into the coops. The cockerel had taken shelter elsewhere. The wind blew stronger still, and the clouds descended until they seemed close enough to touch. It was now almost too dark to see. They found their way back to the kitchen door having barely spoken a word since they'd left it. Evelyn coughed and wheezed like a hag.

"We'll need more water," she said to the boy on the doorstep.

"And some meat," said Lily.

Evelyn looked in the direction of the icehouse but could not see it through the storm.

"I'll get them," the boy said.

Evelyn turned back to him. He was blinking furiously, his eyelashes turned blond from the dust that clung to them.

"Don't worry about the meat. Do you think you can get to the lake before it gets too dark?"

He nodded.

"All right. Be quick. Then we can lock the door and be done with it."

Evelyn went inside and got the lamp. She wound it until it was as bright as it would go and brought it back to him.

"Four buckets should be enough."

The boy nodded again and disappeared around the side of the house, his dark curls whipping in the wind.

Lily sat down at one end of the kitchen table and began shuffling their cards.

THE BOY CAME and went with the buckets of water and the lamp, illuminating their world briefly before disappearing for a fifth time.

"Where's he off to now?" Evelyn said.

Lily didn't reply. Evelyn watched her sister thumbing the cards in the twilight and realized how long it had been since they had sat, just the two of them, at the kitchen table. Eons had passed since the boy had entered the garden. She could hardly remember their life without him, just as she could hardly remember their life with Mama. She had fallen out of practice speaking with her sister even before Lily had gone beyond the wall; now they sat opposite each other as strangers.

"Well. At least you don't need to worry about anyone else coming to the garden," Lily said.

The boy's head floated past the kitchen window. He shouldered the door, which Evelyn had shut to keep the dust out of the house. He was holding two joints of cured meat, one under each arm. He heaved them onto the table and set the lamp down beside them. He sat down and took off his sunglasses and coughed and rubbed his eyes. Lily looked up from her cards and saw what he had brought.

"Oh, good boy!" she said.

"I said we didn't need those," said Evelyn.

"It's all right. I had time."

"Well, we're not eating any of it yet."

"Oh, come on, Evie," said Lily. "In the circumstances, I think we're due a treat."

"It's not meant to be a treat. We'll need to save it in case we're trapped here for any length of time."

Lily sulked and seemed to be in no mood to make dinner, so Evelyn reheated some porridge while her sister and the boy sat in silence at the table. Evelyn set the pan between them. They ate little, listening to the world howling outside the house.

"Are we going to play cards, then?" said Lily.

"I don't feel like it," said Evelyn. "Sorry."

"Suit yourself," said Lily.

Evelyn gazed out at the storm. The dust was blowing horizontally across the window. Lily was probably right. No one could reach them through this. And even if they could, she wouldn't see them until they were on the doorstep. She checked both dead bolts anyway, then went back to her spot at the window.

"What about you then, beast of burden?" she heard Lily say. "Cards?"

She could not hear the boy's answer, but the sound of the cards snapping on the table suggested he had agreed. Or perhaps Lily had decided to play a game with herself.

"Are you scared?" Lily asked.

The boy nodded or shook his head; Evelyn could not see.

"Did you get storms like this in the other place?"

"Yes," said the boy. "All the time."

"You hear that, Evie? Sounds like wherever we go, we'll end up digging ourselves out."

Evelyn raised her eyebrows, the closest thing to a laugh she could manage. She heard the purr of Lily shuffling the deck.

"Did you really dig it out? After the first storm?" the boy asked.

"We did. I can't remember how long it took us. It was Mama who worked hardest. But me and Evie did our bit, didn't we?"

"We did," Evelyn agreed.

"You didn't get hungry?" said the boy.

"Oh goodness, yes," said Lily. "Nearly starved. We just had to ration everything. Papa went and got lots of tins and such. Do you remember that, Evelyn? Fruit and vegetables. I used to guzzle the juice straight from the can. Gosh, yes, I loved it. It's a shame we don't have any this time round. I suppose we can make do with what's in the cupboard."

"Yes," said Evelyn. "We can make do."

She tried to sound upbeat, though Lily did not know the findings of the inventory she had taken, and Evelyn did not care to enlighten her. She looked at the joints of meat on the table and considered hiding them somewhere, for emergencies only, before Lily could get her teeth into them.

32

She would have thought night had fallen were it not for the thin, disturbed strip of light at the top of the window frame. In that strip she could see the dust motes buzzing like thousands of trapped insects. She got up, and the act seemed to take another lifetime. She saw that Lily and the boy were still awake and sitting at the table, but neither was speaking. They hadn't bothered to turn on the lamp. They looked like a pair of ghosts.

The dust was seven or eight feet deep, piled up against the window with such weight that there were filament-thin cracks running across the glass panes. The gap letting in the light was no more than two inches wide. The storm was still blowing, distant and muted.

Evelyn went to the sink and splashed her face with cold water and barely felt it. She returned to her blankets with her skin still dripping. The three of them watched the gap in the window slowly filling until the kitchen was in complete darkness.

"We'll have to go to the floor above," Lily said.

"No," said Evelyn.

"Those windows won't hold much longer. We'll have to get out of here at some point."

"No," said Evelyn. "It's dangerous."

"I know you don't want to think about it," said Lily, "but the boy's been up there. Many times. And he came back with all his teeth and hair. Unmolested by rats. Or monsters."

"I didn't go everywhere," he said quietly, as if still expecting to be punished for it. "But I think it's fine."

Evelyn couldn't bear the thought of it even now. She struggled with that familiar nausea. "I'm staying here."

"Do you want to stay here?" Lily said to the boy.

He shook his head.

"Then that's two against one," Lily said. "Come on. Let's see if we can't get one of these doors open."

"Lily," said Evelyn.

"What?"

"I don't want to see the rest of the house. I'll go mad."

"You'll go mad if you stay down here. And when the window breaks, you'll suffocate."

"But all those things. I don't want to remember any of those things. And remember Mama said—"

"Mama is dead, Evelyn."

"What difference does that make?"

Lily gave her a look of such pity that Evelyn had to bury her face in the blankets.

She called the boy to heel, and they began to rummage

through the pile of garden tools, then opened drawers and cupboards. There was the sound of heavy metal objects being placed on the work surface, then a little gasp of satisfaction from Lily before their footsteps receded to the back of the kitchen. Evelyn heard furniture scraping across the tiles and dared to raise her head.

The boy had hauled the wardrobe to one side. Behind it six sturdy planks of wood had been nailed across the doorframe. Lily held the lamp to the boards, and she and the boy studied them closely, their shadows stretching toward Evelyn, distorted and grotesque. Lily tutted and ran her fingers over the edges of the wood.

"Here," she said to the boy. "Try here."

Lily had taken the poker from the fireplace to try to prize the wood apart. The boy had a claw hammer. Evelyn watched as the boy set to work hacking and levering, dismantling the remaining pieces of her world. Twice the hammer slipped and he caught his fingers, and Lily rubbed them better, whether he wanted her to or not. When it was clear that he was making little progress, Lily returned to the pile of gardening tools and crowed in triumph when she found a screwdriver. Behind them the window clicked and another crack appeared in the glass.

An hour or more passed before they successfully tore the first of the boards from the wall. They had gouged at the nails until the board was loose enough to slip the poker between it and the plaster, and the boy had leaned on it with all his weight and yelped when it finally sprang free. Evelyn caught a glimpse of the dark paneling of the door beyond and shuddered. She half hoped that the sand would come flooding in and suffocate them all there and then, before the door was opened.

"Let's have a little rest, shall we?" said Lily, and seesawed back to the kitchen table. "A rest and something to eat. Can't work on an empty stomach."

The boy followed her, sucking on his thumb and looking back at the fruits of their labors.

Evelyn watched her sister thump a loaf of bread onto the table and cut it slowly into slices. The boy was twitching like a bird again, turning his head toward the door, then the window, then the boards at the back of the kitchen. Lily placed a piece of bread in front of him and then took the good knife to the nearest joint of meat, and with a little fiddling stripped back the outer layer of gauze. She unwound the rest of the material, rolling the meat across the table as she went. Evelyn watched and did not move. She saw the yellow gleam of the severed bone, the dull blueish-red of the preserved muscle. Then the last loops of gauze slipped from its hand, and the fingers slowly opened in the lamplight like the petals of a flower.

The boy cried out and leaped backward, tipping his chair onto the tiles.

"Oh," said Lily. She seemed unsurprised.

The boy had clasped his head in both hands and made a noise that was almost gibbering. Lily tried to set his chair upright and he flinched.

"Come on, silly thing," she said. "It's not still alive."

He took one uncertain step toward the garden tools. Evelyn gave him a stern look. She wondered if it was the same expression her mama had made, when Evelyn had been in the boy's position. Either she was not stern enough, or the boy was not so easily cowed, because he took another step forward and snatched a pruning knife from the pile of tools. He waved it in front of his face as if shooing flies and backed off toward the dresser. Of course it would come to this, Evelyn thought. How could it not.

Lily looked at the man's arm for a moment longer, then came around the table, shushing the boy as if he were an animal. The fingers on the end of the meat brushed against her hips as she passed. She went toward the boy, and the boy swung the pruning knife wildly at her. Evelyn felt something stir in her. She steadied herself and slowly got to her feet.

"Hey," she said, "that's enough."

"It's all right, boy," said Lily, but Evelyn could hear the fear in her voice. "They're from a long time ago. They're not like you and me. These ones deserved it."

She knew, thought Evelyn. She had always known. Just as she had known everything else.

The boy swung his knife again and ran toward the door that led into the buried garden. Dust had crept through the gaps at the top and the bottom. He began rattling the dead bolts.

"Don't be an idiot," said Lily. "You can't open that now." She turned to Evelyn. "Stop him, Sissie, before he does something stupid."

Evelyn grasped the sickle from the table while the boy sobbed and fumbled with the bolt.

"Stop that!" said Lily, and moved as fast as Evelyn had ever seen her move. There was the grinding of grit and metal. Lily grabbed at the boy and tore his sleeve, but the boy flung his arm behind him and shoved Lily backward. Evelyn watched as her sister fell, her body weirdly loose and disconnected, just bones in a bag. She hit the ground hard, and her head bounced against the tiles before coming to rest.

The boy undid the locks on the door, and there was a long,

loud *hush* as the sand and dust poured through the crack. The weight of it forced the door wide open and nearly crushed the boy against the wall, against the coats and hats and sticks that were bundled there. The sand spread over the floor like water until it reached Lily's heels. The boy slid and swam and scrambled over the slope of it, every breath a moan, and kept climbing until, somehow, he had wriggled underneath the lintel of the door and made his way up and out, to his freedom or to his death.

Evelyn looked down at her sister. The lamplight cast her cracked and ancient face in ghastly relief, and the shadows of her fingers curled and uncurled very slowly over the tiles. Lily sighed, but there was no pain in that sigh at all. Tiredness, and perhaps remorse for something; the same kind of sigh she used to make when she curled up in the blankets beside Evelyn after a day's work.

It took Evelyn a long time to get down onto the floor. Too long. By the time she had Lily's head in her lap, there was no breath left in her sister's lungs and the blood in her plaited hair was already cold to the touch.

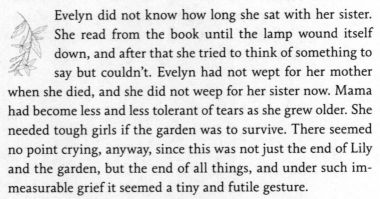

33

Evelyn did not know how long she sat with her sister. She read from the book until the lamp wound itself down, and after that she tried to think of something to say but couldn't. Evelyn had not wept for her mother when she died, and she did not weep for her sister now. Mama had become less and less tolerant of tears as she grew older. She needed tough girls if the garden was to survive. There seemed no point crying, anyway, since this was not just the end of Lily and the garden, but the end of all things, and under such immeasurable grief it seemed a tiny and futile gesture.

In the darkness she lay down beside Lily and held her, the curves of their backs and their bellies fitting snugly to each other. Hours passed and Evelyn found a few words. She whispered a mantra of apologies into Lily's ear: for allowing the boy to stay, for not being honest about so many things, for siding with Mama on so many occasions. She asked Lily again and again: "What shall I do? What shall I do?"

Her sister's body cooled against hers, and she got up, apologizing still, and fetched a blanket to put over her. The remains of the almanac fell out of the folds, its cover too loose because of the missing pages. Evelyn did not pick it up. She went and tried to restart the fire in their stove, but it only filled the kitchen with a pall of brownish, stinking smoke. She lay down again and pulled the blanket over them both. Part of her thought the warmth might revive Lily, as it had Mama.

Their mother had seemed to die and return to life several times over the course of her last months in the garden, going silent and still for days on end, then unexpectedly waking to remind them of some task they had forgotten, or to hurl volleys of salivary insults at both of her daughters or, more often, their absent father. Even after she had gone cold, Evelyn had continued her vigil, adding more blankets, forcing more soup between her mother's stiff lips, not knowing if this was another temporary death. Lily had begun practicing her routine in those days. Evelyn had only really been sure that Mama was dead when the smell became intolerable and her mother's skin began to shrink against the sharp angles of her skull.

SOME HOURS LATER Evelyn heard footsteps overhead and felt as if she were back in one of her dreams. If they had been dreams at all. The steps were careful and deliberate. They crossed the kitchen ceiling, paused above the stove. Then they went to the far corner. Then they came back again and stopped above Evelyn's head.

Evelyn knew it was the boy. No doubt he would come for her, too, unless she found him first. Perhaps this had been his plan all along, to claim the garden for himself, and the others. *He's not dangerous*, she remembered saying, and in the heat of her shame and her rage she felt herself returned to life, as if dredged from the bottom of the lake.

She knew what she must do. She took up the sickle and the lamp and waded through the darkness to the back of the kitchen, where she set to the task that her sister had begun. The boy had taken the pruning knife with him—she would have to be careful about that, she thought—but he had left the poker and the claw hammer behind. She pried and jimmied the boards until her fingers were bleeding, and she felt an unexpected pleasure in the throb of her cuts and blisters. It was good to be working again, she thought.

She removed another two boards and was able to reach the doorknob. She stood for a long time with her hand on the cold brass ball, holding it tightly until it, too, was warm and clammy. She imagined opening the door and seeing Mama on the other side, her face sad and severe as it had been in life, looking down her long nose in disappointment. Then a tanned hand, etched with years of bramble scratches, grabbing her wrist and pulling her almost off her feet toward the kitchen table to be punished.

"I'm sorry, Mama," she said. And then added: "But you saw what he did to Lily."

The knob was very loose and the mechanism seemed to disintegrate when she turned it. The door opened quite easily. She had expected a gust of wind, a howling, the sound of something being released, but none came. Beyond the kitchen it was cold and silent, and there was the same dark, damp, savory smell as the icehouse.

Evelyn stooped under the remaining board, then stood up. She held the sickle to her chest and raised the lamp.

She knew this hallway. She remembered it as if she had passed through it only days earlier, running to the stairs to get back to her bedroom. Such a strange mixture of relief and terror to see it again. It was a little narrower than she had expected, its walls speckled with a combination of damp and mold and a long-lost floral pattern on the wallpaper beneath. The carpet was like moss underfoot. She stood and listened but heard only her breath, reluctantly coming and going. Ahead were doors to the left and the right. Two more beyond that. A dizzying number, and these only what she could see.

A gust of wind struck the house and it shivered and settled. Evelyn crept forward very slowly, listening for the boy every four or five paces but hearing only the house itself.

There were too many *things* here. They cluttered and clogged the corners of the hallway like fungus. Mama had always made sure that the kitchen contained only what was needed—crockery and cutlery and tools for cooking and cleaning and making the fire. Anything that had no use was buried or burned. There were even some very useful things that she had looked upon with suspicion. The windup lamp, for instance, was something that Papa had given Lily. It, too, had gone into the ground when Mama discovered it, but Lily had unearthed it after their mother died and found it still worked. Mama had wanted to throw out the refrigerator and the machine that washed the dishes, but they were too heavy to move.

So many things. Evelyn thought she recognized them all. A low table, pushed against the right-hand wall, with a glass vase furred green and white, and a mug with something like clay at the bottom of it. Lamps with shades of brittle fabric, two on the table and one hanging from the ceiling like a huge half-opened flower. A dish of keys and two heavy plastic pebbles whose function she could not remember but whose smell brought Papa to mind with a painful intensity. Unbelievable amounts of paper, scattered across the table and the floor. Lily had only had her four pieces. Here were at least a hundred more, an embarrassment of riches, and Lily not around to see or make use of them. Glossy sheaves with colorful shapes and pictures of women and men, not men like the ones in the icehouse, but men who smiled and looked healthy. The pages were covered in printed text, like the book, whose meaning she understood only superficially, and in some places not at all.

Evelyn put down the sickle and held the edge of the table to steady herself. She pushed the corner of it into her palm until it left a blueish dent in the skin. She watched the blood rush back, amazed. She was only a few feet from the kitchen door, and already she felt, with a kind of elated terror, that it was the garden that had been a dream, the longest dream, and only here in the house was she truly seeing and feeling things for the first time—the pattern of the wallpaper, the hardness of the table, the coldness of the draft.

She opened the door to her left. She knew exactly what was inside. Or did she? The thought had occurred to her that she was not remembering these things at all but was mapping this house onto the house from the book. But no, here was the playroom and Evelyn knew every inch of it. Horses on the curtains and sagging boxes of board games on the windowsill, against the backdrop of Mama's plywood boards. On the floor, a doll wearing a dress like their mother's ball gown, and something half built in plastic bricks. Reds and blues and yellows. Colors bright and sad.

The ruin of Lily's piano hunched in the corner. Evelyn struck a key, but it made no sound and something scuttled fearfully out from under the strings. She struck another. This one produced a short, dusty note, but even that was enough to conjure her sister, legs dangling from the stool that had seemed monumental to Evelyn from where she was playing on the floor. There was paper here, too. Lily's drawings, people and monsters, jagged and gruesome and funny-looking. Her ballet shoes, hardly bigger than the doll's.

Evelyn lowered herself to the floor and handled each object with great care. She sorted the scattered bricks carefully into piles according to shape and color. The gesture felt very familiar. It was like planting the beds. Or perhaps it had been the other way round, and all her neat rows and circles of flowers were the reenactment.

She looked at the collection of her own toys. How old had she been when that first storm hit? she wondered. Twelve or thirteen years old? The same age as the boy, perhaps. She didn't know. She didn't know how old she was now. Perhaps Lily could have told her. Perhaps it was all in her tally.

Evelyn heard a heavy thump overhead, and her heart felt like it was caught on a fishhook. The room bled and swam, and for a moment she thought she might be dying. Another thump, and rapid footsteps. She waited until the house was quiet again. It was a long time before her nerves settled and her sight cleared.

She still had to deal with the boy. There was much to see and to think about in the house, but she mustn't let it distract her. She wondered what he was doing. She didn't know whether he was looking for her or running away from her. Perhaps it didn't matter. The house was a labyrinth, and she imagined her and the boy scurrying in blind circles, both of them expiring of hunger or thirst without ever seeing each other again.

She got up and went back to the hallway and took the sickle in her hand. It felt heavier than before.

At the end of the hall was a staircase. It was enormous and ascended in two right angles to the floor above. Each stair sagged in the middle like wet linen strung across the stairwell, and most of the banisters had collapsed. There was dust here, too, but a different kind, the dust of long, uncounted years.

"Here, boy," she called aloud. "Here, beast of burden."

Evelyn thought she heard whispering on the floor above, but she wasn't sure if it was the wind or the boy or some other animal.

She tightened her knuckles on the sickle and went up the stairs. She stepped on the edge of the staircase, as she'd done when she was a child, so the wood wouldn't creak and wake her parents. It was necessary now, too, since the center of each stair was so riddled with woodworm it had the appearance of honeycomb.

Halfway up she started coughing and had to rest for a moment, cursing her feebleness. What were the chances of her catching the boy by surprise if she wheezed like this everywhere she went? Maybe, she thought, she should just let the boy find her. She was so tired.

Don't be a brat, she heard Mama say. *We're all tired.*

On the upper landing there was a confusion of footprints in the dust. The boy's. Evelyn stopped and listened again, but the creaking and whispering had stopped. He had come this way many times, and not only recently. Some of the older prints were already fading, and they were crisscrossed with the tracks of birds and squirrels.

Evelyn shone the lamp around. More doors, more rooms, more things. Another table of vases and two picture frames, both face down. She turned them over. She thought they were paintings at first, better than anything Lily had ever done, inconceivably detailed and lifelike. The first was a photograph of just her and Lily. They were outside, in the garden, sitting on the steps of the gazebo. A garden party. One of her father's. Evelyn was sitting up very straight in a floral-patterned dress, looking earnestly at the camera. Lily was beside her, clasping her wrist and burying her face into her sister's blond curls. Evelyn thought she remembered the photo being taken, or perhaps it was the photo that created the memory. Perhaps that was what the house was doing. And in fact, what did it matter, if her memories were true or not?

The next photo had been taken indoors. Her and Lily and Mama and a man who she knew straightaway was Papa. The background was plain, slightly blue, she thought, though she couldn't see properly in the lamplight. The family had been arranged against a screen. The photo could have been taken anywhere. Mama was holding her and her sister, and Papa was standing behind Mama with his hands on her shoulders. None of them looked very happy—Papa in particular. He looked at lot like Lily, with a rounder nose than their mother, a rounder face, a face that Evelyn would have called kind had her mother not informed her that their father was anything but.

And where was Papa now? Dead, too, she assumed. He'd abandoned them at some point, between the digging out of the garden and the boarding up of the house, and after that Mama had forbidden them to speak of him. Forgetting Papa, forgetting the house, forgetting the world from before—it was all the same thing. It was selfish people like Papa who had ruined everything in the first place, long, long before the first storm had hit. Everything poisoned at the source.

Evelyn kept looking at her father's face, and it was suddenly very clear why the idea of another garden was so terrifying to her. It was not just the thought that there were other people out there; it was also that Papa might somehow be with them, that he had survived and found sanctuary and was perhaps searching for his daughters.

Was that so hard to believe? What if he was the one who had sent the boy in the first place? What if he was the boy's friend, on the other end of the telephone? She tried again to count up the years, to calculate if Papa might be alive or dead. She did not even know how long a man was supposed to live.

A sound behind her. She thought it was the boy, turned too quickly, swung the sickle and wrenched her poor, aching back. She staggered in a strange pirouette toward one of the doors on the landing and came to rest holding the door handle. She leaned on it, but the door was already open and she fell into the room beyond. The windows in here were all shuttered and she'd left the lamp on the landing, so she saw nothing of its contents. She crawled slow as stone through the pitch black until she found the edge of something that might have been a chair and then climbed into it, her old joints throbbing.

She sat opposite the door, but nothing came through it. The house was silent save for a trickle of dust from the rafters. Evelyn felt as if the floor was at a slight angle, a ship pitching under the new, unfamiliar weight of a woman and a boy. She waited and waited, wanting him to enter, hoping he would not.

Papa's melancholy face returned to her in the darkness, and she tried with all her might to forget it.

A Departure

They shoveled all morning, if it was possible to call it morning. Night and day were still barely distinguishable. Dishcloths stretched over their noses and mouths and tied at the back of their heads. They guessed where the beds and the paths had been by the furrows and depressions in the dust. The work was thankless, endless. Evelyn felt as if they were trying to make a new world from some primordial clay that refused to be molded and was constantly slipping and drifting in the slightest breeze.

There was the sound of hammering from inside the house. She looked at Lily. Her sister was sitting on the lowest bough of Evelyn's apple tree, reading her book. Dust between the pages. Dust between her fingers and toes.

What's she doing? Lily said.

Evelyn shrugged.

They went up to the kitchen door. The lawn was a series of low dunes, like the brown peaks of a meringue. Evelyn was hungry, but her mouth felt too dry for her to eat anything. She went into the kitchen and found their mother fixing boards across the interior door. The rest of the kitchen was dark, but the sweat on her brow was lit red by the light from a candelabra, making her look like she was working at a forge.

What are you doing? Evelyn asked.

We have to stay in here from now on, her mother said. The rest of the house isn't for us.

What about all our things? asked Evelyn.

I've moved everything we need down here, said their mother, gesturing to the opposite corner.

Evelyn squinted at a shapeless heap of clothes and blankets.

If we're starting again, then we're starting again, said their mother. We don't need all that old tat.

Lily appeared in the doorway.

What's happening? she asked.

Mama says we can't go in the rest of the house anymore, said Evelyn.

Why not? asked Lily.

Stop yapping at me! said their mother.

She hammered another nail, harder than she needed to, into the board. Lily looked at Evelyn.

Why not? she said again. Why can't we go into the house?

Because it is your father's, said Mama. And it's full of your father's things. And his father's things. And every bloody father before him.

Same goes for everything out there, said Mama, flinging an arm in some vague direction. Every man jack of them thinking they're lord of the bloody manor. Well, the whole bloody manor's on fire now, isn't it.

The house is on fire? said Lily.

No, Lily. Don't be an idiot.

Where is he?

Who?

Papa.

Your guess is as good as mine.

Their mother hammered the remaining nails into the corner of the board and came back with the candelabra. She set it on the table and mopped her brow with a rag. She looked thin, swamped by her woolen jumper.

Why are you looking at me like that? she said. Your father left us. Didn't I tell you he would? Didn't I say?

Evelyn nodded.

Is he coming back? said Lily.

Of course he's not coming back. Good riddance. As I said, people like your father are the reason we've come to this. We'll be far better off without him.

Lily started crying.

Why did he leave? she asked.

Because he had no use for us anymore. Just take take take, like every other man. Then off to try his luck elsewhere. Didn't I tell you, Evelyn? Didn't I tell you about the bees? Fattens himself up and then off he goes.

Evelyn had not thought their father looked fat. Not in years. Lily wept and would not be consoled.

You can cry all you like, Lily, he's not coming back for you.

Evelyn held Lily close and felt the coldness of her sister's tears soaking through her pinafore and vest and onto her skin.

Well, for Christ's sake, if you miss him that much, then you can go after him, for all I care.

Their mother got up and blew out the candles. Evelyn stood in the darkness with her sister. In the thin light from the open door she watched Mama forage for something in the dresser and then walk off in the direction of the toolshed, talking to herself.

34

There was bright sunlight at the edges of the shutters and the world outside was very quiet. Evelyn levered herself out of the chair and went over to the windows.

She tried three of the clasps before she found one that was not rusted shut. She opened the shutters and the light poured in and Evelyn cowered beneath it.

She had not expected to see daylight again. It was a long time before she felt able to open her eyes.

The storm was over, and the garden was gray-white and endless. The sand and dust reached the sill of the second-floor window. It was carved into dunes, stretching toward the horizon. Evelyn counted the tops of half a dozen trees, their dry leaves showing only the faintest rumor of greenery. The window looked south to where the lawn had once been. All gone, along with the beehives, and the orchard, and the wheat field, and the wall, and Mama, and Lily. There was just her and the boy to be buried now. She listened for him. Nothing.

She turned and surveyed the room. Three huge, swollen chairs, big enough for her and Lily to sit in together. A fireplace, into which the chimney had collapsed. Shelves, strangely ribbed. The rug, a hunting scene. The portraits, faces to the wall and slashed from corner to corner.

Evelyn went over to the bookcase. She ran her finger over the spines, amazed at how many there were. Lily had always said that there were more books in the house. These ones were nicer than her and Lily's book. They had stiff covers to stop the pages from curling. She slipped some of them from the bookcase and found that many had been devoured by mice and mites and turned to yet more dust when she opened them. But some were still intact. She could read the titles but not make sense of them.

Their book had been a forbidden treat, since Mama had decided that words and books were part of the old world, part of the poison. And now here were hundreds more, every one of them a catalog of sins. She selected another book at random and pulled it from the shelf. A handful of pages fell out and she caught them and read a sentence: *The organ complained magnificently as I passed the chapel door.*

Evelyn could not understand what the words meant, yet they filled her with an oblique, nightmarish dread.

She heard footsteps again, then a noise like something heavy falling. There was a set of double doors at the other end of this room that led, some real or imagined memory told her, into a dining room that also connected with the landing.

She opened them and took the lamp through with her. A

vast table on which dishes and plates lay buried under dust like rocks on a beach. The faintest echo of decay. There were more than four place settings, and Evelyn wondered who else had eaten here. Papa had held parties, she remembered, but that was a long, long time before the storm hit. She trudged to the other end of the room, opened the door, and saw that the landing was empty. There were new footprints leading to the floor above.

"Come here, boy," she called as she climbed. "Come here, beast of burden."

What to do when she found him, though?

The third floor was brighter than the others. Here the windows had not been boarded or shuttered so completely, since it was less likely that someone would try to break into the house through the top floor. The roof was full of holes and Evelyn could see patches of churned and ragged sky above. There were deep mounds of sand and dust on this landing, broken panes of glass, ivy and creepers hanging from the skylights. The wind wailed through the gappy and broken rafters, and Evelyn thought it was the boy wailing, though she could not see him.

She made her way along the landing and found her and Lily's shared bedroom, the beds so small they looked like more toys from the playroom. The walls patterned with birds and animals. A plastic cup full of green scum. The boy's fingerprints over everything.

She found the bathroom with its huge tub, filled almost to the brim now with sand. She had that same memory again, of being lifted from the steaming water and enfolded in a towel so big she feared and hoped she would get lost in it. There was a towel hanging from a rail beside the bath still. The boy had touched this, too. It was stiff and flaky.

She went on, the sickle dangling pointlessly at her side, her arm wrung out like an old dishcloth. She could barely lift it now. The boy could be waiting to pounce on her in any one of these rooms and she wouldn't be able to do anything about it.

Beyond the bathroom was another bedroom. Mama and Papa's, she remembered. Evelyn thought she could smell perfume but knew she was imagining it. The centerpiece was a large and very fine brass bed, sheets and mattress devoured by heaven knew what. On either side was a bedside table. There were photographs on these, too, placed face down like the others.

Evelyn stopped on the threshold but did not enter. A pair of boots poked out from the side of the bed, as if the boy had lain down there to sleep. The boots were not his, though. They were larger, and older.

She leaned on the doorframe for a moment, knowing what she would find if she went only a few paces farther. She dropped the sickle and staggered toward the bed frame. The body was stretched out between the bed and the wall in peaceful repose, like the carved tomb of some monarch. It was a man's body, though little of it remained. The bones were still wearing a set of clothes, thin and shredded and of no color at all. A shirt and jeans and a cracked leather belt. Evelyn looked down at the boots again. She knew whose they were. He didn't look anything like the picture in the pack of cards.

Evelyn came forward and knelt beside the bones. She ran her hands over the dome of the skull. The top was smooth and clean, but at the back there was an uneven hole that admitted her fingers. The stock of his gun was just visible beneath the bed.

The skull grinned at her. The monster in the house. Had Mama locked him in here? Or had he locked Mama out?

She sat against the bed and rested her hand on the dead man's arm and looked up through a crack in the rafters. The clouds had cleared and the sky was a scorched and faded blue. She watched the shadows crawl over the room, the boy somewhere on the edge of her consciousness. Her sweat congealed and she felt as cold and numb as the bones she clutched. Only her throat felt very hot, and very raw, and she realized that she was sobbing now, in defiance of everything that she had been told, for Papa, for Mama, for Lily, for herself, for everyone.

35

Evelyn didn't know if she had slept or not. She had never been so thirsty. Her lips were dry and sticky and tore when she tried to open her mouth.

She heard voices coming from somewhere far beneath her. More than one, but so faint she could hardly distinguish them from the sound of her own pulse. Dream voices. Impossible voices. Definitely not the boy's. She thought of coming home from a day in the garden and hearing Lily humming or muttering to herself in the kitchen. The voices were deeper than Lily's, though, deeper than the boy's, and Evelyn felt them as much as heard them. Like listening to her parents talking through the wall of their bedroom.

The sound of bodies moving carelessly. Someone careering through the house, on the floor below them. She tried to place exactly where the sound was coming from. She thought they were in the living room. Perhaps they had followed her footprints? She imagined them manhandling the books, the photographs. She imagined them finding the kitchen and helping themselves to the jars of honey, to the beetroot and onions that she had pickled only a few days before. And Lily. What would they do to Lily?

Evelyn stood up and felt as if she were floating slightly, all the weight of water gone from her body, leaving her dry and brittle. She drifted to the doorway and listened. Among the voices and the footsteps there was another sound, a continuous pure, low tone.

She picked up her sickle and her lamp and went out onto the landing. Something like a laugh drifted up the stairs, a terrifying sound in that tomb-silent house. She looked at her papa and thought to say something, but nothing came so she left him behind.

She went along the landing in the opposite direction to the one she had come from. Memory or imagination told her there was another door at the end of this floor that led to a different staircase. She found it and opened it. A set of back stairs, just as she'd thought. In a rush of delirium she thought maybe she had the power to imagine whatever she wanted, and it would simply appear. That she was, in fact, still in the larger dream of the garden and was free to create it exactly as she wished it to be. And what if this were true of the world outside as well?

She was on the second floor again in what seemed to be a different wing of the house. She could no longer hear voices but still felt the low vibration through the soles of her feet. The footprints of the boy led chaotically in all directions. She did not follow them. She might take a wrong turn and open a door and find herself back where she had been the previous day, looking into the eyes of the others who had entered the house. There was a mirror opposite the stairwell, and for a moment she thought she saw Mama in it and she looked away, frightened.

She took the stairs down to the ground floor, and found they went deeper still. Stone steps, here, worn and sunken in the middle, and cleaner than the rest of the house for some reason. A windowless cellar. Shelves, mostly empty apart from a few cans of paint, some pots and pans, some machines that she didn't understand. A gigantic white chest pushed into one corner, like a sarcophagus, also empty.

She thought she might climb into it and hide. But then she might suffocate. So what if she did? No, that would make her a coward, like Papa.

Poor Papa. Poor boy.

"Don't be ridiculous," she said out loud.

She wondered if there was a way back to the kitchen from the cellar. She needed to drink something, anything. It hurt to swallow. The air in the cellar was damp, but the top of her nose still burned when she breathed. She'd drink the pickling vinegar if she could. She wondered again if the others had found her jars. Onions and beetroot, eggs from years back still plump and tangy.

She crawled into the corner and put her hand in something wet. She licked her fingers, not caring what it was. The water was grainy and tasted old but not rotten. Damp from the lake, or the spring that fed it. The puddle was too shallow to drink from properly, but she laid her hands in it again and again and sucked at her palms.

The water was quickly gone, and she sat and leaned against the white chest and watched the lamp wind down. She heard a single tremulous breath from the corner opposite her. The air seemed suddenly warmer than it should have been.

"They're here," she said.

There was another sharp, dry breath and the click of a mouth with no saliva. Evelyn spoke again.

"There are men in the house."

"Don't eat me," said the boy.

The cellar was pitch-black. The boy's words burned in the nothingness, colors and shapes as if she'd rubbed her eyes too hard.

"Do you still have the knife?" Evelyn asked eventually, her voice seeming to come from somewhere outside her head.

The boy's clothes rustled.

"We might need it," she said.

No reply again.

"You're stronger than I am. You'll have to kill them."

"I don't want to kill them," said the boy. "I don't want to eat them."

"We're not going to eat them," she said. "We can't eat them raw, anyway."

The boy began to whimper.

"Be quiet," snapped Evelyn.

"It was a person," said the boy in a whisper.

"What was a person?"

"The meat."

"It was a man," Evelyn said. "From before."

"So?"

"We had to. At the beginning. They were trying to take the garden from us. And we had no food."

"It's the worst thing you can do."

"It's definitely not the worst thing."

He went quiet again. Evelyn listened for the others but heard nothing apart from throbbing silence. Perhaps the cellar was too deep, its walls too thick for her to hear. Perhaps she wouldn't know they were coming until they were already upon her.

"Where is she?" said the boy.

"She's dead," said Evelyn. "You cracked her head open."

The boy didn't reply. After a moment or two she heard him crying.

"Stop that." Mama's voice again. "I need you to be strong for when the others get here."

And she realized, after all this, that she did still need him.

"I can't kill them," he said.

"You had no trouble killing my sister."

She waited for the boy to protest, to apologize, but he did neither. Evelyn sat in her silence, her grief. The boy repeated himself.

"I can't kill them," he said. "But I don't want to go with them."

"I don't want to go with them either. So what do you suggest? That I outrun them?"

Evelyn wound up the lamp, and it spilled its light over the cellar floor. Even then, she couldn't see the boy properly. She crawled forward and set the lamp in the center of the room, then crawled back again. He was sitting with his back to the wall and his knees under his chin. The pruning knife was on the floor beside him. He was covered in so much dust that he looked like some crouching gargoyle. His shirt twitched and she heard the sound of something being unscrewed, and she thought, with rising panic, that he was readying some kind of weapon; that this had been a ruse all along and she had made exactly the same mistake as before, foolishly thinking him harmless. But he just raised something to his lips and there was a slurping noise.

"What are you drinking?"

He stared at her in the lamplight, then slid something noisily across the flagstones. Evelyn stretched forward to pick it up. Their father's hip flask. The same one she had taken to him when he had been imprisoned in the icehouse.

She unscrewed it and sniffed the top. It smelled of the lake, and of tarnished metal, with the slightest hint of Lily's potato wine. She drank. Just water.

"Your private supply?" she said.

He must have filled it when he went to collect the buckets.

"Do you have food as well?"

He nodded. She slid the canteen back across the floor, but it didn't reach him. He stared at it for a moment, then at Evelyn, as if expecting a trap. Then he snatched it back, shook it to see how much was left. He rummaged beneath his shirt again and threw her a small piece of stale bread.

Evelyn nibbled one corner. Her teeth met grit, and her mouth was too dry to swallow it. She put the remainder in her front pocket.

"If they find us, what will they do to us?" Evelyn asked.

"They'll take us back," he said.

"Back where?"

"Where I came from."

"The other garden."

"It's not a garden. But yes."

"Why?"

"Because they want to help you."

"We don't need helping." She paused. "We didn't need help . . ."

"They think it's better if everyone's together. They're still finding people. Not as many as before. But they're still looking."

"What's there? In your garden?"

"It's not a garden," he said again. "It's more like a city."

It took a moment for Evelyn to master the visions that this word brought with it.

"And what you said to Lily. You have all those things?"

"Yes."

"So it's just like before."

The boy frowned. "Before what?"

Evelyn didn't know what to say. She found she was trembling.

"Are your mother and father there?"

"I don't know."

"How do you not know?"

"I just don't."

Evelyn thought of Lily and wondered, briefly, if they could have had lives after all in such a place.

"Why did you leave?"

"Because I wanted to. There are better places. I know there are."

"Like our garden."

"Yes."

"You knew we were here?"

The question had never been answered. It had drifted away from them in the chaos, but she would have the truth now, she thought. Even if it meant nothing in the circumstances.

"I found you. By accident. I don't know what else to say."

"What about the telephone? Someone was asking you if you'd found us. Was that them? The people in the city?"

She hated to say it. The word itself seemed to have a thin and bitter taste.

The boy opened his mouth to speak and held it like that for some time. He closed it, rasped his dry tongue over his lips, and started again.

"It wasn't you she was asking about."

"She?"

"My friend. She gave me the phone when she left and I said I'd catch her up."

"Why didn't you leave together?"

"It's difficult. You have to do it in secret. They don't want anyone to leave. They want to keep everyone together and they want everyone to work."

Evelyn thought of Lily again. She'd been right. It seemed work was all there was, wherever you went.

"There's somewhere else, though. A town somewhere near the coast. I mean, I don't know if it's a town. A gathering. She went months ago, with her parents, but she gave me a map and that old phone so she could tell me where to go."

"I saw the map. She told you to come here."

"She told me not to. She told me to avoid it. Every year one or two people try to get to where she is. They all say to avoid this place."

The boy looked at her and did not elaborate. He did not need to. How funny, Evelyn thought, that her mama's legacy should reach so far beyond the garden walls. Evelyn was not sure if she felt pride or shame or anything at all.

"I got lost, anyway," the boy said. "I just walked and walked. And then suddenly the house was here. You were here. I would have died if I'd stayed outside, so I made a choice."

"I don't know if I believe you."

"It doesn't really matter anymore, does it?"

"I saw the message. It said: *Have you found them?*"

"She didn't mean you. She sent that before I even got here. She was talking about some way-markers. Some trees or something. I told you, I got lost. I had to turn off the phone because they'd already nearly caught me once before." He listened for the others in the house. "I suppose she didn't know that they could do that when she gave me the phone. Didn't know they could follow the signal, or whatever they do."

"You should have just kept going," Evelyn said. "Eaten your fill and gone on your way."

"I didn't want to."

"Why not?"

"I liked it here." He paused. "I liked you."

He gave no indication whether this was still the case. Evelyn suspected not.

"You wanted to bring her here, then? Your friend."

"Maybe. I thought about it."

She pictured this. A teenage mama and papa, inheriting the house and the garden from their elderly children. It might even have worked out. How hopeful she'd been when she'd first seen him in the icehouse, long-limbed, straight-backed.

"Well," she said, "too late now."

36

 The cellar was silent again, but Evelyn had the strangest sensation that she was still talking to the boy. The same feeling that she used to get with Lily, that words were not necessary. A shared consciousness, mingling in the middle of the cellar. Evelyn ate her hard corner of bread. It made the roof of her mouth bleed. They passed Papa's hip flask between them, taking smaller and smaller sips.

"You finish it," said Evelyn when it was down to the dregs. She threw it back to him and he dropped it. It clanged like a bell. They both froze in the diminishing echo and waited for someone to come, but nobody did.

They slept on and off. Evelyn's tongue and lips were quickly parched again. She felt light-headed and light-bodied, as if caught in some dry, fierce updraft.

"We'll need to go back to the kitchen," she said finally.

"We can't," said the boy, his voice hardly there. "They'll see us."

"I haven't heard anything. We've been here for hours. Maybe days. They might have left."

"No."

"How do you know?"

"They'll be packing up the house. They'll take everything back with them. They always do."

"We'll die down here if we don't move," said Evelyn. "We need water."

"And then what?"

"And then we wait for them to leave. Or we kill them."

He paused, neither agreeing nor disagreeing. "And after that?"

She thought for moment. Pessimism was a luxury she could no longer afford. She was the only one left, and she would have to speak for Lily, and Mama, too.

"We'll dig it out."

"We can't. You saw. It's ten feet deep."

"Doesn't matter. I'm staying with the garden. I'll dig it out by myself if I have to. Never been afraid of a bit of hard work."

Although, she admitted to herself now, it wasn't just about the work. Work was all she could offer the garden, but Mama had been able to offer something else. Something like the Magic she read about in the book. The line that always came to her: *He just whispers things out o' th' ground.* She thought Lily had it, too, the Magic, though she was work-shy. The garden had come about through the combination of both of those things, and she could only do one of them. She could work. Work had to be enough. But she was tired, so wretchedly tired.

She crawled to the door of the cellar and a little way up the steps. It was silent on the floor above.

"You should go," she said.

"I don't want to," said the boy.

"You stand a better chance than I do. I can't fight them or run away from them."

"Neither can I."

"You're good at creeping around. You've hidden in the house before. Remember how long it was before we found you?"

"I think we should stay here."

"Then I'll go," she said. "We need water."

"Please stay," he murmured.

"Make up your mind," said Evelyn. "You thought I was going to eat you not so long ago."

He didn't say anything to that. Evelyn pulled herself up and felt the blood returning to her legs and feet, thick as treacle. It was some time before she was steady enough to take the three or four steps over to where the boy was sitting.

"Give me the knife," she said.

He felt beside him and handed it to her blade first. She took it gingerly. It wasn't particularly sharp, but it was at least smaller and lighter than the sickle. The kitchen knife would have been better, but that was back on the kitchen table.

"Flask, too," she said. "I'm not bringing back the whole bucket."

He gave it to her. She wrapped the lamp in the folds of her smock and began climbing the steps. The boy was whispering something behind her, but she did not stay to listen.

At the top of the steps she shone the lamp around quickly, then covered it again. She was in the same hallway she had entered when she first left the kitchen. She tried to remember the route she had taken through the house but found herself disorientated. She thought she was somewhere toward the front of the house—or the back, as she and Lily would have called it—where the windows looked out over the lake, but she couldn't be totally sure.

She kept to the right-hand side of the hallway, feeling her way along the bulges and wrinkles in the wall. Nowhere to hide, if someone saw her.

"Ridiculous," she said again, under her breath.

She came across shelves piled with bags and suitcases, all tattered and deflated. The remains of stickers, names and places that no longer existed. Fairy-tale places: Brighton, Paris, Cairo. She looked for India, which she knew from the book, but couldn't find it. There was a sealed door between the shelves, which she remembered, quite suddenly, had been called the luggage entrance.

She turned a corner in the hall, and the air became charged with the voices again. There was a dim pool of light to the left, where the grand staircase led up to the second floor. Footsteps, back and forth, back and forth, the same route over and over, and that low, dread resonance of something outside of her experience.

Her heart felt unhinged. A fizzing down her left arm. She waited and waited.

It seemed no one had come down to the ground floor yet. She stared at the grayness around the foot of the stairs and thought she saw only one set of prints, her own, from when she had followed the boy however many days previously. She shuffled forward, plowing dementedly through the dust. The voices were clearer than ever, like nothing she had heard before—loud, brutal syllables falling through the stairwell.

Evelyn passed by the foot of the staircase, the door to the playroom, and the table with its bowl of keys and piles of paper; then she ducked under the boards into the kitchen.

Everything was as she had left it. The meat was still on the table, fingers languidly uncurled, with the pile of garden tools next to it and the buckets of water that the boy had collected underneath. She went to the table and drank quietly and greedily, water dripping from her chin. She looked at Lily under her shroud. After a few moments she went over and pulled the blanket back and looked upon her sister's face. She was amazed at how little it resembled Lily's now; a strange, distorted effigy.

She heard more thumping, but not overhead this time. Somewhere at the other end of the hallway, on the stairs, coming down to the kitchen. The voices were insistent but indistinct, and accompanied by the low drone she'd heard before. Behind it all, the quiet slither of sand and dust falling from a great height.

Evelyn's arm trembled and sang. Her chest hurt, and her jaw, too. Her lungs were like two flattened bags. She had to close her eyes from the pain. She covered Lily's face again and piled more blankets on top of her, then crept into the corner of the kitchen behind the stove and crouched there, waiting.

She heard two of them come blundering into the kitchen. She couldn't believe how loud their breathing was. A gurgle that reminded her of Lily snoring. They spoke a few words to each other, but they seemed as distant and distorted as they had been on the stairs.

A fierce white light, bleaching the floor, the edges of the table, the upturned fingers of the man's arm. Colossal shadows. Then the men themselves, so large they seemed to hunch under the ceiling. They wore clothes like her mother's overalls and had their own sunglasses, though these were much larger and were attached by an elastic strap around the backs of their heads. They wore masks over their mouths with tubes that looped under each arm to something they carried on their back. Lights were affixed to the center of their head, like a single sleepless eye.

One of them went to the kitchen table. He picked up the arm, studied the end where the elbow had been severed, murmured something, then put it back. The other was standing at the dresser, going through the crockery and cutlery with gigantic gloved hands. He circled the table and went over to the window. It was fractured like a spider's web now, but still held back the weight of the sand. The man peered at it, then saw the bundle of blankets reflected in the glass. He came back and crouched a few feet from Evelyn. The other one was hefting the garden tools from one hand to the other.

"One here," said the figure squatting by the blankets, and the voice was deep and cracked but unmistakably a woman's voice. She peeled back the layers covering Lily's face.

"The boy?" said the one by the table. This one was a man.

"Someone else."

The woman pulled all the blankets off Lily and began to examine her like she had the other items in the kitchen. She took off her thick rubber gloves and replaced them with a more forgiving pair. She lifted one of Lily's earrings on her fingertips and looked for a way to detach it.

The man went out and came back with a transparent plastic box. He went from surface to surface collecting bowls, plates, saucepans, and placing them carefully inside. He picked up Lily's eggcup.

"Look," he said.

The woman looked up, and he held it in the beam of his head torch, turning it slowly in his finger and thumb.

"You seen one of these before?"

She shook her head.

"It's beautiful."

Evelyn's heart felt like a tiny hot coal. There were spasms firing all down the left side of her body. She murmured into her lap. She could not stop herself. A fraction of a breath, but the woman looked up from where she was peering into Lily's half-open mouth and her glass eyes met Evelyn's and the coal beneath Evelyn's ribs flared and the pain was enough to blind her.

"There's another one here," said the woman. "She's alive."

The pruning knife was in Evelyn's left hand, but she couldn't feel the weight of it. She tried to lunge at the woman, but there was that white heat again and she gasped and fell forward onto the floor.

"You're all right," said the woman. She thrust her hands under Evelyn's side and tried to roll her over. Evelyn was aware of nothing but each agonized heartbeat, and each fearful lull in between.

The woman said something to the man, and he went to the door and shouted. The loudness of his voice was unbearable, abominable.

"You're all right," said the woman again. "We've got you."

The man came back, and Evelyn felt a prick like a bee sting somewhere on her body, she could not say where, followed by a lush and delirious coolness. She lay on the floor next to her sister and found that her vision had returned. She looked at the dangling flex of the electric light, without its bulb, and found it new and fascinating. Her heart ached dully but had stopped writhing. It seemed not to beat at all.

"We've got you," the woman kept saying, over and over. "We've got you."

They lifted her onto something like a tarpaulin. Evelyn felt herself being lifted from the floor and carried from the kitchen. No, she did not want this. Even in the disarming bliss of whatever they had put in her veins, she knew that. She groaned and rolled over.

"We've got you," said the woman again.

Evelyn shuffled on the stretcher. She felt tiny in the company of the huge man and woman. A tired child, being carried up to bed. She maneuvered her face next to the woman's hand and opened her mouth and sank her teeth into her wrist.

"No, no," said the woman, and gently nudged her away. "Come on. You're safe. We've got you."

The woman and the man passed her clumsily through the doorway, which was still half boarded up. They carried her down the length of the hallway, past the playroom. The door was open, and Evelyn could see someone had disturbed the toys she had so carefully arranged, and she hated them for it.

There were a few moments of discussion at the foot of the stairs. Twice more Evelyn attempted to get up from the stretcher. The woman pushed her firmly back down the first time; then the man did, without interrupting their conversation. She did not try a third time. Her breathing was shallow and her pulse was weak. The sharp pain in her chest was gone, but her skin prickled and she felt nauseated. She turned slowly on the tarpaulin again to see her surroundings and then looked up the stairwell. There was another huge head looking down over the banisters above. Only three of them? She thought she'd heard more. Perhaps someone had already gone to the cellar.

The man above called to them and they started up the

stairs. Evelyn again had the distant sensation of the house pitching and yawing like a boat. When they reached the turn in the staircase, the man overhead shouted more urgently. He was pointing and seemed to be agitated, and deep beneath the waves of whatever medicine they had given her Evelyn registered this but did not feel agitated herself. She watched as he ran to the other end of the landing, felt the stairs ahead of her give way, slowly at first and then all of a sudden, and the man who was carrying the front of her stretcher disappeared through them and let go of her and her head lolled over the ragged hole where the staircase had collapsed. There was a great cloud of dust and more shouting, and beneath her the man now howled in pain.

The woman who had been at her feet abandoned the stretcher and went down to help her injured colleague. Evelyn lay curled on the hard angles of the staircase, as if she had fallen there from a great height. She could not see the second man anymore. Beneath her the injured man continued to cry out, and the woman sifted through the debris and heaved the timbers aside.

Evelyn was aware of something tugging at her feet. The stretcher slid to the foot of the stairs, and on each step it felt as if a different part of her came loose. When she reached the ground, she continued to slide, apparently of her own accord, back into the darkness of the hallway.

The boy appeared. He knelt beside her and poured water from the hip flask over Evelyn's face, then let her drink some. She couldn't feel herself swallowing. She couldn't feel anything. She saw and she heard but thought little and moved less; in the world, but not of it.

The boy gathered the top end of the stretcher in his pale

fists and began to haul it slowly across the carpet. He pulled Evelyn back to the kitchen, whispering to her all the way, and though she could make no sense of his words, he seemed to be trying to reassure her.

The house drifted past her, the open doors, the furniture, the wallpaper, and she felt nothing now, a mere witness to it all.

37

There was the clink of bottles and jars. The boy was piling things up on the stretcher, between Evelyn's arms and legs, around her ears.

"What are you doing?" she said, or thought she said, but he didn't answer.

There were times when he seemed to leave the kitchen completely, or perhaps he just went beyond the edge of Evelyn's senses. Then he would return and give her water and food—bread and beans and vegetables that tasted earthy and slightly rotten. Still he added to their supplies. Jars, tools, clothes, shoes, blankets, most heaped on top of her, some collected in Lily's shopping bag. She felt the pages of the book flutter against her forearm.

"What are you doing?" asked Evelyn again. Her heart

ached more when she tried to speak, but only when it hurt did she know it was still there, still beating.

"We're leaving."

"Where are we going?"

He leaned over her and put a finger to his lips. She heard the voices of the man and the woman again.

"We have to be quick," said the boy. "And very quiet."

"There are seeds in one of the drawers," said Evelyn.

"What?"

"There are seeds in one of the drawers."

The boy went back to the cupboards and drawers, and she could hear him opening and shutting them, but she didn't know whether he had heard what she had said.

At some point the boy decided they were ready and closed the sides of the stretcher around her like a cocoon, leaving only her head and shoulders free. He attached a rope to the head-end of the cocoon and began to pull it out of the kitchen.

The procession moved down the hallway, and Evelyn watched the dead bulbs of the electric lights pass overhead. She felt as if she were resting on her funeral bier. The boy dragged her past the opening to the staircase. The woman was tending to the man's injuries behind the piled ruins of the stairs and did not see him pass with his strange sledge piled with trophies.

They came to the entrance to the cellar and passed this, too. The boy moved slowly and with great effort, pausing after each step. Evelyn's bier slid and stopped, slid and stopped, slid and stopped. They reached the back stairs. The boy started to haul the tarpaulin up to the second floor. He seemed to rest for hours on each step, gasping for breath. The provisions he had loaded into the tarpaulin along with Evelyn's body began to spill out and down the stairs, and he had to run back and forth

collecting them. Some he put back in the bier; some he stuffed
into the pack on his back. She witnessed this, too. She did not
remember him having a pack like this.

Eventually they came to a set of ragged curtains that pooled
on the floor next to Evelyn's head. The boy opened them and
there was light.

Shouting erupted from the floor below. Only the woman's
voice, though. The boy hissed and swore, and from somewhere
in the depths of Evelyn's head rose Mama's voice telling him to
wash his mouth out with soap.

The boy strained at the window. It would not budge. More
shouts and footsteps on the stairs, on the landing. The frame
gave a little, and he opened it to the world beyond. He had to
unload everything from the bier and pass it through the window, then pull Evelyn through afterward. She was aware that
he was panicking but found it hard to panic herself. She felt
herself being passed through the gap and then laid to rest softly
in the dust. It was piled up to just beneath the windowsills of
the second floor. Ten feet deep, maybe twenty. The boy placed
her back on the stretcher, then continued pulling and did not
look back.

The day was golden. Morning or early evening, Evelyn
wasn't sure which. The sun was not far from the horizon, but
she didn't know if she was looking east or west. It seemed large
and kindly and it warmed her bones. She turned her head
slightly. The pain in her chest waxed and waned.

There was a beauty in the emptiness. A wondrous calm after the noise and violence of the house. The dunes rippled and
glittered like the surface of the lake they had replaced, punctu-
ated with treetops. Their leaves had shrugged off a good deal
of the dust and showed muted green above the surface of the

desert. Evelyn thought she recognized the arrangement of them. Chestnuts and cedars mostly. They were facing west then, and it was evening.

For some reason she thought she might see their chickens scratching in the dust. She looked for the tops of the beehives. The rough dome of Mama's grave. All her years caring for these things, and it was as if they had never existed at all.

The boy took a route that was not directly west, but more southwest, and Evelyn soon saw dry leaves and branches passing above her. These were not evergreens, but beech and oak and sycamore, the trees that had lined the burn, and she knew that the boy was taking the old path of the stream toward the edge of the buried garden.

She gazed up at the heavens from her cocoon, and the sky blushed and turned blue and the branches became less and less distinct. Where the trees ended, the boy stopped and sat cross-legged in the dust. He offered her some water and brushed some of the dust from her eyes and nose. She drank gratefully. He opened one of the jars that he had loaded onto the bier and fished out a pickled egg. He ate half of it and gave the other half to Evelyn. The vinegar was so sharp it made her heart ache again.

"I think the sea is this way," said the boy.

Someone had gone to the coast, the boy had told her, but Evelyn could not remember what he had said. She remembered something else, though, from much longer ago. A memory that had taken firmer root. In the book, people went to the sea to get better. They went to the seaside. Perhaps this was what the boy was thinking.

Mama had always said the sea had turned black a long time ago. But Evelyn did not know how much she believed Mama anymore.

She closed her eyes in assent and the boy didn't say anything else. He sat beside her through the night as the enormous arc of stars passed silently overhead.

At dawn the boy got up and tied the bier to his waist again and started walking while it was still gray and freezing. The trees were gone and the garden was gone. A world behind them, and a world before them. The endlessness of it all. In the east the sun rose, as it had always done, and its light fell upon them both without judgment.

An Ending

Time became complicated. Neither a line nor a circle. A coil, perhaps. Repeating and repeating and yet converging on something nonetheless.

Their mother dealt with visitors, few and far between as they were, and when she found she was too old the responsibility was given to Evelyn. Every time Lily was hounded inside the house under some pretense or other. Not that Lily would not have managed. They were both taller and stronger than their mother by now, and their mother's moods were wilder, as if rising to meet the challenge.

She demanded to see the almanac every morning, right up to the end. Evelyn would wheel her out into the sunshine, and she would pore over it for hours with both sets of glasses perched on the tip of her nose, unable to read a word, declaring the day's tasks from her jumbled memory rather than from what was written in front of *her. She told them to bury the telephone, the piano, though both had been locked away and forgotten. She told them to make a nest for Eddie. He'd be returning soon, she said. He couldn't come back to nothing, could he? Once she informed them that it was time to burn the whole garden. That they would be starting again the following morning. Evelyn and Lily conspired to keep her happy and agreed to everything she said when they were with her. They cut up her food and cleaned her bib. Sometimes she asked for Lily to push her around the garden in the chair, but by the time they reached the bottom beds, their mother was usually screaming and Evelyn would have to drop everything and take over from her sister.*

I can't stand her! Mama would say. I can't stand that bloody woman!

Most days Mama was asleep by midafternoon. While she dozed, Evelyn and Lily talked about what might come to pass.

On one inexplicably cool day their mother slept until past noon. It was the first morning Evelyn could remember when she had not been working from dawn. She and Lily went out into the garden and sat on the lawn under a sun so small and pale they might have mistaken it for the moon. The dew dampened their dresses, and Lily ate blueberries straight from a bush. Their mother was no longer keeping an inventory of everything that was grown and harvested in the garden.

What do we do when she goes? asked Lily.

What do you mean?

What I said. What are we going to do about the garden?

We'll look after it.

Do you think we can?

We're doing all right. It might be easier without Mama to look after as well.

I suppose so. It's like having a child, isn't it.

They were quiet.

So you want to stay, then, Lily said.

I don't understand.

I mean you'd rather stay here than go out there on an adventure.

Evelyn watched her sister plucking the fruit from the bush. Her hair fell in two matted curtains on either side of her head, and Evelyn could not see her expression.

What exactly do you mean by an adventure?

Just to see what's going on out there. See what happened to everyone.

There's nothing out there, Lils. Nothing worth seeing. I told you.

Papa's out there. Maybe he's still wandering around looking for us.

I can't tell if you're joking.

Lily turned and grinned.

Yes, I'm joking, she said. She squeezed a blueberry between her fingers, and the juice ran bright as blood down her palm and the inside of her wrist. Evelyn watched. Her own blood had not come that month, or the month before. She did not know why, and she did not expect any answers from her mother or her sister.

Stop it, she said.

What? said Lily.

Come on, said Evelyn. Don't waste them.

That same night Evelyn and Lily slept on either side of their mother, as they always did, their bodies touching, arm to arm and thigh to thigh. In the blank hour before dawn their mother sat bolt upright and looked at the ceiling. Evelyn sat up beside her.

What is it, Mama? she asked.

Her mother shushed her and stayed perfectly still, looking and listening. Evelyn waited and eventually asked again:

What is it? Can you hear something?

I can't sleep with him crashing around up there!

Who?

Your father! Night after night. Never gives me a moment's rest.

Lily got up on the other side and put a hand on their mother's shoulder.

Papa's not here, she said. *Papa left. A long time ago.*

Mama looked at her, and then turned back to Evelyn as if to check Lily was telling the truth. Evelyn nodded and put the backs of her fingers to her mother's forehead to check her temperature. Mama lay down again and fell back into whatever black and torturous state she called sleep.

Evelyn and Lily were awake for the rest of the night, but did not speak. In the morning they remembered their mother's words, but by then there was so little time left, and they readily explained them away as the ravings of a woman hours from death.

A Beginning

She watched the man coming barefoot over the dunes with a basket of flowers. When he saw her, he stopped and smiled and then quickened his pace. He scrambled up the side of the mound where she'd been waiting, and she sat in his shadow looking out at the breakers.

"This is very adventurous of you," he said.

She inclined her head, just so he knew she'd heard him.

"Aren't you cold?"

"I'm all right," she said. The wind tugged at the last of her hair, white and so thin it might as well not have been there at all.

He sat down beside her and put the basket between them. She pawed through the contents. Blackthorn, celandine, silverweed, bitter vetch.

"I found some scarlet pimpernel as well," he said. "But I'm keeping that for Lily. Sorry."

She looked out over the sea and thought how much she would like to go for a swim again. It had been years. She knew the waves would knock her down before the water was anywhere near deep enough, and besides, she was too old for swimming. Too old for anything. The man was surprised she'd even made it the hundred paces from her house to the dunes.

The sky was all torn clouds and glimpses of sunlight. One of them scattered a few raindrops upon her forearm, few enough for her to count, and then blew inland. She shivered.

"Do you want my help getting back?" said the man.

By way of an answer she held out an arm, and he took it and helped her up. She seemed to be almost the same height standing as she was when seated. They went very slowly, the man putting on a good show of patience as her slippered feet plowed through the sand.

There were other houses besides hers, more shelters than houses, but the residents were out working in the fields. Inside, she got straight into her bed and sat with her hands folded in her lap. She watched the man close the little wooden door behind him and stoke the fire. The room was very small and heated up quickly. He put the kettle on and waited for it to boil.

"Where is Lily?" she asked. "Rehearsing?"

The man smiled, and she knew she had got something wrong.

"She's out with her mother," he said. "Digging potatoes, I suppose. Not what I'd choose to do on my birthday, but there you go."

She laughed and then said: "Sorry."

"For what?"

"I got confused."

He shook his head. "It's all right. My fault really."

Evelyn found she was increasingly confused these days. The man's daughter shared a name with her sister, but only that. The little girl was redheaded and willowy. She was quiet and shy and slow to laugh. Everyone around here was slow to laugh, Evelyn thought. There seemed to be a violence to laughing out loud, but sometimes she longed for it. She longed for her sister to make fun of her.

"She'll like those pimpernels. Very pretty."

"They're her favorites."

"My Lily liked them, too."

"I know. I remember."

The kettle began to boil. The man filled a mug and brought it over to her. She sipped it at once and let the tea scald her because it was good to feel something. She watched him going around the shelter, arranging the rest of the flowers in jam jars for her, an echo of something that had happened a long time ago. Or perhaps something that was going to happen. That was another source of confusion. She was sure by now that time wasn't simply a line that ran in one direction. Having a young Lily running around only seemed to confirm that.

While she watched him, she realized that he was stirring more than one memory in her.

"The last time we celebrated Mama's birthday, we got her flowers," she said.

He exchanged one stalk of celandine for another, then turned. "Yes?"

"Papa had forgotten. Or perhaps he hadn't. It wasn't as if we could go anywhere and buy her a present, or a card, or a box of chocolates." She lingered on those last words, tasting their sweetness. "Lily and I remembered, at any rate. We decided we would collect bunches of flowers for her as a surprise. Well. She was surprised. And she was furious. She screamed like billy-o at both of us. Locked herself away for days. We could hear her crying through the bedroom door. Poor Mama."

She paused. A gull landed on the roof and pattered about.

"She wasn't angry about the flowers being cut," she said. "I think she was just sad. So desperately sad. That her life should have shrunk so much that the contents of the garden were the only thing we could offer her as a gift. She would have liked some chocolates, I suspect. Some other nice thing."

She thought for a moment and tried to remember everything all at once.

"She didn't even want to stay in the beginning," she said. "Strange to think, when I remember her at the end. She'd been a dancer, you know. Like Lily. Like both our Lilys. Did I ever tell you that? Perhaps I did. I'm sorry. I often wonder why she stayed at all. But then sometimes I don't wonder at all. I suspect she loved him. I suspect they loved each other."

She paused again.

"Yes. I am full of suspicions about those two."

She sipped at her tea. Her throat was sore from talking so much and she coughed. She felt like a husk. The man looked like he didn't know what to say. Eventually he said:

"I can put some honey in that if you like."

"No, it's all right, thank you."

"Hives are just out there."

She shook her head.

The man's daughter appeared in the doorway. She took a

step backward so that only her head was visible. Evelyn knew she scared her. She dared not think what she looked like these days.

"Hello, Lily," said the man. "Are you coming in?"

The girl shook her head.

"Come on, silly."

He went out and scooped her up and brought her inside.

"Look what I found." He showed her the scarlet pimpernels. "For you."

He offered them to her, but she was already holding a single muddy potato in her hand.

"Oh. I see. You've already got a birthday present."

The girl nodded.

"That's our dinner, is it?"

She nodded again.

"Can Evelyn have some?"

The girl clutched her father's neck. She nodded a third time and then turned her face away.

"Well, that's very kind of you," he said. "Shall we go and cook it, then?"

The man dipped as he went out under the low lintel of the door.

Evelyn stayed in the bed. The wooden walls were thin and she could hear the man talking to his wife and daughter in the next shelter along. The woman had been out in the fields and said the harvest was good. There would be enough for everybody, the man thought. Evelyn heard the woman go outside with her daughter, and she stood there pointing out seabirds while the man cooked their supper. Somewhere the bell of the garden's one goat rang out in the dusk, a lonely but reassuring sound.

She hadn't moved an inch by the time the man came back. He put a plate of fried fish, potatoes, and onions on her side table. He had cut everything up into tiny pieces for her, but she wasn't sure she had the energy to raise a fork to her mouth.

"You could come and eat with us if you like," he said.

"It's all right," she said.

"Or we can come through and sit here. Keep you company."

She shook her head. Outside, the sun had gone down, and even with the tarpaulin up it was very dark in the shelter. The man wound up the lamp for her and set it down next to the plate. He looked awkward and uncertain. Almost as he had when she'd first laid eyes on him.

"Well," he said, "let us know if you need anything."

He went out and returned to his family.

Evelyn slid down into the bed without touching the food. There were other people talking now, each shelter like a radio set transmitting into the night sky. She directed her attention to the man and his daughter again. He was putting on a funny voice.

"*Two pieces o' meat an' two helps o' rice puddin'!*" he said, and she laughed.

"It's been ages since you read her any of that," the woman said.

"There's hardly any of it left," he said.

"You could read it tonight."

He agreed, and once they'd finished their supper, he read to them both. "*There is no one left . . .*"

Evelyn listened. The story made even less sense to her now, with so many gaps. The man didn't know the order of some of the pages, it seemed, but she didn't mind. If her own recollections had no order, then it hardly seemed necessary that the book should. She liked the words and phrases more than the larger story anyway. She hoarded them like jewels.

She heard them go to bed. They talked of their daughter and of the work that was still to be done. Long after the family had fallen asleep, Evelyn lay on her back with her eyes wide open, as she often did, since sleep did not come easily to her, and she watched the stars drifting through the gaps in the roof and listened to the sea coming in and going out, coming in and going out.

Acknowledgments

Thanks to Liv Maidment for her faith, guidance, vision, and friendship; to Jane Willis for her encouragement in the very early days; to Kirsty Dunseath, Sally Kim, Daphne Durham, and Lara Hinchberger for their editorial sensitivity and insight; to everyone at Doubleday UK, Putnam, and Penguin Canada for their immense industry and enthusiasm; to Sarah Day and Mary Beth Constant for copyediting par excellence; to Beci Kelly and Chris Lin for the magnificent cover art; to Titus and Carrie, Jamie and Beth, the Erskines, Luke Benedict, and Sarah Schulman for giving me various spaces to write in; to Dave and Mary, Verity, Emerald and—especially—Chris for listening and reading and offering kind and galvanising words; to Karen Bowling, for the gardening tips and so much more; and to Laura, for everything.